MIDNIGHT JEWELS

Tzvi White

P·U·B·L·I·S·H·E·R·S
New York · London · Jerusalem

Copyright © 1992

All rights reserved.
This book, or any part thereof,
may not be reproduced in any
form whatsoever without the express
written permission of the copyright holder.

Published and distributed
in the U.S., Canada and overseas by
C.I.S. Publishers and Distributors
180 Park Avenue, Lakewood, New Jersey 08701
(908) 905-3000 Fax: (908) 367-6666

Distributed in Israel by
C.I.S. International (Israel)
Rechov Mishkalov 18
Har Nof, Jerusalem
Tel: 02-518-935

Distributed in the U.K. and Europe by
C.I.S. International (U.K.)
89 Craven Park Road
London N15 6AH, England
Tel: 81-809-3723

Book and cover design: Deenee Cohen
Typography: Devorah Rozsansky, Rivky Kaminsky
Cover illustration: Gregg Hinlicky

ISBN 1-56062-187-7 hard cover

PRINTED IN THE UNITED STATES OF AMERICA

Attribution

This work contains many discussions pertaining to Jewish *hashkafah*. Many of the metaphors, analogies and examples appearing in these discussions were taken directly from the *shiurim* of Rabbi Avigdor Miller of Brooklyn, with his kind permission.

1

LIGHT WISPS OF CLOUDS DANCED HIGH ABOVE THE DOWNtown skyline. Bold skyscrapers rose in the distance, while Cahill's renowned Centerplex could be seen close by. From the Chief's ninth floor conference room in Police Headquarters, Dr. Binyamin Beck surveyed the hundreds of pedestrians below, scurrying about like busy little ants. From this height, it was easy to keep track of the movements of many people simultaneously. Maybe, Dr. Beck thought, Hashem put skyscrapers into the modern age to give people a clearer image of what the world looks like from Heaven. It was a lesson to humankind to realize that everyone is watched from Above at all times.

"If only I could see all the criminals from here," imagined Beck, "maybe we'd have a chance of breaking this robbery string."

He combed his fingers through his beard. It was an old nervous habit he had acquired when he was studying for his doctorate in atmospheric chemistry. Somehow, the feel of the beard helped him think better.

Beck peered outside at some roof work proceeding on top of the building next to Headquarters. It was only a seven-story building, so Beck could stand against the floor-to-ceiling glass windows of the conference room and see the work area as though it were being staged in front of him. A huge crane with an arm at least a hundred feet long had somehow found its way up here.

It was still early, and there was only one workman on the site, making some adjustments underneath the crane's cab. He was a tall fellow, wearing a bright red and black plaid shirt. Beck could see that he had long black hair drawn into a ponytail.

Ponytail on a man, Beck observed to himself with obvious distaste. Beck reflexively thought of long hair on men as a sign of wildness, rebellion, do-your-own-thing—an ultimately self-destructive attitude that *Yiddishkeit* would not tolerate.

"Why do people have to do weird things?" Beck mused aloud. Then he chuckled. "Outside of the Torah world, my full beard, black suit and black hat must also look weird."

Beck watched as the man with the ponytail straightened up and walked over to a pile of steel beams near the edge of the roof. A minute later, he was joined by another, shorter workman wearing denim overalls over a bright yellow shirt.

They're awfully close to the edge, Beck noted to himself. I wonder if *Halachah* would require a *maakeh* around that roof during the period of construction. It's a long way to the sidewalk if either one of them falls off. He felt a stab of nausea just thinking about the possibility.

Suddenly, Beck noticed the two workmen face each other and exchange words. From their postures and wild gesturing, they seemed to Beck to be quarreling heatedly. All at once, they both flung their arms straight ahead and pushed each other backwards with force. The man with the ponytail stumbled and began falling toward the brink of the roof.

"Oh, heavens!" Beck gasped as he pressed his palms flat against the glass.

He watched speechlessly as the man in overalls dove for his partner and clutched his shirttail. Just in time, he prevented the ponytail man's lurch toward a grisly death.

What idiots! Beck fumed to himself. Just incredible idiots!

He was stupefied by the nearly disastrous scene he had just witnessed, and he watched with dismay as the two men hurried behind the crane and out of his sight, still arguing vehemently with each other. For a moment, Beck stood transfixed at the window, waiting to see if the men would reappear.

From the direction of the airport, a 747 jet lumbered upward into Beck's view of the horizon. The huge plane sliced through the fleecy clouds like a champion skier schussing through a mountain of white snow with self-assured aplomb.

The view of the distant clouds turned Beck's thoughts to the month he had just endured aboard a university vessel in the North Pacific Ocean and the Bering Sea, researching the flow of gases between the atmosphere and the oceans. He had been smart, he congratulated himself, for taking three weeks of leave in order to recoup from the voyage and spend time with his family.

Besides, he reflected, he had never viewed his doctorate, nor his research position, as anything more than simple vehicles through which Hashem provided his *parnassah*. Indeed, he was better known for his role as president of Cahill's internationally famous East Cahill Citizens Patrol. In ten years, the Jewish community in East Cahill had built the ECCP into the largest and most effective organization of its kind.

Through a decade of cooperation, Beck pondered, he had developed a warm relationship of mutual respect and support with most of the top brass of the Cahill Police

Department. He had discovered many exemplary human beings behind those crisp uniforms and official insignias.

"My, you look pensive this morning," Chief Vincent interrupted Beck's thoughts.

"Oh, hi, Chief," said Beck. "These plate glass windows in your conference room really afford a wonderful view. I was just thinking about all the robberies we've been having in the last two months. Even our precinct in East Cahill hasn't been immune."

Chief Ronald Vincent, a thirty-two-year veteran of the police department, had worked his way up to the top through years of conscientious service. He was a man of high principle, quick wit and imagination, attributes that served him well in dealing with a department of nearly six thousand uniformed officers and a metropolitan population of one and a quarter million citizens. Despite the taxing hours and heavy responsibilities, the Chief obviously relished his position.

"Now, Doc, you know we're doing all we can to make some arrests," said the Chief. "But right now we don't even know that all the robberies are related. We have descriptions of at least eight different suspects and five getaway cars. In fact, the only common denominator is that they seem to be keeping the victims' credit cards."

"I know," Beck replied. "That's the kicker. Usually, a robber takes cash out of the wallet or purse, and then discards everything else, including the credit cards. Of course, it could all be just coincidence."

"Come, you two," boomed a voice from across the room. "Let's get the meeting started."

Beck reminded himself that he had come to Headquarters this morning to attend the monthly Citizens Advisory Council meeting. Too bad, he thought, that the chairman was sick. That meant the vice chairman would run the show today. Horace Grimm, a stodgy, phlegmatic lawyer from South Cahill, was vice chairman of the Council only because no one else wanted the job. Dr. Beck disliked much of his social philosophy. Grimm had defended many practitioners of various loose lifestyles whose civil rights had allegedly been breached.

When it came to dealing with crime and immorality, Beck regarded much of the American establishment as cowardly, too insecure to reward what's right, and too lily-livered to punish what's wrong with enough force to keep it from happening again. Beck's social-political-theological view of the world did not have many fuzzy lines or gray borders.

For sure, thought Beck, Grimm was a coward if ever there was one. Beck, entirely without malice, had once drawn Grimm's attention to a cockroach on the floor of the Headquarters cafeteria. The man's reaction was astonishing—total loss of speech, quivering, near convulsive tremors. Grimm was a huge ball of a man. His three chins and rolls of midriff blubber enhanced Beck's image of Grimm as a hypocrite who was only out for Number One. There was no love lost between the two men, and they both knew it.

"We've got a lot of business to attend to, and I know the Chief has another meeting this morning," said Grimm loudly, so the other Council members already seated around the table could hear. Grimm's smugly crinkled nose and pointed barb were plainly meant to imply that Beck had nothing else to do with his time. There was little Beck could do but swallow his pride.

Beck had taken a seat opposite Grimm, his back to the windows. He was sitting next to Don Farringdon, an appliance repairman by vocation, who had become very active in the large, mostly lower class communities of west and southwest Cahill. Beck felt a certain respect for the man. He was always polite and well spoken, and had invested years of enormous energy into helping his neighbors. Since Grimm was still shuffling notes, Beck and Farringdon took the opportunity to exchange greetings.

"Will you have a moment after the meeting?" Farringdon asked quietly.

"Assuming our good friend doesn't get carried away with himself," Beck replied, nodding toward Horace Grimm.

"Good morning, Chief, and ladies and gentlemen," Grimm began with formality, as impressed with his newfound position as the *nouveau riche* are with their wealth. "As you know, our Chairperson is ill today. We certainly wish her a speedy recovery."

Grimm stopped to clear his throat, which patently did not need clearing.

"The first item on our agenda this morning is to discuss the rise in the number of incidents of police brutality around the nation. Of course, we haven't experienced this type of conduct in Cahill—or at least the press hasn't uncovered it yet!"

Grimm paused for maximum effect.

"Chief Vincent," he resumed, "maybe you can tell the Council the steps being taken to ensure that similar excesses don't occur in our department."

Beck was just about to jump to Grimm's challenge ahead of Vincent, when someone's beeper went off. By the time Beck realized it was his own pager and fumbled under his jacket to turn off the offending device, he had become the center of attention. One glance at the LED readout, though, made Beck forget all the present company. It was Chet calling, and he had entered a 3, their prearranged code indicating an emergency. Casting a "Too bad, Charlie" look at Grimm, Beck mumbled something and left the room to find a phone.

The call went through right away. "Yeah, Chet, what's up?"

"Benny, we've had another robbery in our neighborhood, and this one's a humdinger."

Officer Chester Carter, an outstanding veteran of the Cahill Police Department, had been assigned eight years earlier as a neighborhood officer to work with the East Cahill Citizens Patrol. The assignment was a dispensation granted to many of Cahill's neighborhoods, and Beck had capitalized on their officer by building numerous community programs around his position.

"Cough it up, Chet. Don't keep me dangling from skyhooks."

Sometimes, Beck was annoyed by Carter's sense of drama.

"Benny, do you remember Mrs. Stein? The eighty-two-year-old lady whose purse was snatched two weeks ago? Remember she picked Puppy's photo off the mug shot cards?"

"Go ahead," Beck urged. He often wondered how these crooks came up with such aliases.

"Well, two nights ago Mrs. Stein was coming home about seven-thirty, and as she was walking toward her front steps, a man about twenty years old came up from behind and demanded her purse. Mrs. Stein says he had a knife. She was carrying her purse under her coat, but she handed it over to him right away. Then the scoundrel lunges and stabs her in the left abdomen. She's at Mount Hope Hospital right now, and the doctor's saying she won't make it!"

"Whew!" Beck exhaled. "Who took the report?"

"Officer Greene. He's one of the rookies on Sergeant Gilling's squad. I was out of town yesterday, so I didn't catch wind of it until the Sarge called me this morning, or else I would've told you about it yesterday."

"That's okay. If Greene is in the station now, see what you can get out of him. I'll meet you at Mount Hope in fifteen minutes."

Beck returned to the conference room and whispered apologetically in Vincent's ear, "Sorry, Chief. Chet just gave me some bad news, and I've gotta go. I'll call you later."

As he gathered his papers, Beck inwardly rejoiced at having escaped Grimm's homilies on American injustice. Facing the assembled Council members, he said in a sugary voice, "I apologize, ladies and gentlemen. I have an emergency to attend to, but I'm sure Mr. Grimm will keep a productive meeting going until the Chief has to leave."

Wondering if this return shot had hit the mark, Beck turned back to observe Grimm's reaction. He was greeted by a terrifying apparition. There was Grimm, speechless, face puffed out grotesquely, eyeballs bulging, lower jaw hanging open. Beck's first thought was, "Heart attack!" Just as he was about to dash around the table, Grimm, who was by now making unintelligible gurgle-choke sounds from his gullet, began pointing his index finger in front of him. He was trembling so badly that Beck could see the fat shake like jello. He looked like Mount St. Helens three seconds before the top blew.

Everyone's gaze followed the direction of Grimm's pointing finger out the plate glass. What followed was a shout and a mad rush for the windows. On the adjacent building, the workman in overalls was hanging on for dear life to the end of the tall crane's cable. He was already forty feet off the roof, and the cable was still being spooled upward at full speed! And there was no one in the cab to stop it! In another instant the man would be mangled as the cable was pulled through the massive pulley at the top of the crane. *His only option was to let go!*

2

CHIEF VINCENT SPRINTED FOR THE DOOR.

"Mack!" he barked to his aide, Major MacDougal. "Disaster on the roof of the Long Office Building next door! Get Fire to respond, and I also want the whole building sealed off immediately. No unauthorized persons on the roof until CID has been up there."

The Chief, always a man of action, had set his resources in motion even before he knew the doomed man's fate. Returning to the conference room, he discovered the Council members in a state of shock. One glance out the window told him why.

Evidently, the workman had swung the cable like a pendulum, just far enough to clutch one of the crane's arm struts right before he would have been crushed by the pulley. Vincent saw him now, seventy feet above the roofline, his arms and legs hugging the very top of the crane, like an infant monkey clinging to its mother when confronted by a menacing tiger. Assuming the man did not pass out from his trauma, the Fire Department would be able to get him down in one piece.

Major MacDougal produced a pair of binoculars, but Vincent, relieved to see the disaster avoided, waved them off. Sirens were screaming in the distance.

"Mind if I look?" said Beck rhetorically as he picked up the glasses. Fortunately, the morning sun was not in his eyes as he focused up at the lucky workman.

"Unbelievable!" Beck exclaimed to himself. "He's just a boy! Couldn't be more than eighteen, tops."

Beck could see the young man's short-cropped hair and the sun sparkling off a gold tooth. Beck lowered his gaze to the cab of the crane, which was still in the morning shadow cast by Police Headquarters.

"Hm," he mused, as he handed the binoculars back to MacDougal. He jotted something in his notebook.

"*Oy vey!* I'm supposed to meet Chet in ten minutes!" Beck muttered. He looked around to say goodbye to Vincent, but the Chief had left the room again.

Beck opted for the stairs, and bounded down two at a time. He knew he was as graceful as a walrus on a Slip-n-Slide, and the jolts certainly strained his unexercised limbs, but people had been known to turn into stone waiting for the elevators in Headquarters. Besides, this was no time to pamper his dignity. If Mrs. Stein were still conscious—why hadn't he thought to ask Chet about that?—she could unlock the whole puzzle of the robberies.

Beck reached the lobby level and opened the door to enter the Headquarters garage. He had parked the ECCP Command Car on the first aisle. Despite his rush, he felt a stir of pride as he eased himself into the plush surroundings of their organization's well-equipped vehicle. The new car smell still lingered in the suede upholstery. The sleek white vehicle was marked prominently with blue and yellow reflective stripes along the entire length of each side. The large ECCP logos affixed smartly to each door complemented the rooftop emergency light bar and spotlight.

With a parting wave to the sentry, Beck sped onto the street and quickly entered the freeway.

"Benny to Dovid," he called over the radio. "Can you copy?"

Baruch Hashem, he thought, they had installed a twenty-five watt amplifier in the Command Car, enabling him to radio the office from most points in the city.

"Go ahead," crackled the reply.

Dovid Berg, a young man of twenty-one, had joined the ECCP staff the previous year to help coordinate the many programs and activities.

"I'm on my way to Mount Hope to visit someone, so I'll be a half hour late. Any messages that can't wait?"

"Just one. Judge O'Brien would like you to call. Do you have his number?"

"Probably, but the only way I'll reach my notebook right now is if I jump into the back seat, and Rusie might not like me performing that stunt at sixty miles an hour." Rus Beck, affectionately known since childhood as Rusie, had been married to Beck for nearly twenty-five years.

"I doubt if the insurance company would like it either," chuckled Dovid. "O'Brien is on 3-6-9-4. See you in a while."

"Thanks," Beck signed off.

It was just past nine a.m. He might still be able to catch the judge before court started. He lifted the mobile phone to dial.

Over many years of assisting crime victims and pursuing criminals through the courts, all of the Circuit Court judges in Cahill had become familiar with the East Cahill Citizens Patrol. Beck saw the judges as one of the key elements in their fight against crime, and he had built many bridges of friendship with most of the judges.

"Judge O'Brien's chambers," said a stiff female voice on the other end of the line.

Beck could tell she was a new secretary. It usually took a year or more before they shed their cloned robot voices and took on something of the personalities of the judges they worked for.

"This is Dr. Beck with the East Cahill Citizens Patrol. The judge phoned me a while ago, and I'm returning his call."

"One moment, please."

Beck knew it was never a moment. Unfortunately, he was paying air time, and the ECCP was not rich.

"Hi, Benny," Judge O'Brien came on the line. "I've only got a minute, but I wanted to let you know that Mark Lowery is going to be in my court next Monday—a week from today—for a VOP hearing. I remember from last year that you all are interested in his case."

"We certainly are, Judge," Beck replied. "We weren't directly involved in the case, but I remember the name Lowery. Didn't he pull a robbery in one of the fast food places?"

"Good memory, Benny. It was at Woody's."

"Oh, right. Listen, Judge, I really appreciate your alerting me. We'll be there. How's your wife and family?"

"Just fine, and thanks for asking. We'll have to get together so I can show you our Grand Canyon pictures. Sorry I can't chat now, but I've got to go on the bench."

"Right. Have a good day."

Beck was often amazed at how much consideration they received from the courts. It helped to be a religious person in this environment, he thought. Even in the topsy-turvy morality of the late twentieth century, the old, traditional principles of right and wrong still commanded an instinctive respect. When a *kehillah* stood up against wrongdoing in responsible ways, under the guidance of *gedolei Yisrael*, it demonstrated that it was on Hashem's side. Hashem would reciprocate and stand up for such a *kehillah* in its times of need.

"*Oy!* I've got to get off here." Beck had been lost in reverie and almost missed his exit.

Mount Hope Hospital, just four blocks from the freeway, was one of the city's largest hospitals, and only two miles from the *frum* community. When the *eiruv* was built twenty years earlier, it had been extended to include Mount Hope.

The excitement in Headquarters this morning had energized Beck. Now, as he walked briskly from the parking lot to the hospital, the melancholy prospect of visiting a seriously injured, elderly Jewish woman sobered him. Mrs. Stein's rights had been violated, and he was determined that someone would pay dearly, the indulgent American establishment notwithstanding.

Chet Carter was pacing near Room 602 and saw Beck emerge from the elevator. He gesticulated vigorously, but Beck was obviously lost in thought. Carter had worked with Beck long enough to recognize the older man's philosophizing moods. Beck called it his "*mussar* mood," and they often joked about it. One time Beck had collided headlong with a wall in JFK airport because he was so engrossed in teaching Carter how the existence of *Olam Haba* could be proven from a watermelon.

Carter's long strides carried him quickly through the hall toward Beck, until he was close enough to emit in a loud hush, "Benny! Down here."

"I could've given birth waiting for you to show up," Carter ribbed. "Lose your way, or something?"

"Sorry," Beck took the challenge. "The Chief held me up. He wanted to promote you this year, but I convinced him you're earning too much money as it is."

The joke was transparent. Beck's views on the miserably low salaries of the police officers were well known in City Hall.

Beck was glad Carter had helped clear away his distractions. They had work to do.

"Actually, Chet, we did have some excitement at Headquarters this morning. Ask me later. By the way, how is she?" Beck nodded his head down the hall in the direction of Room 602.

"Same as you would be if someone stuck a knife five inches into your abdomen! The only vitals he hit were the spleen and edge of the intestine, or else she would have died on the spot. She's had a lot of internal bleeding. She's lucky to be alive."

It was more than luck, Beck thought to himself. History does not merely unfold at random. *Hakadosh Baruch Hu* orchestrates every detail of every event throughout the universe, including this sad encounter between Mrs. Stein and her assailant. May He have mercy on the poor woman, Beck mentally added. The gruesome specter of a five-inch penetration made him shudder and reawakened his anger.

"She was conscious," Carter continued, "and fully coherent during the ambulance transport right after the assault, but she's been in and out of consciousness ever since. Greene couldn't give me much, and now that Homicide has taken over the investigation, I really can't get involved in it."

"Why not?" Beck sounded a little irritated.

"Department rules. Sorry, boss. I'll be able to keep up with their findings, but I will not be able to do much myself."

The police department's Homicide Section was a crack squad of experienced and dedicated detectives. Unfortunately, along with many other departmental units, the staff size had remained constant as the case load had risen over the past decade. Beck was not optimistic that Mrs. Stein's incident would get the attention he wanted for it.

"You know Lt. Furnas, don't you?" Carter asked, referring to the commanding officer of the Homicide Section. "Why not give him a call and ask him to push the case?"

"Good idea, but I think I'll go through the Chief. It'll carry more weight." Beck tried not to abuse his relationship with Chief Vincent. However, he did not want this case given short shrift.

"I did check with the crime lab," Carter added. "Mrs. Stein was carrying a brand new handbag, but they couldn't lift any usable fingerprints. Other than a couple of curly red hairs caught in the bag's snap, it was completely empty."

Beck was slightly startled as the door to Room 602 opened and a middle-aged woman stepped out. She was wearing a dark blue suit, with a white, satin kerchief tied neatly around her neck, setting off her long dark hair.

"Sorry, Benny," Carter whispered, "I forgot to tell you that Mrs. Stein's daughter was in the room with her."

Beck's eyes widened. "Whoa! Let's not let this fish get away."

"Cute," Carter retorted. "What else could I expect from someone who just spent a month at sea?"

"Quit it," Beck ordered. "She's headed this way. Maybe she can tell us something. *I'm* not bound by department rules, am I?"

"No comment," Carter retorted.

By now the woman had come abreast of the two men. She was crying softly. Age had etched a few telling wrinkles above her cheeks.

"Excuse me, ma'am," Beck caught her eye. "My name is Dr. Beck. I'm with the East Cahill Citizens Patrol, and we work together with the police. This is Police Officer Carter."

The woman glanced at the two men. They could see she was too distracted to be suspicious.

"I'm Mrs. Holland," answered the woman in a weak

voice. "I'm Mrs. Stein's daughter."

"I know," Beck sought to reassure her of his authenticity. "How is she?"

"The same. I just thank Heaven she's still alive. Maybe there's hope." The woman was severely distraught.

"I know you must be quite worried," Beck tried to comfort her. "We have to stay up here, and I don't want to keep you, so maybe we'll just walk you to the elevator."

She seemed to appreciate the support.

"There's only one thing we've been trying to get more information on," Beck added in an offhand tone. "Do you know what your mother had in her handbag when it was taken?"

"Officer, that was a brand new bag," she said.

Beck smiled inwardly. He could have passed for a rabbi, maybe, but he looked as much like a policeman as an Eskimo looks like an Irishman. Her mistake would make the conversation easier.

"I gave her that bag for her birthday two nights ago at dinner," she continued. "All she put in it were her wallet and checkbook. The police found the bag and her checkbook lying by the curb down the street from her house, but the wallet was gone. Fortunately, she only had a couple of dollars in it."

"That really was lucky," Carter jumped into the questioning for the first time. "Did she have anything else in the wallet?"

Carter's sleuthing instincts had made him quickly forget departmental rules. He was a born bloodhound, Beck chuckled to himself.

"Well, just her credit cards. Several years ago, I convinced Mother to drop all of her credit cards except Visa. She also loves to shop at Macy's, so she kept that one, too. I reported both of them stolen yesterday morning."

The two men sensed that she was talking freely now. She seemed relieved just to have interested ears listening to her.

"I can imagine how much this thing weighs on your mind," Carter pressed on. "Could I ask you just one more thing?"

They had arrived at the elevator. Beck punched the down button, and when it failed to light up, he pushed it again, just to make sure that the gnomes in charge of elevators received the summons.

"Of course, officer," Mrs. Holland replied. "I'm okay, and I want to help you as much as I can."

"Well, it's terrific to hear you say that," Carter encouraged.

Beck knew that Carter was fishing for a lot more than met the eye. He had studied Carter's style for years. Interrogating perpetrators of crime, Carter could be ruthless. Beck just *knew* that he must keep a set of sharpened bamboo sticks hidden somewhere in the station house. However, when talking to victims of crime, Carter conveyed genuine gentleness, sense of caring and helpfulness. Right now, he was trying to give the overwrought woman all the support he could muster and still extract some information from her.

"I was just curious to know exactly what time you gave your mother the handbag two nights ago," he said.

Mrs. Holland raised her eyes in thought for a moment. Beck noticed the puffy bags of exhaustion under her lower lids.

"Let's see," she answered. "We had dinner together—just the two of us—at the Coachman. Even when my husband was alive, it was always our annual tradition to take Mother out for her birthday. I had prearranged for the waiter to surprise Mother with a birthday cake for dessert. He was Chinese or Korean or something, so he sang 'Happy Birthday' with an oriental accent. We had a good laugh from that.

That must have been about seven o'clock. And then I took out the present. I had wrapped it in some lovely paper and taped a pink satin bow to the corner. Mother lost her evening bag several months ago, and she was self-conscious about using her regular bag when she was dressed up. In fact, all she brought to the restaurant were her wallet and checkbook. Mother is very fastidious and proper. That's why I was so excited about giving her a new bag. It was really beautiful, but then this thing had to happen..."

The elevator arrived.

Good timing, thought Beck to himself. Her tongue is going Mach 2, and the way she's headed she'll be mired in an emotional minefield any second now.

He viewed all female sentimentality as mawkishness. The only exception was his wife. Ironically, her feminine emotionality only stirred his affection for her; but with other women, he had no patience. He knew it was his shortcoming, and he tried now to do *teshuvah*. He berated himself for not empathizing more with Mrs. Holland and forced himself to feel her anguish. *Yiddishkeit*, he knew, demanded that a person train even his thoughts and emotions.

"Chet, would you please hold the elevator a second," Beck directed. He handed a business card to Mrs. Holland. "Here's the number for both myself and Officer Carter. Our beeper numbers are on here, too. If there's anything we can do for you or your mother, please call us anytime, day or night. We want to do everything we can to help you."

"Thanks for understanding." Mrs. Holland sounded genuinely appreciative as she tucked the card into her purse. She stepped into the elevator while Carter held the door back for her.

"Oh, yes, and one more thing," Beck added. "Do you have a Book of Psalms at home?"

"Why yes, I believe I do." Mrs. Holland was puzzled.

"Good. Recite Psalm 130 every morning with a lot of feeling until your mother is well. It'll help."

A look of confusion flashed across the woman's face. For the first time in their conversation, she seemed to realize that she had been talking to an Orthodox Jew.

"Thanks, officer, I mean, rab— . . . uh . . ." she stammered, and let the sentence die. "Oh, and I almost forgot, I wanted to tell you something else. It probably doesn't mean anything, but earlier this morning, when Mother was semi-conscious, she kept repeating the word 'daisy,' or something like that. I really couldn't make it out so well. Anyway, thanks again for your help."

She disappeared from view as the elevator doors converged like the waters of the Yam Suf. Beck was left wondering whether they were on the Jewish side of the doors, or the Egyptian side.

3

"HM . . . DAISY," BECK PONDERED, STROKING HIS BEARD and glancing sidelong at his companion.

"Don't look at me, boss," Carter said. "You know something I don't know?"

"Not at all. It's just that subliminal facts sometimes spill out of a person when they're in that halfway state of consciousness. It might be significant. Anyway, what're your plans now?"

Carter hesitated a moment. "I'll probably go home and run some errands. You know, I had asked the Sarge to call me if any more robberies took place in the ECCP area, so he woke me up at six o'clock this morning with Mrs. Stein's incident. That's why I'm not even in uniform now. I just rushed over."

Beck looked Carter up and down and mentally thanked Hashem for this intensely dedicated officer. Carter was a big man, nearly six feet tall, thirty-five years old and in good physical shape. His black hair and bold features perfectly suited his image as the quintessential police officer. The eight years he had worked with the East Cahill Citizens Patrol were the most productive of his career. He had shared incalculable hours of patrol with over a thousand members of the Jewish community, enduring endless boredom as well as occasional crises. He had resolved countless safety problems in the neighborhood and had won the collective heart of the entire citizenry.

They, in turn, had provided him with the support that no other officer enjoyed anywhere in the city. He could rely on an army of volunteers for any project, or tap into a deep well of information to support any investigation. Above all, he was constantly buoyed by the heartfelt admiration and gratitude of the close-knit community. He had always been a workaholic, but other veteran officers had burned out where he had not.

For his part, Binyamin Beck had invested considerable effort in helping Carter adjust to Jewish customs—their ways of thinking, eating, talking, dressing—in short, their whole way of life. Beck had heard Carter admit that when he was first detailed to the ECCP, his overriding fear had been a slip of the tongue that would offend the community—a "colorful" word or a joke that would be considered inoffensive in "normal" company. As Beck had predicted, though, experience had taught the officer that he had nothing to fear. Indeed, common Hebrew and Yiddish terms had become a natural part of his regular vocabulary.

Besides, Beck reflected, the Jews were a sensitive people, innately respectful of authority, highly self-disciplined and self-motivated. The cohesiveness of the Orthodox community in Cahill was legend. It enjoyed the benefit of a powerful but sensible and altruistic leadership in the persons of the congregational rabbis, whose words carried enormous weight among the people.

"Listen, Chet," Beck wrenched himself back to the present. "How about if you check into the station at three this afternoon, pick up your radio and come over to the office right away. I'd like to have a think session for an hour before you have to leave to set up for this evening's patrol.

Meanwhile, try to get some shut-eye. Put off your errands, if you can. I need you rested and with your brain in gear." Beck flicked a knuckle at the elevator's down button again.

Carter's eyelids drooped slightly at the mere mention of sleep. The recent robberies in the area weighed heavily on the minds of both men.

"As long as I'm here, I'm going to do the *mitzvah* of visiting the sick," said Beck. "Maybe there's something I can do for Mrs. Stein. See you at three."

"Okay," Carter responded, as he stepped into the elevator. "But make sure you give me a call if something comes up."

He's a jewel, Beck reflected as he ambled toward Room 602. We owe a lot to the Cahill Police Department. To link neighborhood officers in tandem with citizen organizations is surely a mark of how innovative and progressive our police force is.

Beck stopped in front of Room 602 and collected himself. He was anxious to see Mrs. Stein, perhaps even to ask her some questions, but he also reminded himself that he was engaging in the *mitzvah* of *bikur cholim*. Beck knew he was no *tzaddik*, but he tried nevertheless to focus his concentration.

He straightened his tie and rapped lightly on the door, then opened it enough to slip inside. As he closed the door most of the way, the room's sterile hospital odor seemed particularly strong. Although the surroundings were bright and well decorated, the cold look of the modern architecture and spotless furnishings struck him as antiseptic and lifeless. Only a pot of begonias, topped with a stuffed, satin heart, softened the stark ambience.

Beck tiptoed to the bed. Mrs. Stein lay nearly lifeless, an IV penetrating her left arm and a ventilator tube in her nose. Her sallow, sickly pallor made her seem far older than her eighty-two years, while her full head of white hair made her appear ghostly. Beck's heart went out to her. He would have willingly borne some of her pain himself. To his surprise, her eyes were partially open, but he could not tell whether she was conscious.

He edged closer to the bed and bent over the woman. She lowered her dull gray eyes to look at him.

"Are you feeling better?" he said softly, encouraged that she was aware of his presence. He remembered that she was hard of hearing and repeated the question much louder. "Are you feeling better, Mrs. Stein?"

He felt like a fool. What did one say in a situation like this? He saw a bowl of ice on her food tray.

"Would you like a little piece of ice?" It seemed disrespectful to talk so loudly to a woman whose life was in the balance.

She shook her head ever so slightly. She could not speak with the ventilator in place, and probably would not have had the energy to talk in any case. He would have to ask yes-or-no questions.

"The police told me it was a short man who robbed you," Beck opened the subject rhetorically.

She nodded. He did not know how far he should press her. Obviously, her health was the paramount consideration.

"He was a young man without a beard, wasn't he?" It was a safe guess, and Beck wanted to establish a level of rapport with her. She barely nodded her affirmation.

"Did you see if he got into a car afterwards?"

She nodded again.

"Was he alone?"

She shook her head.

"Oh, another man was in the car, too?"

She concurred.

Beck wondered how much he should push the distressed woman. The need to raise his voice only doubled his guilt and his apprehension that he had no business holding this conversation in the first place. But he suspected that Mrs. Stein would have been eager to communicate had she felt stronger. He wanted to know more about the other man in the getaway car. Probably the driver.

"Was he short, too?" Beck ventured.

This time she barely shook her head "no." Beck could see she had shifted her eyes to stare at his beard. She appeared to be struggling inside, as though she wanted desperately to communicate. She was tiring, but he figured he would try one more question. He took a deep breath and mustered his courage.

"Do you know what 'daisy' means?"

But the woman's eyes had closed. She was either asleep or unconscious again. He relaxed his shoulders and sighed with relief, as though he had just crept across a bed of fresh eggs without cracking one.

"Hashem should give you a *refuah shelaimah*," Beck whispered.

He adjusted the cover, which had partially slipped off the bed, and stepped lightly toward the door. He opened the door quickly and was startled to find himself face to face with a large, scowling man about thirty years old.

Beck's heart jumped to his throat. It was the man with the ponytail! The one who had been on the roof of the Long Office Building this morning. His deep-set black eyes and prominent, hooked nose gave Beck the shivers.

Beck composed himself instantly. He would try to bluff.

"Can I help you?" he said with authority.

"Er . . . no . . . Ya know this ol' woman?"

He had a rasping voice. The scowl had disappeared, and Beck sensed he was trying to play innocent.

"I'm a close friend," Beck fibbed, "but what business is it of yours? What's your name?" Beck was suddenly concerned for Mrs. Stein's safety. He wished that Carter were still around.

"I was jes' visitin' a gal nex' door here, an' I heared loud talkin' in this room as I was passin' by."

Beck knew the man was lying. "Well I suggest you continue on your way," he asserted authoritatively.

Beck stood in the doorway until the man had disappeared into the elevator. He went to the nurses' station and related the entire incident to the head nurse. She immediately summoned the head of hospital security, and Beck reviewed the details for him once more.

"Please keep an eye out for Mrs. Stein," Beck addressed the nurse. "Here's my card. If you don't mind, please give me a call if that fellow comes back, or if any other suspicious people come around. Mrs. Stein has already lived through enough trauma."

"Thanks for alerting me, Dr. Beck," the nurse replied. "We'll try to keep someone in the room as much as possible."

Beck's apprehension was hardly assuaged. These crooks would stop at nothing, he was convinced. He paused once more at Room 602 and poked his head in. Mrs. Stein was sleeping peacefully.

"*Hakadosh Baruch Hu*, please watch over her. You know that everything we do is merely *hishtadlus*. Please help the police catch these ruthless villains, and bring Your righteous justice down on their heads."

Descending in the elevator, Beck snickered at himself. Who was he that Hashem should listen to his *tefillos*? Well, maybe in the merit of their *kehillah*, a *kehillah* where people exerted themselves incessantly on behalf of each other, Hashem would "exert" Himself on behalf of Mrs. Stein and everyone else in their community.

Beck was still shaken by his confrontation with the ponytail man. As he started the Command Car, he was sorry he had not tailed the man and tried to get his license plate number. The guy was somehow connected to Mrs. Stein, Beck was sure. Mrs. Stein had indicated that the driver of the getaway car was tall. Maybe it was the ponytail man. Wouldn't that be some coincidence!

Beck punched the radio mike button. "Benny to Dovid."

"Stand by," came the radio reply. "I'm on the phone."

"That's okay," Beck transmitted. "I'm on my way over, if this red light will ever change. See you soon."

Beck glanced at the dash clock and began planning the rest of his day. He ought to call Rusie and coordinate with her. He needed to test Miriam for her *Navi* exam tomorrow. She was the sixth of their nine children, a bright and sensitive child. She was becoming a young lady, too. It was rewarding to watch each of the children metamorphose into responsible adults. He should also call Chief Vincent as soon as he reached the office.

H-o-n-k! Beck was wrested from his thoughts. He looked at the light. How long had it been green? He stepped on the gas, embarrassed. There must be a long line behind him now, he imagined. He glanced in the mirror.

Oh, no! His heart leaped. The ponytail man was right behind him!

"XNC422," he noted on the dash clipboard, his adrenalin racing. "Well, at least I got his tag. Red Camaro. I wonder if *he* tailed *me*! But then why did he honk and give himself away? On the other hand, maybe he wasn't the one who honked. Could've been someone two or three cars back. I don't like the smell of this whole thing."

Beck watched in his mirror as the Camaro turned at the next intersection. Now that the man had been discovered, was he making himself scarce? Or was it just another coincidence? Beck was still puzzling through the morning's events when he entered the ECCP parking lot. He drove to the end of the lot, near the side door that was leading to the Patrol's office, but all the parking spaces were occupied. Backing up, he finally pulled into an empty slot near the driveway.

The building's owner was a *frum* businessman in the community, and he permitted the ECCP to occupy a third-floor office virtually rent free. It was to his benefit, of course, because it meant that one or more policemen were in the building almost around the clock.

Beck climbed the stairs slowly and entered the office which had become such a busy nerve center over the years. They had renovated the premises themselves when they moved the ECCP headquarters here four years earlier. Beck had designed the office as one large, open room to facilitate interaction among the staff. The hardwood floors, original oak doors and moldings and soft mushroom color of the walls lent a coziness to the surroundings. Rusie had also insisted on sewing draperies for the tall windows, and she had selected an off white material spattered with pretty, lavender wisteria blooms. The total effect of the ambience quickly put visitors at ease. Over the years, a long parade of police commanders, FBI officials, judges, politicians and other public servants had tramped up for meetings.

"Hi, Benny," Dovid Berg greeted Beck. "Coffee's fresh."

"Oh, thanks, Dovid."

He looked over at the young man sitting at a tawny oak desk. Dovid always wore long-sleeved white shirts, and lately had begun wearing only black or dark slacks.

"Anything new?" Beck inquired.

"Not much. Rockland sent us a nice donation. You know I've been after them for a year."

"I know," replied Beck. "How much?"

"Two thousand."

"That's great!"

Dovid was a handsome fellow, with jet black hair and a neatly trimmed beard. He was endowed with copious energy. He had been doing more and more fundraising for the ECCP, and Beck was proud of his progress. Not only did it help the organization, but Beck noticed that the more the young man dealt with the public, the more he blossomed with self-confidence and maturity.

Dovid had not come from an impeccable background. His parents lived in some wealthy, assimilated community in California, and he had no other relatives other than a distant cousin and her family in New York. Beck tried to give Dovid frequent encouragement.

"Listen, Dovid, will you do me a favor. Get hold of Owen Cunningham. He's a District Attorney. Tell him I'll be at Mark Lowery's Violation of Probation hearing in front of Judge O'Brien next Monday. I assume it'll be at nine-thirty, but just confirm it with him. Also, can you get out the file on Lowery and stick it in my box. To be honest with you, I don't remember the case, and I'm going to have to read through it before the hearing."

"Sure," Dovid said. "You also have a message to call Mr. Farringdon. He said he saw you this morning."

"Thanks. I like that man," Beck remarked. "The grass doesn't grow under his feet. Say, what's this?" Beck had picked up a neon pink flyer from his IN box.

"Oh, I'm glad you saw that," Dovid said. "That came in the mail to my house yesterday. It's an announcement of an Israeli folk concert next week, and they mention that Isaiah Golan will be the guest performer. I knew him in my former life. He's a Hebrew Christian missionary. How did they find my address, that's what I want to know?"

"Dovid, they have all kinds of devices. They could've gotten it from your parents."

Dovid was an only child. His father had retired from a very successful precious metals brokerage firm that had taken him all over the world. Both Dovid and his mother had often accompanied his father, especially when he went to Europe. That was where the teenager had become entangled in Christianity.

He once related to Beck his emotions the first time he entered a cathedral in Munich. It was on Neuhauserstrasse, a block inside the Karlstor Gate. Dovid remembered that the grandeur of the building had taken his breath away. He remained inside for two hours, spellbound, awed by the majestic surroundings and the formality of the service. When he stepped back out into the prosaic streetscape, the anticlimax was palpable. The experience had set the scene. Not long after Dovid's family returned to California, the boy went to a Hebrew Christian convention.

"Benny, when I look back, I see how lucky I was that I was accepted at the university here."

"Not lucky," Beck corrected. "*Hashgachah pratis.*"

"Okay, you're right," Dovid said, rising to his feet. "Hashem was watching over me. I didn't realize that I had been dragged into a cult. I had even lost my will to think. Things were hammered into us so many times, and from so many different angles, that it became our entire world. If someone raised a problem, we were programmed to close our minds, to give pat answers that skirted the question, or just to walk away. Certainly, we were not allowed to question the theology that had been drilled into us.

"In fact, if Rabbi Marcus hadn't asked me to help him put up his *sukkah* two years ago, I would still be licking the dirt off Golan's boots. I had never heard of a *sukkah* before then. I helped for two hours, and we got the walls up. The next day, Mrs. Marcus called to invite me for *Yom Tov*. I still can't tell you why I accepted the invitation. We had been admonished to stay away from religious Jews, but somehow, her invitation seemed so innocent.

"I stepped inside their *sukkah* on the first night . . . the beautiful pictures, festive decorations, candles, the smell of pine . . . the children dressed like royalty . . . the courtly table set with silver and china . . . the crystal decanter brimming with rich, purple wine. I was thunderstruck!"

Beck could see that Dovid was worked up. He had never spoken much about his past before.

"Benny, do you know what that elegant scene—that grand *sukkah*—reminded me of? *Munich!* Here was all the splendor and glory of religion *outside* the church building! Such majesty! Such aristocracy!

"All at once, it hit me that the Munich cathedral was just a facade; all the glitter was merely tinsel. Stripped of its trappings, it was only an impersonal museum, a stadium with salaried players in fancy uniforms—and I was nothing but a spectator. The show was thrilling, but it left little room for audience participation. The *sukkah*, on the other hand, was not only magnificent in its beauty, but it was lovingly occupied by the royal party who had created it.

"And the Marcuses took it all in with the nonchalance of a duke's family in their own palace. I had to fight back my tears, right in front of all those children."

Dovid had walked over to the window next to Beck's desk and stood watching the cars flit by on the boulevard.

"That's very interesting, Dovid," Beck commented, "and I can see your point. Every *baal teshuvah* has his own story to tell. I think yours is one of the most moving I have heard."

Instantly Beck was sorry he had opened his mouth. It broke the spell and made Dovid feel self-conscious.

"Sorry, Benny, I didn't mean to unburden myself on

you. It's just that when that flyer jumped out of the mailbox at me, I was abruptly confronted by all those horrible ghosts of the past."

"I can imagine," Beck reassured him with a light touch on the shoulder. "But I don't think you have to worry about it. When something like that arrives, just pitch it in the trash. You know I could use some of that coffee after all the excitement I had this morning." He wanted to get the spotlight off Dovid.

"Why, Benny? What happened?"

"Dovid, you'll never believe it. In fact, I still have trouble believing it. I had a front row seat this morning watching a young man nearly get killed."

"What!" Dovid jumped. He whirled around to face Beck, his eyes opened wide.

"Just what I said." Beck proceeded to describe the entire incident of the man who narrowly escaped mutilation and certain death at the top of the big crane.

"Wow!" exclaimed Dovid. "That's a real freak accident."

"Well, to be honest, I'm not convinced it was an accident, although it's not really my business. I'm sure the police will check it out. The Chief had CID up there within minutes. Actually, I'm going to give him a call and see if there's any information they can release. Meanwhile, why don't you see if you can dig out the Lowery file?"

Beck finished pouring his coffee and glanced through three letters on his desk that Dovid had prepared for his signature. He lifted the phone and punched the numbers to Chief Vincent's private line.

"Chief Vincent's office."

"Hi, Major. This is Benny Beck." Beck liked dealing with Major MacDougal. He was a paragon of efficiency. "I was going to bother the Chief, but since you answered, you probably have as much information as he does. I was wondering what happened in that crane incident this morning?"

"Dr. Beck, the best we can tell, it was an unfortunate accident. The cable take-up reel somehow slipped into gear. There wasn't even anyone in the cab at the time. That young man was standing on top of a ten-foot scaffolding, but we're still not sure why he was holding onto the cable. Anyway, he's safe and sound now."

"Major, you don't know the name of the company doing the repair work, do you?" Beck probed.

"No, I don't. Would you like me to find out?"

"It would be great if you could. I'm sure the papers will report it this evening, but if you find out before then and have a chance to give me a call, I would certainly appreciate it."

"Of course," MacDougal replied. "By the way, we did get the identity of the victim. Are you interested?"

"Sure," Beck said, as he picked up a pencil. "What's the name?"

Beck gripped the receiver as MacDougal said, "Mark Lowery."

4

"WHAT!" BECK CRIED, THEN CAUGHT HIMSELF. "SORRY, Major, I thought I recognized the name, but I was confusing it with someone else. Listen, thanks for the information. Let's hope we never have to witness another horror like that one."

"I'll second that. Have a good day," MacDougal said as he hung up.

Beck set down the phone slowly. "Dovid, I smell a rotten fish, but I can't identify the species. MacDougal said the fellow who was almost killed on the crane this morning is Mark Lowery."

"Jumpin' Jehosaphat! Benny, could it be the same guy?"

"We'll find out next Monday, I guess," offered Beck, "because I'm going to be at the VOP hearing. Now I'm *really* curious to see his file. Would you mind getting it out while I call Mr. Farringdon back?"

Beck picked up the telephone message with Farringdon's number, but his thoughts were on Lowery and the crane accident. If Lowery had been in trouble before, he was most likely still associating with bad company. Beck's experiences over the years had brought him to the unhappy conclusion, "once a criminal, always a criminal." The prisons certainly did nothing to reform their guests. "Prison Rehabilitation" fell in the same pack of euphemistic lies as *"Arbeit Macht Frei"* and "Government of the Proletariat."

Maybe Lowery was mixed up in drugs. Maybe one of Lowery's good "friends" worked for the same roofing company and had tried to do him in. Beck did not know much about heavy construction equipment, but it seemed absurd that dangerous machinery would be built without multiple safeguards. How could a motor just "slip" into gear spontaneously? The police ought to take this more seriously. At least, they should consult with the manufacturer to determine if such an accident *were* plausible. Beck wondered if there was a manufacturer or dealer nearby.

His thoughts were interrupted by a facetious voice on the other end of the line.

"Kelly's Pool Hall. Eight Ball speaking." Beck had dialed Farringdon too mechanically.

"Sorry," Beck muttered sheepishly. "Wrong number."

He dialed Farringdon again, this time with closer attention.

"Hello, Mr. Farringdon? This is Benny Beck."

"Oh, hi," Farringdon replied. "Thanks for calling me back. Say, if you don't mind, I'd rather you call me Don."

"Sure," answered Beck. "I'm sorry I ran out of the meeting this morning, but we had a little crisis back here that I had to take care of. That was some accident we witnessed this morning with that man on the crane, wasn't it?"

"Scary. I don't think I've ever been so shaken up, and you're talking to someone who fought in the jungles of Vietnam. I've got an urge to send that fellow a bouquet of roses just to congratulate him on still being alive. I bet he felt like death warmed over. I wonder who he is."

"Ha!" Beck appreciated Farringdon's metaphor, but he decided not to offer any information.

"Say, Benny, can you hold on a minute? One of my salesmen is having a problem. I'll be right back, okay?"

"Sure," Beck replied. "Take your time."

Muzak floated through the phone receiver as Farringdon put Beck on hold, but it failed to register on his mind. Farringdon's words, "congratulations on still being alive," resounded in Beck's ears.

It sounds egotistical, he mused to himself, but maybe Hashem orchestrated Lowery's brush with death just so little old Binyamin Beck could learn a lesson. In truth, *Hakadosh Baruch Hu* rescues *every* human being from so many life threatening events every day, but we are as oblivious to the dangers as a dog crossing a highway, and no more grateful for the successful passage. How many polio or typhoid viruses invade my body in a year, and are instantly pounced upon by the miraculously accurate immune system that the Creator designed in me? How many poisons are cleansed from my tissues every minute and sequestered in my bladder and bowels for elimination? It's a pity that the human excretory system is involuntary. Were toxic nitrogen elimination a conscious act, I might be more grateful to the One who engineered this lifesaving machinery. When I leave the bathroom, I should be as ecstatic as a man who endured ten years on a dialysis machine and suddenly received the rapturous news that a kidney donor had been found. It is a gift to be able to go to the bathroom and discharge my functions normally. Why do I just zoom through the *Asher Yatzar* blessing? I should say it with intense conviction, as though I had just been snatched from calamity—because, indeed, I was!

The Muzak switched to a grating rock beat. Beck winced with annoyance over this intrusion into his reverie. He moved the receiver away from his ear.

And how many drunk drivers, he continued to himself,

do *not* smash their cars headlong into mine during the course of a day? When I arrive home from work each evening, I ought to leap out of my car and immediately bend my knees to the Benefactor Who saved me from the lunatics inhabiting the roadways. And when a friend's infant suffers the woeful tragedy of a SIDS death, *rachmana litzlan,* does it enter my thick skull to thank Hashem the next time *our* baby wakes up from his naps? Why do I blind myself to the millions of miraculous rescues Hashem performs for me in a lifetime?

In truth, every morning, after I rattle off *Modeh Ani* by rote, I should take a deep breath and say, "Hashem, I really mean it. I love You. Thank You so much for returning my *neshamah* and allowing me to live another day." I should be delirious with joy when I awaken each morning. I am mortgaged for life to Hashem with the debt of gratitude I owe Him.

Beck's mind began to conjure up an image of Lowery clinging desperately to the top of the crane. As Beck peered through the narrow tunnel of the binoculars' field of vision, Lowery seemed to stare back at him intently with woeful, importuning eyes. Beck saw Lowery's mouth open wide.

"Benny! Benny!"

The cry seemed to float towards Beck from remote space, piercing his heart. What could he do to rescue the young man? It was a hallucination, Beck knew, because it was impossible to hear Lowery through the glass panels and at such a distance.

"Benny! Benny!" came the distant, feeble plea once again.

Beck shook himself back to reality. The cries were coming from the phone receiver.

"Hello, Don . . . Yeah, sorry, I didn't have the phone to my ear. Everything okay with your salesman now?"

"Not really," Farringdon said, "but that's not your problem. Sorry I put you on hold for so long."

"Not at all," Beck replied. He was still moved by the vision of Lowery begging him for help. He tried to pull himself together.

"By the way, Don, we were discussing the crane accident. Do you remember seeing anyone else on the roof at the time? My attention was riveted so much on that poor fellow, I didn't notice whether other workers were around."

It was not exactly true. Beck had looked hastily, but he had not seen anyone else.

"As a matter of fact, there was someone, Benny. You don't mind me calling you Benny, do you?"

"Of course not."

Farringdon continued. "What actually happened was that about a minute after the accident, a workman appeared on the roof near the cab of the crane. He must have been on the other side of the crane's pad at the time of the accident, where we couldn't see him. Mrs. Jamison was standing next to me, and I remember wondering aloud to her why the guy hadn't jumped in the cab and stopped the cable. Probably, he didn't know anything was happening until it was too late."

"Interesting," Beck pondered. "You don't remember what color shirt he was wearing, do you?"

"How could I forget!" Farringdon replied. "Bright red. Why do you ask?"

"Well, I hope we never have another Council meeting like that one," Beck dodged Farringdon's question. "Thank Heaven, the fellow is safe."

"Amen," Farringdon seconded. "Anyway, the reason I called you was to see if I can twist your arm."

"Go ahead. What's up?" Beck replied.

"You know I live in the Rockford Hill neighborhood in southwest Cahill. We're right on the border with the

Western Police Precinct, and I've been doing a lot of community work over the years in West Cahill."

"I know, Don. Believe me, your reputation has preceded you. You deserve a lot of credit for taking on a very tough job."

"It is tough sometimes, but it has its rewards. I'm not complaining."

Beck knew Farringdon was not one to pity himself.

"What I wanted to discuss with you," Farringdon continued, "is the possibility of launching a citizens patrol in West Cahill along the lines of your group. Do you ever try to help other communities start their own patrols?"

"All the time," Beck answered. "At least a half dozen times a year, if not more. Is there a particular neighborhood you have in mind?"

"Yes, the Wicomb area. It's infested with drugs, violence and near anarchy. Mostly tenement-style living, besides the public projects. The few remaining homeowners and stable residents in the area are frightened and totally frustrated. I've got a group of them meeting tomorrow night in the Wicomb Multi-Purpose Center to discuss the crime situation. The Community Relations sergeant will be there from Western Precinct, but I wanted you to come and plant the idea that they might start an organization like the ECCP. Even if they don't run actual patrols, they could at least operate a successful victims' assistance program like you have. My goal is to help that neighborhood get organized to the point where they can advocate for themselves."

"Don, I'm all for it," Beck said. "You know the old adage, 'Where there's a will, there's a way.' Well that's the whole story when it comes to citizen-based crime fighting. What time's the meeting?"

"Six o'clock. I apologize for the short notice, and I really appreciate your participation. Do you know where the Wicomb Center is located?"

"I've got a good map," Beck replied. "Don't worry, I'll be there, and I'll bring some of our materials. Let's see if we can galvanize them."

"You're a champ," Farringdon said in parting.

Six o'clock would be fine, thought Beck. He would have ample time to return for his *Gemara shiur* at eight. Only the most pressing ECCP business ever interfered with his *shiur*.

He swiveled his chair around. "Dovid, I've got an assignment for you. What do you know about construction equipment?"

"Let's see, Benny. When I was in third grade, my parents gave me an Erector set for making straight A's."

"Cut the clowning," Beck said with mock gruffness. "This is serious. You are about to become an expert on heavy construction cranes. More precisely, I want you to help *me* become an expert. I need to learn more about Caterpillar construction cranes. I'd like you to find the nearest dealer and set up an appointment for me to visit him. I'm willing to travel out of state, if there's no dealer nearby. But the closer to home, the better."

"Okay, boss. I'll start on it right away. Also, I stuck the Lowery file in your box a minute ago."

"Great," Beck responded, as he picked up the manila folder. The notation "Lowery, Mark" appeared in black marker on the index tab. He opened the folder.

"Incidentally, when you call about that crane . . . That's okay, go ahead and get the phone," Beck interrupted himself as the telephone rang.

He was delighted they had hired Dovid a year ago. The young man was intelligent and reliable, and required little supervision. What separated the ECCP from other citizens patrols in the nation, besides its sheer size, was that everyone in the organization undertook his role as a *mitzvah*, a religious obligation, and not a mere civic contribution. Dovid had been *shomer mitzvos* only a couple of years, but this compelling sense of duty had already rooted itself firmly as the driving force in his life. He also possessed sterling *midos* and a good measure of common sense. Beck had occasionally discussed with Rusie some possible *shidduchim* for Dovid, although Dovid claimed he was not yet ready for marriage.

"It's for you, Benny," Dovid said. "Line two. Vivian James, from Mount Hope Hospital."

"Hey, that's the nurse I talked to on Mrs. Stein's floor. Thanks, Dovid."

Beck picked up the phone, "Hello, this is Dr. Beck."

"Dr. Beck, this is Vivian James, the head nurse you spoke to at Mount Hope a little while ago. I wanted to let you know that the gentleman you described returned about twenty minutes after you left. When I confronted him, he said he had made a mistake and was on the wrong floor. I watched him leave, but I notified security anyway, and they said they will call the police. Do you suspect this man of something specific?"

"I'm not sure, Mrs. James." Beck wanted her to keep her guard up, but he did not want to tell her everything he knew.

Now he was worried, though. Mrs. Stein was not attended every minute of the day and night. Anyone could come in and unplug her, and in two minutes' time, she would be dead.

"Thanks for calling me. If you don't mind, I'm going to urge Mrs. Stein's family to get a full-time private nurse to watch her. Does the hospital allow that type of arrangement?"

"Of course," the nurse said. "In fact, we welcome it. Makes our job easier. As long as she's certified, you don't even need permission."

"Excellent. We'll be in touch. And thanks again for your eagle eyes."

"It's my job."

Beck leaned back in his executive chair and brusquely raked his fingers through his beard. He was angry. So much of his time was consumed by criminals. They were violating his right to liberty and the pursuit of happiness, which he defined as the happiness of learning Torah, and the freedom to teach his children the proper way of life.

Crime fighting was a frustrating job. Beck wished the justice system could be streamlined. He longed for the good old days, when the citizenry was afraid of the police. One cop could keep a whole neighborhood in order with just a billy club. Troublemakers knew he would use it, too. Now, it was the police who feared the criminals, and for good reason. So many outstanding officers had been tragically mowed down in the line of duty. They were heroes, true, but their efforts seemed almost quixotic sometimes.

Beck tugged hard on a knot in his beard until a hair was uprooted. He winced. There was no longer a question in his mind that Mrs. Stein's robbery—and perhaps all the recent robberies—were connected to Mark Lowery, the ponytail man and maybe the roofing company. He was glad that Chet and he would be talking this afternoon. There was a lot to talk about.

"Okay, Dovid," Beck finally voiced his deliberations. "I'm no *posek*, but I don't see how we can be lenient when lives are involved. Remember I told you about that guy in the crane incident wearing a ponytail? I forgot to mention that I saw him nosing around Mrs. Stein's room in the hospital. The head nurse tells me that she saw him back there again. Dovid, I'm very concerned about Mrs. Stein's safety. I'll talk to Major Toffat about trying to pick that guy up, and at least get his I.D. I hate to disturb Chet at home, but I need to find Mrs. Stein's daughter and prevail upon her to hire round-the-clock nurses to watch her mother. In fact, I think I'll ask Chet to make the contact with the daughter himself."

"Can I suggest something else?" Dovid responded. "Why don't we get a full time ECCP watch on Mrs. Stein's room until the family makes its own arrangements?"

"Now you're cookin' with gas," Beck said, delighted with Dovid's initiative. "Excellent idea. Why not make some calls off the emergency standby list and round up about five volunteers? Explain the situation to them. I'd suggest three-hour watches, starting as soon as possible. It's Room 602 at Mount Hope. Hopefully, we'll only have to do this through tonight."

"Gotcha, boss," Dovid said enthusiastically.

"That's what I like about you, Dovid. *Zrizus!*" Beck encouraged.

He had long ago discovered that Dovid only needed to be instructed once—if even that much. The rest he figured out on his own, and carried the ball from there.

"Meanwhile," Beck remarked, "I think I'll surprise Rusie and show up for lunch. She deserves more attention than she usually gets from me. People don't realize how quickly this organization would disintegrate were it not for the eager support she gives us all. I'll be back at three. Chet and I are going to review the robbery situation."

Beck put on his black hat. He hoped Rusie would be pleased that he came home for lunch. He liked to spend time with her. She was always interested in the Patrol's affairs, and often he relied on her intuition, even when it clashed with a simple reading of the facts.

Beck stopped at Super Kosher and loaded two heaping bowls from the salad bar. He selected Rusie's favorite dressing, checked through the line and headed home.

The Becks lived on Millbank Row, in the heart of the

frum community. Millbank was only four blocks long, bejeweled with forty-three *shomer Shabbos* families, including two hundred and forty-four children under the age of eighteen—and several more on the way. The Beck's home was the last one on Millbank, a large red brick structure three stories tall, with an expansive porch wrapped around the front and half of the sides. It was typical of the charming, sprawling, turn-of-the-century vintage houses that populated much of East Cahill.

As Beck turned into the driveway, he immediately noticed that most of their wide front lawn had been mowed.

"Now, why did she do that?" he muttered aloud, feeling guilty that Rusie had undertaken one of his chores. "She's probably exhausted now."

He stepped out of the car and gathered up the Super Kosher bag. Climbing the wooden steps he had built long ago to the kitchen in back of the house, he muttered a heartfelt thanks to Hashem for his *eishes chayil*.

Rusie was a highly self-controlled woman, who generally exuded happiness and cheer. But just in case she had experienced a difficult morning, Beck thought, he should be prepared to sympathize with her. If she should hurl a grating word at him, it was only to vent frustration, and he should have enough *seichel* to keep his big mouth shut. A lump of anticipation arose in his throat. He steeled himself as he reached for the doorknob.

"Hi, Binyamin!" Rusie greeted Beck with surprise. Then she saw the salads. "Oh, did you come home for lunch? Yossi's ready for his nap. Let me put him to bed, and then we'll sit down. It's so nice to have you home!"

"Fine," he said. "I've got an incredible story to tell you when you're ready. The most amazing thing happened this morning."

As she left the room to get a clean diaper for the baby,

he added, "By the way, thanks a million for mowing the lawn for me. But if you do it again, I'll give you three demerits."

He heard a delighted laugh issue from her retreating figure.

Yossi had seen him walk into the kitchen and crawled over to him. He stood himself up and held onto Beck's trousers. Their ninth child, and only son, he was nearly a year old and had always been attached to his father. Beck picked him up and hugged him, then hoisted him and balanced him standing up on the palm of his hand. Yossi broke into a broad grin and clapped his pudgy hands. It was an unusual trick Beck had discovered with Sara, their oldest, when she was only four months old, and he had developed it with each of the children in turn. It created a special bond between them. Guests were either amazed or appalled by the unique performance.

Beck put away his hat and jacket and sat down in the breakfast nook off the kitchen. Staring at the unfinished pine utility shelves he had built for Rusie, he noticed the ancient wallpaper peeling away from the corner. It reminded him once again that the financial strain of their big family left few extra resources to fix up the house.

"Probably better this way," he reflected. "It forces us to downplay *gashmius* in a society where *gashmius* has become an ideal, a goal of life, a false prescription for happiness."

"Sorry I took so long," Rusie said when she returned. "I couldn't find the baby's blanket."

She opened the salads and passed one to Beck, along with a fork, napkin and glass of milk.

"Oh, you got the garlic and honey dressing," she noted. "Thank you."

"Nothing but the best—for the best," he replied, as he loaded a forkful into his mouth.

"You wanted to tell me what happened this morning,"

she reminded him with excited curiosity.

Beck swallowed the food in his mouth and took a drink. He then related the events of the entire morning—Lowery's hair-raising escape, what Carter and he had learned from Mrs. Holland, his one-way conversation with Mrs. Stein, the ponytail man and the call from the head nurse.

"Whew! That's overwhelming," Rusie exclaimed. "I'm emotionally drained just listening to you spill it all out. I can imagine you must be exhausted."

"It really does seem like a fast action movie, doesn't it?" Beck replied. "It was a series of crises, one right after the next. What do you make of it all?"

"Why are you asking me?" Rusie responded. "You're the Sherlock in this family, not me. You really think it's all related? The string of coincidences is too long to be plausible. There are so many players, and so many unknowns. I find it all confusing. I just don't like the sound of this man with the ponytail. And if he's the one that stabbed Mrs. Stein, what's to stop him from doing the same to you, *chas veshalom*, or to anyone else who gets in his way? You know, Binyamin, you really ought to call Rav Feinman and ask his advice before you send Patrol members to watch Mrs. Stein's room. I don't think it's right to put Jews in danger."

Beck had not considered Rabbi Feinman. All major decisions in the ECCP, and many of the minor decisions, were made only under Rabbi Feinman's guidance. Rusie was right, at least on that count.

Beck made a weak attempt to cover his oversight. "I hate to bother the Rav. Besides, the scoundrel who stabbed Mrs. Stein was short, and this rogue with the ponytail is tall. I don't think there's much danger. Remember that he just slinked off when I confronted him, and he did the same again when the head nurse confronted him."

"Yes, but you always tell me that all criminals are

cowards," Rusie countered. "So if he's a coward, that just proves he's a criminal, and therefore he's dangerous."

Beck was trapped by female logic. If he diagrammed her argument, it would look perfect. But there was a flaw somewhere, he was sure. How could a person be a sneaking coward and a brazen danger at the same time? He had learned long ago the futility of attempting to straighten out her mental processes. Besides, over the years, he had been right no more often than she. He considered what a dynamo she could be if she learned to think more rationally from his example and combined that logic with her own acute intuition. Of course, look how much grief he could have avoided in his own life had he learned the art of intuition from her and combined that intuition with his own logical processes. Maybe, he imagined, that is why Hashem wants a man and a woman to spend their lives together. He stuffed a big cherry tomato in his mouth to prevent himself from speaking.

"Look, I'm not saying you're wrong," Rusie soothed. "I just think we ought to consult the Rav. How about if I call him for you? I'll give him all the information and see what he says. Hopefully, I'll be able to reach him this afternoon, and I'll call you after you're done talking with Chet."

"Great idea. That'll be a big help."

Just one more example, he realized, of how much he and the ECCP depended on Rusie. She deserved more public credit, but his sensitivity of her *tznius* kept him from putting her in the limelight.

Rusie changed the topic. "By the way, have you been in the new dry cleaning place on Benbrook Road?"

"The one that opened a few weeks ago?" Beck said. "No, I haven't."

"I know you're going to think I'm crazy," Rusie continued, "but I'd like you to go in there and talk to the owner."

"About what?" Beck wondered what he was being dragged into.

"No, I mean, just tell me what you think of him."

"Rusie, what are you talking about? How am I supposed to just pop in, a total stranger, and strike up a conversation for no reason whatsoever? Why? What's wrong with the guy?" Beck knew she was withholding information, and he wanted to know more before he barged in on someone.

"I've got it," she offered. "Rochel, Avigayil and Miriam have *Shabbos* dresses that need dry cleaning. I'll give them to you, and you can drop them off on your way back to the Patrol office."

Sara and Esther, their two oldest daughters, were married and living in Yerushalayim. Since Naomi, the next child, had left for seminary in Bnei Brak, Rochel, their eleventh grader, had accepted the mantle and responsibilities of the "oldest" child. She and her next two younger sisters had recently attended a former teacher's wedding in New York.

Beck noticed that weddings were usually followed by costly visits to the cleaner. Just one of the many mysterious correlations of nature.

"How about if I do it tomorrow?" Beck answered. "I want to stop at the bank now, and I have to meet Chet soon. But you still haven't told me what's wrong with the owner of the dry cleaning place. What am I supposed to be looking for?"

Rusie hesitated. "Well, I'm really not sure. I went in there yesterday to drop off the winter sweaters. The owner— I assume he's the owner, at least he was the one that stood behind the counter—is a tall man in his early or mid-forties with a full head of hair. He seemed preoccupied with other matters, like he wanted me out of the store as soon as possible."

"Probably has a lot of headaches from starting the new business," Beck suggested.

"Maybe," Rusie acknowledged. "But I also got the feeling that my entrance had interrupted something . . . something he didn't want me to know about. When I put the ticket on the countertop, the fan blew it off, so I started diving around the end of the counter to catch it. You should have seen the man leap, like I was invading his territory or something. I just wonder if he was concealing something behind the counter that he didn't want me to see."

They were both silent a moment.

"The truth is, it's none of my business," Rusie admitted. "And I really don't care what he does with his store. I guess I wouldn't have brought up the whole subject, except . . ."

"Except what?" Beck urged her.

"I don't know. Just a creepy feeling the place gave me, Binyamin. I'm not a suspicious person by nature, you know that. But I left that store feeling I had just been in contact with something sinister."

"Sort of like *tumah*," Beck offered. "Intangible but real."

"That's right."

"You didn't see anyone else in the store, did you?" Beck asked.

"As a matter of fact, there was a young lady working by the conveyor racks. Hourly worker, I presume. Probably about twenty years old. She was putting bags over hangers. A pretty, blonde girl, dressed casually but neatly. She almost looked Jewish. She started coming over to the counter at one point, but the owner shot her a poisonous scowl, and she stopped in mid-stride and turned around. I pretended not to see, I was so embarrassed for her. She glanced over at me a minute later, when I was waiting for change. She had the most forlorn look I have ever seen. I could've picked up a hanger and poked that man's eyes out."

"*Midah keneged midah,*" Beck laughed.

"No," Rusie added, "that girl looked like she hadn't smiled in months. I don't think it was just an isolated incident between the two of them."

Beck was never comfortable with the layers of interpretation his wife put on the people and events of her daily life. From one look at a young woman, how was it possible to extrapolate her history over the previous months? To his chagrin, her extrapolations were not always off the mark.

"Okay," Beck conceded defeat. "I'll take the dresses in tomorrow morning and see if I can strike up a conversation with this devil. How do I recognize him?"

"He has dark brown, straight hair, sort of long. He's clean-shaven, with a mean looking cut on his jaw, like someone had gashed him with a knife. He was wearing one of those large gold rings with the block initials C.H."

"Now look who's playing Sherlock. You really noticed details," Beck declared. "Fair enough, I'll try in the morning. I'm going to get my stuff and go back to the office now."

Rusie took the disposable utensils into the kitchen. Beck said a hasty *brachah acharonah,* then immediately regretted his insipid *kavanah.* He chastised himself, "When will I learn to recite *brachos* with enough feeling to show Hashem I really appreciate the food He gives me? I wish I could school myself to be instinctively afraid of Hashem's Name. Then I would never launch into a *brachah* without thinking first."

He gathered his folder, with several telephone messages Rusie had taken for him earlier.

"I'll be home for dinner," he said to his wife on his way through the kitchen. "Thanks for sharing lunch with me."

"Thank *you,*" she responded. "I wish we could do it more often. Remember you wanted to stop at the bank."

"Oh . . . right. I almost forgot." He sent an impulsive thanks Heavenward for this *ezer kenegdo.*

5

WHEN BECK ARRIVED AT THE ECCP OFFICE, HE NOTICED Carter's car already in the parking lot. He had never known a policeman to be late for an appointment. Punctuality was their trademark.

Beck opened the heavy outside door to the building and started up the stairs. The ECCP had been the only occupant of the third-floor premises for the past four years. They enjoyed the increased security, knowing that the only visitors to the third floor were on Patrol business. They had even been granted permission to install a steel door where the second floor hallway ended in the steps to the third story.

When Beck reached the third-floor landing, he was startled to encounter a stranger emerging from the Patrol office. The man had a wild, slovenly appearance, with a balding pate and a long, scraggly beard. A ghoulish scar stretched from his right temple nearly to his nose, conferring a Frankenstein appearance on him. Beck estimated he was not more than thirty-five, although his wizened hands and stooped walk made him appear older. He shot a dour frown at Beck from under lowered eyebrows as he brushed past. A barnyard reek emanated from his ragged denim overalls. Beck watched him disappear down the steps.

"Who on earth was that?" Beck addressed Carter when he entered.

"Oh, hi, Benny," Carter rejoined. "You mean the phantom that just walked out?"

"The same," said Beck.

"I don't know. He claims he was looking for a doctor's office. I guess he was shocked to walk in here and find a policeman staring at him. Is there even a doctor's office in the building?"

"No, there isn't," Beck answered emphatically. "Did you ask his name?"

"No, I just told him he had the wrong place," Carter said.

"Chet, if you don't mind, would you chase him and see if you can get his I.D. There's been too much trouble lately, and I'm jittery. Remember, I don't wear bulletproof armor like you cops do."

"What's the matter? You been talking to Rusie again? You should follow my example and not discuss business with your wife."

Chet and Renee Carter had been married for eight years and had two young sons. Renee had always been haunted by a fear that her husband would be injured on duty. They had a longstanding agreement to avoid discussing his police activities so as not to unbalance her fragile equanimity.

"And *you*," enjoined Beck, "should heed my request to collar the apparition that just left this office. He may *look* like Farmer in the Dell, but there have been too many disturbing coincidences today to suit my liking."

Carter responded to the urgency in Beck's voice. "Yes, sir! I'll be right back up. Save some coffee for me."

"Maybe I'm overreacting," Beck sighed, turning to Dovid after Carter left. "I'll have to apologize to Chet for being so strident. The truth is, Rusie did plant some strong misgivings, probably more than I should have allowed."

"No, Benny, you're more than justified," Dovid said in support. "I didn't like the way that fellow's eyes roamed around the office. In fact, Chet had some difficulty convincing him to leave."

"Now my suspicions are really fanned, Dovid. Let's see what Chet unearths. Well, what's new on your front?"

"Plenty," Dovid said. "First of all, Major MacDougal called with the name of the roofing company that you requested. It's called Tip-Top Roofers. After we finished talking, I looked them up in the phone book. Would you believe they are located right here in the Spartan Industrial Park? They're one of the firms on the west side of the tracks."

Beck voiced surprise. "No kidding! This plot is getting too close for comfort."

He had grown very protective of the neighborhood they served. He felt disgraced whenever criminal elements infiltrated the area, as though he were personally to blame.

The Spartan Industrial Park was built on the edge of the East Cahill neighborhood. It was an old development embracing five winding concourses of austere, cement buildings, leased by more than forty companies. However, a major tract had never been improved and was overrun by a sprawling, tangled woods. Sequestered in this area, a few businesses were accessible only via a gravel road from the west side of a double set of railroad tracks.

Beck drew his fingers through his beard, cogitating on MacDougal's information.

"Dovid, will you do me a favor? I'd like you to take your own car and drive over to Spartan. See if you can locate this Tip-Top outfit, and sketch a little map of the road for me. Also, if you spot any cars on their lot, jot down the tags. You have to avoid suspicion while you're snooping, so don't stop. I'd also like you to drive into the main section of Spartan and pinpoint any footpaths that enter the woods."

"Sure, Benny," Dovid said. "You want me to leave right away? I've still got more messages to give you."

"I'm sorry," Beck apologized. "I didn't mean to rush you out. Actually, why don't you wait until Chet returns? You can go while he and I are conferring. What else have you got for me?"

Dovid sorted through his notes. "Okay. Next item regards Caterpillar. You have an appointment with a Mr. Devone at State Line Equipment and Supply Company in Martinsburg, at noon on Wednesday. He's actually an authorized Caterpillar dealer. Very helpful gentleman. He gave me detailed directions. The place is located just outside Morgan's Ferry, and it takes about two hours to get there. Interstate highway most of the way."

Beck looked over Dovid's shoulder at the directions. "Wonderful. How did you stumble on this place?"

Dovid grinned. "If you hang around Binyamin Beck long enough, you learn a few things. Try it some time."

"Okay, Funny Boy. You said the appointment is for Wednesday? He couldn't make it tomorrow?"

"No," Dovid replied. "He's closed on Tuesdays."

"I'll tell you, Dovid. Wednesday is not going to work, because I promised Mr. Farringdon I would attend his community meeting Wednesday evening. That's at six, and I don't want to feel rushed when I'm with the Caterpillar dealer. I wouldn't mind meeting him when they open on Thursday, if he's available. I could catch the early *minyan* and leave here by six-thirty in the morning."

"Fine," Dovid said. "I'll call him back to change the appointment. Now, one more message. Your wife called to say that she reached Rav Feinman on the first try, and he says we should proceed with the watch on Mrs. Stein's room. I've already recruited three volunteers, starting at four o'clock this afternoon."

"Terrific," Beck beamed. He meant the compliment for both Dovid and Rusie. "At least *something* is clicking. Seems like so many things have gone wrong today, like the world's out of control."

"*Bitachon,* Benny," Dovid remonstrated. "The world's never out of Hashem's control."

Beck set down the pen he had taken out of his breast pocket and looked silently at Dovid for an instant.

"Thanks," Beck said quietly, with sincere appreciation. "I needed that *mussar.*"

He walked over to his desk and collapsed into his chair. Leaning back with his coffee, he took a sip and stared thoughtfully at the ceiling, gently curling his fingers through his beard like a school of fish swimming lazily through a quiet pool. Finally, he sat up and pushed himself around to face Dovid again.

"You know, Dovid, you're right. Life viewed through the eyes of Torah is a serene comfort. Take my case, for instance. If I remind myself that *Hakadosh Baruch Hu* orchestrated today's events, step by step, that the movement of every object, every atom, every electron, was decreed by Him, then there is no room to be insecure, or apprehensive, or discouraged. The entire world, including myself, is piloted by omnipotent Hands, and nothing—literally *nothing*—can go wrong. I am merely an actor on the stage of life. The script, the players, the props—everything has been predestined and ordered by the Almighty. Whatever happens to me is good and right, by definition. Every Jew should feel that way. It would preclude a lot of stress-induced heart attacks."

A puzzled expression advanced across Dovid's face. "Wait a minute, Benny," he protested. "That's pretty extreme, isn't it? Are you saying that we're just robots? G-d is a puppeteer and we are simply dangling helplessly at the ends of strings? What happened to *bechirah,* our own free will to choose right from wrong?"

Beck sat up straight. He hardly noticed the coffee that sloshed out of his cup as he plunked it on the desk.

"Now pay attention, Dovid. Try to shed all that Sunday school trash that was dumped on you in your childhood. Let's understand clearly, once and for all, that the name Almighty is not just an honorary title we give to G-d, like His Highness, *chas veshalom.* We mean precisely what we say— G-d is ALL MIGHTY. That means His might, His absolute will, sweeps the breadth and depth of the vast universe. *Nothing* escapes His infinite grasp, down to the most minute detail. Let that sink in.

"G-d has no boundaries and no form. He has no front and no back. In *Olam Hazeh,* this world, man has no inkling whatsoever of G-d's attributes, because our pygmy intellects are strapped into a world of finitudes. Only in *Olam Haba,* the world to come, can one begin to perceive G-d's infinite essence."

Dovid was alert. "Benny, all you're saying is that it's impossible to have *bechirah.* You've put me in a straitjacket and suffocated me. If G-d's unconditional control extends into every spatial and temporal nook and cranny, I have no leeway to choose to be righteous or evil. With all due respect, Benny, I think you're off the wall!"

"Now we're getting somewhere, Dovid. I see you agree with me."

"Huh?" Dovid was annoyed. "Maybe you should change the batteries in your hearing aid. I said that I *dis*agree with you."

"On the contrary," Beck responded unruffled. "If we honestly accept the concept of G-d's omnipotence, your inference is correct—we are puppets and we have no free will. That leads us to another fundamental principle of

Yiddishkeit, namely, the most incomprehensible miracle that exists in the world. G-d voluntarily retracts His omnipotence just enough to concede us the ability to choose between right and wrong, the *bechirah* to do *mitzvos* and *aveiros.*"

Beck paused to allow Dovid time for cerebral digestion as the quartz wall clock ticked off fifteen seconds. He heard a car door close and glanced out the window. Carter had returned.

"It seems to fit," Dovid said aloud. "At least you got rid of my problem."

The two men fell silent, each one enveloped in his own thoughts. Beck asked Hashem for *mechilah* if he had erred in his explanation. He was no *rebbi,* and his learning was limited.

"It's as deafening as a silent movie in here," Carter burst in. "Anyone alive?"

Dovid jumped up, inspired. "Benny just gave me a nice gift, Chet. Here, let me try it on you. See if you can answer this question. If G-d is omnipotent, is it possible for Him to make a mountain so big that He cannot lift it?"

"Wha-at!" yelped Carter. "I walk out for five minutes and come back to find a couple of loonies capering around the premises."

Beck stood up. "Good, Dovid. How would you answer that riddle?" He threw the question back at Dovid. Carter, he knew, had contemplated the subject about as much as he had pondered long term variations in the orbit of Pluto.

"I figure it's a nonsense question," Dovid replied. "If Hashem exerts absolute control over every atom in the universe, there's no such phenomenon as moving a mountain. Hashem simply wills ten billion atoms to exist as a mountain in a certain location. If He wants to move it, so to speak, whether a millimeter or a hundred miles, He merely wills the atoms to stop existing at the former coordinates and start existing at the new coordinates."

"Boffo!" Beck glowed. "You're very close to hitting the nail on the head. It's a principle we refer to every morning in *Shacharis*, when we say, '*Hamechadesh betuvo bechol yom tamid maasei bereishis.* In His goodness, He renews the works of Creation every day.' Hashem renews creation every instant of time. Every subatomic particle in the universe, and every measure of energy, exists at this instant because Hashem wills it into existence at this instant. The next instant, Hashem wills everything into existence again, and so on and on, instant by instant. What He does not will into existence again will not be *mechudash*, will not be renewed, and will therefore cease to exist."

Carter had stood stock-still in the doorway during this intellectual exchange. The baffled expression on his face clearly proclaimed his preference for police work over philosophical discourse. He was nobody's fool, but his predilection for the practical had never allowed him any pleasure in abstract discussions. Beck saw him start to open his mouth to speak, but Dovid interrupted.

"Right," Dovid resumed the floor. "So, moving this hypothetical mountain—however big it is—does not require Hashem to hoist it up and *shlep* it across the landscape. All He has to do is will it into existence at Point Y at Time Beta, whereas just before, at Time Alpha, He had willed it into existence at Point X. To our human eye, it appears that the mountain moved, whereas in fact they were two separate mountains—two distinct creations at two sequential instants in time. Now we've eliminated the paradox, because there is nothing illogical about Hashem's creating a mountain at Point X right now, and then creating another mountain at Point Y at some future instant."

"Dovid, you're a genius," Beck marveled. Out of the

corner of his eye, he saw Carter's jaw drop. "Of course, your mountain riddle can be answered in other ways, too. For instance, sizes, weights, motion and other boundary problems are all based on the human experience of finiteness in the world. In truth, these concepts have no meaning when applied to Hashem, just as red, blue and green have no definition for a blind person. Again, then, the mountain riddle is reduced to nonsense."

"Hold it, guys," Carter finally spoke up. "Can I just get an edge in wordwise?"

"One second!" Dovid exclaimed, ignoring Carter's plea. "There's another nonsense aspect to the mountain riddle. If Hashem can make a mountain infinitely large, occupying all of space, He obviously cannot move it, or else it was not occupying all of space in the first place."

"Well, that's a mathematical problem," Beck answered, "and it really has nothing at all to do with G-d. Even an atheist . . . hey, Chet, where're you going?"

The policeman had started out of the room, muttering to himself. "Sorry, gentlemen," he said. "I think I came to the wrong office by mistake. That'll teach me to park without looking at the address first."

Beck refilled his cup. "Okay, come back here, you knucklehead. Let's get down to business. Dovid and I won't tax your cerebrum any more. Promise."

Dovid smiled knowingly at Beck. He picked up a pad of yellow notepaper and said, "I'm leaving to check out Tip-Top Roofing Company. See you guys later."

"Okay. Make yourself inconspicuous. Will you please close the door on your way out?" Beck reached for a paper towel to wipe up his coffee spill. "What did you find out from our farmer friend, Chet?"

"Zilch. He gave me the slip," Carter reported, gratified that he still had a role in Beck's world. "He vanished before

I reached the parking lot. I took the car out, but I couldn't locate him. I wonder if he heard me coming and ducked inside the building. I probably should've scouted the first floor before going out for a drive."

"Too bad," Beck said. "I wonder what he was up to. He may have been trying to get the lay of the office."

"I reached Mrs. Holland," Carter changed the subject. "She was frightened by your story. I tried to calm her down, but I also urged her to hire a nurse for her mother. She said she would definitely do it."

"Fine," Beck approved. "Meanwhile, Dovid's got a volunteer crew sitting by her room through the night. Do you think she'll have a nurse there by tomorrow?"

"Oh, for sure. She hopes to arrange for a nurse by tonight, but I don't think it'll happen quite as fast as she wants. I'm going to inform her of the ECCP guard. That should put her at ease a bit."

"I hope so, Chet. Now, let's get down to business. First, let me fill you in on my exciting morning."

Beck described the crane incident, adding the information from MacDougal. It was the third time he had related the story, yet the terror and suspense were still fresh in his mind. It would take an animal, he thought, not to be horrified by the imminent death of another human being.

"Wow!" Carter exclaimed. "You guys certainly have exciting meetings, don't you?"

"Believe me, it wasn't planned. I told you I confronted the ponytail man in the hospital," Beck continued. "What I didn't tell you is that he was right behind me when I drove out of the parking lot, and I got his tag. XNC422. A red Camaro."

"What! And you've been roosting on that nest egg?" Carter was excited. "Hold on and I'll get a listing on the tag."

He keyed his mike. "Six Charlie thirty-three."

"Six Charlie thirty-three," acknowledged the dispatcher.

"Can I have a listing on a red Camaro, tag X-ray, Nora, Charles, four two two?"

Carter began drumming his fingertips on the desk. "It's a good thing no one's life depends on this info. She may not call me back for ten minutes."

"There are worse things in the world," Beck soothed. "Meanwhile, you heard that I delegated Dovid to spy out Tip-Top Roofers. Major MacDougal told us that they are the company doing the roofwork next to Police Headquarters. Turns out their place of business is right here in the Spartan Industrial Park. For the time being, I'm operating on the premise that they have a lot to do with Mrs. Stein."

"Six Charlie thirty-three," crackled Carter's radio.

"I'll be a monkey's uncle. Thirty seconds," Carter noted to Beck. "Must be a record."

He picked up an index card to write on and depressed the mike button again. "Six Charlie thirty-three."

"X-ray, Nancy, Charles, four two two, red Camaro, listed to Robert Eberhart, white male, six foot two, D.O.B. four-sixteen-sixty-one, 7203 Highland Hills Drive."

"There you have it, Benny," Carter flipped the card over to Beck. "At least we don't have to call him 'the ponytail man' any longer."

"Eberhart," Beck said. "Fine, now suppose we try to plot all the robberies we've sustained over the past month."

"I'm way ahead of you, boss," Carter replied, smiling with manifest relish as he drew a folder from his briefcase. "Behold, Exhibit One, a map of the ECCP area. The numbers on the red dots indicate the chronological sequence of the incidents and are keyed to the table on the next page. There's an obvious pattern."

Beck was impressed. "Chet, I see you that didn't get much sleep this morning after all."

Carter grinned. "You'd be surprised at what I can do in my sleep. Take a look. There have been a total of nineteen robberies in the last ten days. We're getting plastered by these goofballs. You see the common denominators? Sixteen of the incidents occurred between 1900 and 2100 hours. In all sixteen incidents the assailant was short, with the same general description. Getaway cars were used in at least ten of the incidents—blue Ford Escort in four cases, a red car, unknown make, in one case, and unknown description in five other cases. A knife was wielded in eight of the incidents. Remember when we were discussing these robberies last week? We noticed that the assailants are keeping the credit cards. That pattern is still holding, including Mrs. Stein's robbery. Clearly, my next job is to find out if and where any of those cards were used after they were stolen."

"Right," Beck agreed. "Maybe we're dealing with some kind of credit card ring. But nowadays most merchants obtain approvals on credit card purchases, so the card is worthless once it's reported stolen."

"We'll see," Carter said. "I do agree with you that we're dealing with a ring. I'm sure all these incidents are related, and from the victims' descriptions there are at least three, maybe four different suspects driving the getaway cars."

"That works against us, Chet. The more diverse the suspects' descriptions, M.O.s, locations and so forth, the more difficult it is for us to anticipate the next incident. I think you should convey the pertinent information at roll call each night until this thing clears up. Maybe we'll get lucky and one of our units will spot something."

"Good idea, Benny. I'm going to grab some dinner and then come back to set up for patrol."

Beck tilted his chair back, and stroked his beard for a few seconds. "Do you think you'll have any leads on those credit cards by tomorrow?"

"It depends. The police reports usually list credit cards taken during a robbery if the victim can supply that information. Some reports even note account numbers. You can always tell a good cop by the reports he writes. If I get some cooperative operators, I'll be able to lay my hands on a lot of information over the phone from the credit card companies. But if they insist on formal requests, or even subpoenas, it could take days or weeks."

"Perish the thought," Beck shuddered. "The political establishment has vandalized this country with the notion of blindly promoting individual rights above all. I ask you, sir, which is more important, defending the lives of who knows how many potential crime victims or protecting someone's credit card history?"

Carter protested, "I'm not blaming them. I wouldn't want someone prying into *my* credit account."

"That's because you've been brainwashed along with the rest of the nation, Chet. Let's stack the privacy of your credit account against Mrs. Stein's life. Which is more imperative?"

"If you put it like that," Carter conceded, "obviously the lives of the victims come before citizens' right to privacy."

The cop sat down at his desk and slipped a stack of documents out of his drawer. He hit a key on his computer and waited impatiently as the ECCP Crime Analysis program was loaded.

"Unless, of course, you're one of today's ruling radicals," Beck continued, "in which case you have probably lost sight of the paramount value of human life. Why do you think G-d originally created millions of beetles, millions of birds, millions of each species on earth—except for man. He formed only one man and one woman. We must understand the unique preciousness of humans. G-d created us in His image and breathed into us a measure of His absolute perfection. That means we resemble Him in some critical ways, and we possess a degree of His infinite perfection and holiness. The human being embodies a sanctity shared by no other phenomenon on earth, dead or alive. Our faces are fashioned by G-d and shine with a reflection of G-d in them. When we wake up in the morning, we should scrub our faces, like an adulatory servant polishing a statue of his master. And when we see another human being suffer, it ought to tear our hearts out, because it is an image of G-d, as it were, that is aching.

"A whole gallery of so-called legal defense unions jockey for the privilege to squander millions of dollars a year defending the rights of murderers. For them, humans have no more G-dliness than the sidewalk ants they squash underfoot. They may profess to go to church or temple, but they're all atheists."

Both men were tired and edgy. Carter slapped the ESC key hard to exit his program and stood up in frustration.

"I'm sorry, Chet," Beck finished. "I didn't mean to jump on you. I just bristle at people's upside-down priorities."

"That's an understatement, boss. I should've known better than to pipe up when you were in a *mussar* mood. I'll say one thing, no one can accuse you of wobbling in your beliefs. Not that I disagree with a word you said." He added the last comment for safety's sake.

"We need a break, Chet. Maybe when we clear up these robberies we'll celebrate. Now if you'll excuse me, I want to finish this letter to the Parole Commission before *Minchah*. You're leaving now?"

"Yeah," Carter responded, grabbing his briefcase and police radio. "And by the way, Benny, I think *you* are the one who needs some shut-eye." He winked, but Beck sensed irritation in his voice as well.

As Carter closed the office door behind him, Beck

interlocked his fingers tightly and twisted his palms inside out, in an attempt to vent his tension. Then he sat down in Carter's chair and stared blankly at the drab gray computer screen in front of him. He sipped his tepid coffee, listening to the drone of Carter's car as he drove off.

He leaned back in the chair and again raked his fingers through his beard. Strangely, as he closed his eyes, a ghost of Horace Grimm materialized in his mind. Grimm, the quintessential opportunist, he snarled to himself. A profligate vulture who had amassed a fortune by defending criminals of the most heinous stripe. A dissolute hypocrite whose compassion was never stirred by the suffering of the wretched victims of his clients. He promoted himself as a champion of the oppressed blacks, browns, reds and whites, but green was the only color he truly loved. He, Binyamin Beck, who believed with a palpable conviction that men of all races were created by an omnificent G-d, harbored a much more sincere pathos for the plight of the downtrodden than that inflated miscreant who unthinkingly believed that man was descended from apes in the jungle. What fraction of his lawyer's wealth did Grimm donate to the poor, Beck wondered. Was it anywhere near the ten percent that Jewish law requires as a minimum?

The telephone's abrupt jangle exploded Beck's contemplative mood. He jolted upright and hastily picked up the receiver.

"East Cahill Citizens Patrol."

There was a silent pause, followed by a sandpaper voice. "If you know what's good for you, keep your nose to yourself. Otherwise, we'll put you where the old woman is." The line clicked dead.

Beck hunched forward instinctively and hung up the phone. He was all attention, his weariness completely evaporated. He immediately lifted the receiver again, listened for the dial tone, and pressed 57 to activate call tracing. When the recorded confirmation message ended, he searched through the electronic rolodex on Carter's computer, found a name, and pressed the F2 key to activate the call.

"Carla Jones's office. May I help you?" said a pleasant voice on the other end.

"Hi, Joan, this is Benny Beck with the East Cahill Citizens Patrol. Is Carla in now? It's a semi-emergency."

"I'm sorry, Dr. Beck. She's providing testimony in the Legislature today regarding our new long distance billing procedures. Can I possibly help you with something?"

"Maybe. I just received a threatening phone call, and I activated a trace on it. Can you find out who placed the call?"

"Sure. What's your number?"

"543-2222," Beck said.

"Fine. I'll call you back this afternoon."

"You're a tremendous help. I really appreciate it. If I'm not here, you can leave the information with Dovid."

Another solid friend, thought Beck. Ordinarily, a customer had to complete three petition forms and wade through twenty layers of bureaucracy to identify a traced call. The ECCP had cemented many strong friendships over the years, focusing a broad network of people, agencies and programs, stirring in its own phalanx of dedicated citizen volunteers and creating a potent dynamo that had dramatically reduced crime in the area. It was all Hashem's doing, of course, but they were the magnificent vehicle through which He acted.

Still, Beck realized, he was no policeman, and he was vulnerable. The Patrol's telephone number was unlisted—how had the caller discovered it? The farmer! He must have snitched some ECCP literature when Chet wasn't looking. Or even read the number off the phone. Beck was more suspicious than ever.

He was also frightened. Maybe he should wear a bulletproof vest, at least until the plague of robberies abated. True, armor would not thwart a sharp knife, but it would protect him from the handguns being used by criminals.

Rusie was right, he trembled, these people would stop at nothing. Letter bombs, booby traps, explosives rigged to the ECCP Command Car—their options were unlimited. What was to prevent someone from storming into the office right now and blowing his brains out? He certainly had no desire to be put where "that old woman" was.

On the other hand, he had no intention of backing off the investigation. He was engaged in the *mitzvah* of saving a life, and Hashem would surely protect him.

Then why did he suffer such a dreadful sense of gloom? Whence his premonition of impending danger? An abject darkness seemed to descend on his mind. If only his *emunah* were stronger. He shuddered uncontrollably.

"*Bitachon*," he steadied himself, goosebumps rising on his neck. "No matter what happens to me, Hashem is doing what is best for my *neshamah*. Meanwhile, my job is *hishtadlus.*"

Wait! Did he hear the steps creaking just now? He held his breath and listened. Yes! There was definitely someone stealing up the stairs, making as little noise as possible. No footsteps, just the boards squeaking. Now he heard tiptoes on the third floor landing, outside the office door. His heart skipped a beat.

The squeaking stopped. Beck imagined the muffled breathing of someone on the other side of the door. He was immobilized by the suspense pounding on his brain.

Suddenly, as Beck heard the knob click, the instinct of self-preservation burst through his paralysis. He rocketed himself out of the chair and raced for the door.

6

IT WAS TOO LATE. THE DOOR SWUNG OPEN, AND IN PRANCED Dovid Berg in his stocking feet, carrying a pair of shoes coated with mud.

"Whoa, Tonto," Dovid said, as Beck almost leveled him. "You look like a tornado unwinding at top speed."

Beck stopped just short of flattening the young man. He felt like screaming and smashing his fist through the plaster wall, just to relieve his extreme tension.

He was also embarrassed, and he yielded to his human impulse to cover up by jumping to the offensive.

"What in tarnation are you doing without shoes?" he shrieked, red-faced. "This is no playground!"

Dovid was astonished, and he shrank backward with his mouth agape, not knowing the crime he had committed to warrant this vicious attack. He stood speechless as Beck struggled to control himself.

A moment of tense silence passed. It seemed like an eternity. Beck finally recovered and lowered his voice, as well as his bellicosity. "I'm terribly sorry, Dovid. I was really nervous. I couldn't imagine who was sneaking up our stairs."

Dovid forced out a half-hearted chuckle, just to break the ice, then instantly swallowed his contrived smile.

"I'm sorry, too, Benny. I know you've been under fire today, and I should've been more considerate. I got my shoes all muddy while searching for footpaths in those woods, and I didn't want to drag the gunk into the office."

Beck's adrenalin was still surging. He thanked Hashem that all was well. This time he closed the door and locked it. Enough surprises for one day, he thought.

"It's okay, Dovid. Why don't you get yourself settled." He wanted to provide both of them time to calm down.

"So tell me what you discovered," Beck invited after a few minutes. "From the appearance of your shoes, I'd guess you had some adventure."

He felt miserable and ashamed for having pounced on Dovid so aggressively. Dovid was still young and tender. He hoped Dovid would loosen up quickly.

"Have you ever ventured into that area of Spartan?" Dovid inquired.

"Once, a number of years ago. I chaperoned the kids there to sell chocolates for the Beis Yaakov P.T.A. Boy, was that a mistake. It was one big junkyard."

"It hasn't changed a bit," Dovid replied. "I hope I didn't pick up any nails or glass in my tires. Do I earn credit for *mesiras nefesh?*"

"Your tires do. Anyway, did you get any information?"

Dovid gingerly set his shoes on a paper towel and extracted a sheet of notes from his pocket. He laid it on the worktable.

"Here's the map I made. The main entrance is located here. The road leading in is nearly a half mile long and fairly straight, except for one sharp turn, about a quarter mile in from the entrance. The road surface is loose gravel and terribly bumpy the whole way, with some pretty mean potholes, like the Marines had dug in. There's not a lot of room to maneuver, either, because the trees grow right up to the edge of the road in many places. I certainly wouldn't recommend a visit there at night. You could easily get stranded if a wheel fell in one of those gaping holes. Tip-Top is positioned right here, where the road takes another hairpin turn to the south. They've got a two-story clapboard building here, set back a little from the road. Looks like an ancient structure, but it must be their office. The only other building is a quonset hut warehouse. The doors were open to the warehouse, and I could see stockpiles of various roofing materials. It looks like a *bona fide* business."

"Did you observe any people or cars?" Beck interrupted.

"Not so fast, Benny. One thing I noticed was that there was no heavy equipment around, no cranes or lifts or that sort of stuff."

"That doesn't necessarily mean anything. If it's a small outfit, they may prefer to rent equipment on a per job basis. Some of those machines are very expensive to purchase and maintain. Besides, maybe all their equipment is being utilized at job sites right now."

"Okay, I'll give them the benefit of the doubt. Now you asked about cars. There were only two vehicles parked by the clapboard building, which I assumed is the office. One was a red Camaro, license plate XNC422, and the other was a blue Escort, tag number RNT333."

"Whew!" Beck whistled. "Matches the descriptions of the getaway cars employed in the current robbery string. The Camaro belongs to the ponytail man. His name is Robert Eberhart, by the way."

"I see you and Chet have been busy while I was gone," Dovid commented. "As I was driving by the place, I glimpsed one man standing at the window, although I couldn't distinguish his features. I kept moving, as though I were headed for the next business along the drive, but in reality, I just turned around and doubled back.

"When I drove around to the main section of Spartan, I parked at the far end of the parking lot, past the last building, and explored the woods a bit on foot. You can't see Tip-Top from that vantage, but I stumbled on one trail leading off at approximately this point."

Dovid indicated an arrow on the map.

"Here's where I fell into trouble, because I slipped on a root and landed with my right foot firmly planted in a mud hole beside the trail. As I was extricating that shoe, my other foot slipped, so they both ended up resembling the bottom of a swamp. I'm still not sure where the trail emerges, because I retreated once I freed myself. However, from that viewpoint I was already able to glimpse Tip-Top through the trees, so I assume the path leads out somewhere near their property."

"Terrific, Dovid. Excellent information. This is a very big help. And I apologize for causing you to bear so much on my account. I didn't realize I was assigning you to a war zone. Why don't you get cleaned up so we can go to *Minchah*? I'll shut down the printer and forward the phone."

Another burden willingly borne by Rusie, thought Beck. When the office was unoccupied, all calls were forwarded to their home. The public expected and received service virtually whenever they called, be it six in the morning or eleven at night.

The two men locked the premises and headed downstairs. It was a marvelous convenience to have a *shul* next door. They caught the early *Minchah* at four each afternoon.

Beck felt exhausted as he entered the *shul*. He shuffled mechanically toward his seat and virtually collapsed into his usual place. He dared not close his eyes, for fear of dozing. He did not expect to have much *kavanah* for this *davening*. If he managed to concentrate at least on the first *brachah*, his *tefillah* would be a success, he thought.

He was surprised that his *kavanah* held strong once he rose for the *Shmoneh Esrei*. "*Re'ay na ve'anyeinu*," he began the *brachah* of *geulah*, "*veriva riveinu!*" he continued pleadingly, punctuating his words with a fistblow to the bench in front of him. "See our anguish, and fight our fight for us." He added the thought, Hashem, please fight our fights for us, and deliver us from the enemies who threaten our *kehillah's* peace and welfare.

It was not his usual *Shmoneh Esrei*. He was rarely demonstrative, and he often envied the Jews who displayed such soul stirring *kavanah*. He suddenly became aware of a neighbor's sidelong glance. He felt self-conscious and hurried through the rest of the *tefillah*. If he had possessed more energy he could have pretended to be a *tzaddik*, but not today.

By the time he arrived home, Beck had had enough of the outside world. He just wanted to be with Rusie and the children. He entered via the back door and closed it tightly, as though locking out the world. In the back of his mind, he knew that the telephones would not let them avoid their responsibilities to the community. He recalled Mark Twain's facetious wish that all mankind might eventually be gathered together in a Heaven of everlasting peace and bliss—except the inventor of the telephone.

"Abba's home!" shrieked four-year-old Brachah, as she scrambled through the kitchen and nearly bowled him over.

He picked her up and awarded her a big hug. He was sure that he derived more pleasure from the exchange than the child did. These were the wages of *tzaar gidul banim*, he thought. *Olam Hazeh iz a gutte zach!* This world is a good thing! One does not have to wait for *Olam Haba* to receive reward, he rejoiced in his mind.

"I love you, Hashem," he added silently.

Basheva came moping in afterwards.

"What's the long face for, Basheva?" Beck tried to cheer her.

"I banged my knee on the table." She lifted her right knee for Beck's inspection.

He patted it reassuringly, considering what he should say. She's in the second grade, he thought. Old enough to understand. "How does your other knee feel?"

She was puzzled, but answered honestly, "It's fine."

"Okay," he said. "I want you to concentrate hard on your good knee and how nice it feels, and thank Hashem with all your heart for that one good knee. Now don't think about anything except the pleasant feelings in this good knee, okay?" He gently squeezed her left leg.

She glanced down at her left knee with consternation on her face. He could not tell if she was following his advice or not. He tousled her hair, but only slightly, not wanting her to think he had ridiculed her. He was serious, whether she realized it or not. He prayed this would be one of those childhood experiences that she would carry into adulthood, when she could employ it to best advantage.

"*Eizehu ashir, hasameach bechelko,*" he quoted to her quietly. "Who is considered rich? One who is content with what he has." And he gave her a little kiss.

Rusie had prepared hamburgers for dinner. She was a fantastic cook. Her hamburgers typified her style—bigger, tastier and more creative than anything Beck had sampled anywhere.

"Avigayil, you're sitting next to Yossi tonight, so it's your job to keep food on his tray," Rusie assigned their ninth-grader.

It was a delight to watch the baby devour his food. He possessed a ravenous appetite, and attacked his portions like a famished lion. They joked that he could not bear to have his stomach below the three-quarter mark. All the children had gone through that stage as babies.

Beck was sometimes unable to eat with the family. Meetings with judges, police, politicians and other communities often had to be scheduled in the evenings. When they did eat together as a family, Rusie always pushed him to reserve some of the table conversation for *mussar* and *hashkafah*. She was his *yetzer tov*. They had discussed many ideas over and over, from different angles. The two parents were proud that the girls had absorbed so much, especially the older ones.

Beck addressed all five of the girls, praying that he would choose the words to reach each one on her own level. "Kids, isn't it a miracle that *Hakadosh Baruch Hu* invests each person with an appetite? We know when we're hungry, and we know when we're full."

"Without even thinking about it," added Rochel. "It's involuntary." Her eleventh grade science class had just finished a unit on the digestive system.

"But I'll tell you an even bigger miracle," Beck continued. "All that food Yossi is gobbling will be chopped up by a most efficient food dicer, broken down by extremely complex digestive agents, converted into nutrients and stored energy by a miraculous chemical factory and distributed with pinpoint accuracy to exactly the right places throughout his growing body where each chemical compound is required.

"Now I just happen to have with me the latest version of the human metabolic pathways chart."

He winked and unfolded a poster-size sheet displaying thousands of chemicals, enzymes and arrows in green, blue, purple and red. To the uninitiated, it was an impressive jungle of nonsense.

"It's an entire laboratory," Beck added. "A hundred Dow Chemical plants, each one two blocks long, could not begin to reproduce even a fraction of what goes on in *each cell* of your body. And don't fool yourself. This is just the tip of the iceberg. New reactions and new pathways are being unearthed all the time. That's why they issue a new chart each year. Actually, we know from the Torah that the information and complexity contained even in a single cell is infinite, because it was designed by an Infinite Engineer. This chart represents just a little drop recovered from the vast ocean—the paltry efforts of scientists groping in the dark."

"And it's all involuntary," Rochel repeated.

"You already said that," Basheva pointed out. Her knee troubles were a thing of the past.

Beck quickly assumed the floor again. "It's worth repeating, Basheva. Rochel's right. The fact that our metabolism proceeds automatically is a very big *nisayon* for us. Do you know why?"

"Why?" several children chorused simultaneously.

"You see, Yossi has no inkling of the miracles we are discussing. Maybe in eight or ten years he'll have enough *seichel* to recognize the millions of miracles Hashem arranged in his body. But by then, he will be so accustomed to those everyday events, they will never strike him as miracles, and he will not realize the need to thank the One Who created those miracles. If we were born like Adam and Chavah as adults with full *seichel*, we would be dumbstruck by the myriad unmistakable miracles happening every second of our lives. Instead, Hashem designed us to enter this world without knowledge. He pulled a dark veil over our eyes. It's our job in life to tear away that veil, to acquire knowledge and to recognize the truth."

Rusie finished apportioning the food and joined the conversation. "I'll give you a practical example of what Abba is saying. We think that light helps us observe the world better, right? But isn't it true that light actually blinds us? After all, only at night can we see the stars and the vastness of the universe. The 'light' of *Olam Hazeh*—knowledge of the physical world—is deceptive. It blinds us to the fundamental truth underlying that knowledge."

"Ha-ah!" Avigayil gasped as she lunged for the baby's high chair. She was not in time to restrain Yossi from upending his tray. A trail of french fries and ketchup dribbled down the left side of his head, while the major portion landed with a splat on the floor. He looked at Avigayil, then at the others, with a nonplused expression, as if to say, "Is anything the matter?"

"Don't laugh at him," Rusie ordered, struggling to suppress a smile. "If he thinks it's a game, he'll never learn what's right."

Rusie had earlier cleaned up the baby's lunch, which had suffered a similar fate. After wiping Yossi's head, she plopped him on the floor, legs straddling the wayward meal.

"Best vacuum cleaner around," Rusie announced.

The children took their mother's quip as license to ignore her earlier warning. Everyone broke into merry applause. The baby had no idea what was so entertaining, but not wanting to be left out, his face burst into an expansive grin, and he began emitting squeals of delight.

Beck was the first to finish the meal. He sat back and savored the delicious aftertastes that lingered on his palate.

Thank You, Hashem, he thought, for that satisfying meal and the incredible wife who made it for me. And thanks also for helping Rusie and me teach the girls about Your *chessed*.

Out loud he said, "Ima sure knows how to take care of us, doesn't she? Great hamburgers! By the way, didn't someone tell me that there's no school this Thursday and Friday?"

"Right," Miriam cheerfully explained. "It's intersession." They all enjoyed school, but everyone welcomed the breaks.

"Well, Miriam, since you volunteered so quickly, how would you like to go on a little excursion with me Thursday morning?"

"Hey, that's not fair," the others clamored in protest.

But Beck wanted to spend time with Miriam. The drive to Martinsburg would give the two of them an opportunity to talk quietly together.

"Actually, it's just for the morning," Beck downplayed the trip in order to minimize the others' envy.

Avigayil commented, "We've all had our turn in the past, and I'm sure Abba will be going other places in the future."

Each one of their children possessed particular *midos* in which they shone. Avigayil had developed an admirable trait of accommodating herself to whatever fate Hashem dished out to her. It would be one of her most valuable assets in marriage, Beck thought happily.

"You kids help Ima clean up, please," he said as he washed *mayim acharonim* and *bentched*.

"Rusie, I'm going to the office now. I have several letters to write to David DePaul at the Parole Commission. We've got three criminals scheduled for parole hearings this summer, and I want to be certain they have our input on file."

State law provided for community input on parole decisions, but few groups bothered to contribute, unless a specific criminal had been given wide notoriety in the press. The ECCP was unique in providing input on the parole decisions on every criminal caught in their neighborhood. The practice effectively added twenty-five to fifty percent to the actual sentence served by each prisoner.

"I'll be back at ten fifteen, after *Maariv*," he added. "By the way, Rusie, remember we talked about the new dry cleaner on Benbrook Road? If you don't mind, I'd rather not drop in there until next week. I'm two months late with our service report to the Police Department, and I must spend several hours working on it tomorrow. Sandy even made a comment to me the other day, and it doesn't make us appear very professional."

Beck noted Rusie's reaction closely. If her qualms about the dry cleaner were strong enough, he would not postpone the visit, but he would rather channel his attention to the robberies before involving himself in anything else. There would be plenty of time in the future to check out the dry cleaner. Besides, he still harbored the nagging belief that he was sticking his nose where it did not belong. Even if the proprietor had been rude to Rusie, that did not make him a criminal. Would discretion not dictate that they merely patronize another establishment?

"Sure, Binyamin. That's okay. There's no rush on the dry cleaner."

He detected her disappointment, but judged that she was solid enough. What a *mentch*, he thought.

When he reached the ECCP office, Beck ascended the stairs and let himself in. He flipped on the lights, locked the door behind him and even snapped the deadbolt in place. He was here alone and still haunted by vestiges of his scare with Dovid earlier in the day. He looked at the clock.

"Eight o'clock already. Patrol's on the street by now. I think I'll radio Chet to let him know I'm up here by myself."

He deactivated the telephone forwarding, then lifted an ECCP radio from one of the bank of chargers he had affixed to the wall in the utility closet.

"Dr. Czar to Watch Commander." He preferred to use his "handle" on the air. It helped to maintain a sense of formality and discipline in the radio conversation.

"Watch Commander," came the reply. Carter and he

had hand-picked approximately forty of their best volunteers to command each night's citizen squad. Beck was not positive who this particular Watch Commander was, but it sounded like Shmuel Greene.

"I just wanted to inform you I'm working late in the office tonight, and I'm here by myself. I'll leave the radio on, so if there's something I can do to help you, let me know."

"Ten four."

Beck sat down at his desk and stared at the nearly empty pot of coffee. Tomorrow there would be mold growing on the surface if he did not wash it tonight. He hoped he would remember.

The stillness of the office contrasted bleakly with the noisy bustle of the family dinner he had just left. The office now seemed almost sterile, augmenting Beck's feeling of loneliness. He rose and stepped over to flip on Carter's desk light, as though the added illumination would drive out the ghosts of solitude.

Beck set the radio on the edge of his desk and turned the volume on low.

Years ago, Beck used to marvel at a policeman's sixth sense—the ability of an officer to tune out the continual chatter on the police radio and give his undivided attention to another conversation. But let the officer's name be called on the air, and he would spring up like a hare blundering into a den of wolves. Through years of practice, Beck had also acquired that instinct. Right now, the dialogue on the ECCP radio registered only on his subconscious. To him, the thick silence of the office still resembled a tomb. He wondered if he were the only one in the building. There had been no other cars in the parking lot when he arrived.

He began the first letter to the Parole Commission. The case concerned a Mr. Trent Hugh, a twenty-four-year-old tramp who had accosted many elderly homeowners in the area and threatened them if they did not pay him for lawn services he claimed to have rendered. He was a liar, but his large physique and booming voice intimidated the victims. One night, the ECCP caught him stealing a rake, and Carter arrested him. The charge was so trivial that it would ordinarily have never been prosecuted, but Beck pressured the District Attorney. He also wrote the judge a letter, aggrandizing the widespread terror that Hugh had wrought among the senior citizens. Beck knew that the judge especially despised crimes against the elderly, so naturally, that was the focus of the letter. The judge sentenced Hugh to six months in jail. For stealing a rake! Now Beck was writing the Parole Commission to urge that Hugh not be paroled before completing his sentence.

Beck finished two of the three letters he wanted to compose and stood up to stretch. His eyes fell on a manila file folder in his box, and he reminded himself that he had never reviewed the Mark Lowery file.

He opened it now. Yes, he did recall this case. Lowery was only sixteen at the time, but he had been tried in the adult court because he used a handgun in the commission of the crime. He and an accomplice had held up Woody's next door to Super Kosher. Were it not for the ECCP, Lowery would have escaped scot-free. A Patrol unit observed the two youths dashing out of the restaurant and jotted down the license number of the getaway car. Lowery's confederate was also sixteen, but since he did not wield a gun, he was tried as a juvenile.

What idiocy! Beck fumed to himself. Because he didn't carry a gun, the law regards him as just a wayward little boy. He was a full partner in the crime, and he ought to face the same consequences as his associate.

Let's see what Judge O'Brien gave Lowery, Beck thought as he sifted through the forms. Here's the disposition. Eight years, all but one suspended. Now that's unusual. O'Brien never suspends more than fifty percent. I wonder what he saw in Lowery to give him such a break.

It was a satisfactory disposition, though, Beck reflected. A suspended sentence was commonly misunderstood as a meaningless slap on the wrist. Experience had taught Beck that no judge gave quarter to offenders who violated probation. The ECCP's tactic was simple. If a criminal had been stupid enough to operate in the Patrol area before and now was re-arrested, they would immediately haul him back to court. The judge unfailingly imposed the entire suspended portion of the sentence. Lowery's hearing next Thursday would be a kangaroo court, Beck mused. The remaining seven years of his sentence were as irreversible as Achashveirosh's royal decrees.

I want Chet to attend Lowery's hearing also, Beck thought. I wonder what he did to violate probation? I'll write a juicy letter for the District Attorney to present to Judge O'Brien. Lowery will have plenty of time for his hormones to subside before he walks the streets again!

He scribbled a note and clipped it to the file. As he tossed it toward Carter's IN box, a corner of the folder struck the radio balanced on Beck's desk, knocking it flat. Against the background quiet of the office, the loud smack grated on Beck's ear and reinforced his sense of loneliness and isolation.

Suddenly, Beck sat upright and cocked his ear. His radio instinct reacted to an urgent, raised pitch in the transmissions. One of the units was blurting messages very excitedly, almost shouting into his radio.

". . . he jumped into the passenger's side of a red car! Sorry, I don't know car models . . . Looks like a sporty type of car . . . I didn't get a look at the driver. They're speeding off in the direction of Bucknell Parkway."

"Keep calm, Unit Five. I can barely understand you, you're talking so fast." Carter's authoritative voice came over the air. "Once again, where did this occur?"

Beck was pleased to witness their training pay off. ECCP rules of operation dictated that Carter assume command from the civilian Watch Commander during emergencies.

"6205 Blake," Unit Five reported more evenly. "The victim is lying on the ground now. I can't tell how badly she's hurt. Permission to get out of my car to help her?"

"Absolutely not!" Carter ordered. He added, "Any unit that gets out of his car is fired from the Patrol. Besides, I've already radioed for an ambulance, and you'll just be in their way . . ."

There was a brief silence, then Carter's voice came on again. "Watch Commander to Units Three and Four." He was organizing his troops. "Be on the lookout for a red sports car, short male in the passenger seat wearing a green baseball cap. Get the license number if you can, but I don't want any chases. Just observe from a distance. Unit Four, cover Bucknell Parkway, and Unit Three, start scouting the area south of Bucknell. We're way up by the County right now, but we're headed that way as fast as we can."

Beck grabbed the radio off his desk, dialed the volume knob up a quarter turn and scrambled for the door. Just on a hunch, he was going to station himself across from the west side of the Spartan Industrial Park.

Chet seems to have forgotten what I told him this afternoon about the Tip-Top outfit, he thought. He couldn't resist the thought that maybe he would be tonight's hero.

He scrambled down the stairs and raced for his car. Jumping inside, he clicked on the police scanner installed under his dash and listened to Carter signal for police back-up. If they were lucky, the helicopter was not on another assignment and would be summoned to help out.

Eyes alert, Beck drove as fast as he dared. Spartan was only ninety seconds away, if the lights cooperated. As he scurried through the end of a yellow signal at Harrington Avenue, he felt a glow of triumph mixed with a tinge of guilt.

"Thank You, Hashem, for pushing me safely through that light," he said appreciatively. "Now please help us catch these crooks. And watch over the poor lady lying on the ground."

After all these years, he had still not learned to accept the unspeakable emotional and physical damage done to victims of crime.

"In another year or so, the memory of this incident will have faded," he muttered, "and this woman will have become a mere statistic in our files. But at the very least, Hashem expects me to feel pity for her during her time of travail. That's the fence which keeps a Jew from becoming a self-centered buzzard like Horace Grimm." He felt his teeth gritting together.

When he reached Spartan, he bounced over the tracks, swung to the opposite side of the street and pulled onto a dirt shoulder about a hundred feet from the gravel entranceway to the Tip-Top property. He turned off his headlights and checked that all four doors were locked. He detected no lights, nor any hint of motion, on the undeveloped tract of Spartan.

"I'm sure I beat them here," he commented optimistically to himself. "Now, let's hope they show up."

The night's blackness enveloped him like a heavy shroud, the nearest street lamp thoroughly obliterated by the thick trees overhanging the roadside. He stared intently at the bushes next to his car, wary lest someone be crouching there, but the undergrowth was so dense that it was impossible to discern anything. He felt suddenly vulnerable.

"Unit Three to Watch Commander!" The blast of his

radio startled Beck. He had raised the volume too high.

"Go ahead," Carter ordered.

"I've got him in sight!" Unit Three's feverish excitement was palpable.

"You've got the red car in sight? Where is he?"

"Headed west on Cote Street... I'm a half block behind him. I don't think he sees me!... He's coming up to the stop sign at Bucknell. I see the green baseball cap on the one fellow! The driver's much taller, looks like ... a woman, I think ... or a guy with long hair ..."

"Get off the mike!" Beck fumed to himself as he listened to the radio transmission. Unit Three had not released the radio button, and no one could transmit until he did so.

"The license plate, Unit Three—get the plate number!" Carter barked with impatience when Unit Three finally ended his transmission.

Beck suspected that Carter would have given anything to be in a police cruiser right now, so he could tear up the tarmac. He's determined to net this fish, dead or alive, Beck thought.

"I'm trying, Watch Commander," Unit Three answered with exasperation. "Good ... Now, if he holds at the stop sign a second, I'll be up on him ... Right. The insignia across the trunk says Camaro ... Don't move... Okay, here we go ... The license number ... It spells ... DAISY!"

7

"KEEP HIM IN SIGHT!" COMMANDED CARTER. "WHERE IS HE now?"

"Oh my gosh!" Unit Three yelped. "He just darted out between two cars and came within an inch of getting clobbered. He turned left."

"You mean he crossed the median, Unit Three?" Carter fired back.

"Affirmative, Watch Commander. I'm waiting for traffic to clear. There's no way I'm going to stick my neck out like that idiot—I don't care who he is."

Huddled in his dark car, Beck's excitement had grown during the radio conversation, but Unit Three's last remark now snapped him back to reality. Carter was directing civilians, not police, and he was responsible for their safety. Carter was still too far away from the scene to have any hope of intercepting the getaway car. Beck heard on the scanner that two police units were responding to Carter's backup call, but they were both on the west end of Sector Two, at least a mile away. Whereas the ECCP fielded a patrol car every few blocks, the Police Department could ill afford such a luxury. Meanwhile, the helicopter was assisting an attempted homicide call at the opposite end of the city and was unavailable. As Unit Three's delay by the stop sign stretched out, Beck's hopes of an arrest began to fade.

"Dr. Czar to Watch Commander," Beck radioed.

"Watch Commander," Carter responded. "Have you been listening to the excitement?"

"Of course. I jumped in my car right away. I didn't inform you earlier that Dovid saw that Camaro in the Spartan Industrial Park this afternoon. I headed over to Spartan as soon as I heard Unit Three's report, and I'm here right now, but so far there's no activity."

"Good thinking, Dr. Czar," Carter relayed. "I forgot about the Spartan connection. But don't get your hopes up, because they turned left on Bucknell, which means they're headed away from you."

"Unless he saw Unit Three on his tail, and now he's trying to give us the slip," Beck replied hopefully. "I'll stick around here for a while. By the way, I guess we know what Daisy means now."

"That's not the half of it," Carter replied. "Don't you realize what this means?"

"No, what?" Beck was curious.

"Boy, you *must* be tired," Carter radioed. "We'll discuss it tomorrow. Remember, we're on the air, and who knows if these knuckleheads have a scanner and are listening in on the conversation."

"Unit Three to Watch Commander."

"Go ahead."

"I finally made a left onto Bucknell, but then I hit the red light at Parker. I'm cruising the streets south of Bucknell, between Parker and Townsend, but it looks like they may have escaped."

"Unit Four, please join Unit Three in that area," Carter directed. "We're finally approaching the vicinity, too, but I think we're going to proceed further east on Bucknell. Let's give it another fifteen minutes, and if nothing comes up by then, resume regular patrol positions." His businesslike orders barely concealed the disappointment in his voice.

Carter was right, Beck thought. The Camaro was not likely to come to Spartan. The crooks were probably trying to vacate the area as far and as soon as possible. He was on pins and needles, but he would sit tight a few more minutes. The blackness of the night permeated his bones.

"Actually, I'm pretty stupid," Beck said to himself. "If the crooks show up here and spot me, I'm a goner. My only defense is a radio. Big deal. So Chet will know to come and collect my corpse."

The thought of his vulnerability made Beck shudder. He wondered what beasts might be closing in on him at this very moment. He wished he had the Command Car's spotlight so he could pierce the thick soup of darkness.

Without warning, the bushes beside his car parted suddenly, and a crouched shadow loped out. Beck's adrenal glands instantly discharged a megadose of hormone, jamming his heart up to full speed.

A half second later, too late to pre-empt his endocrine system, he recognized the silhouette as an innocent raccoon. It was carrying a fruit in its jaws. Or was it a chunk of meat? No, now Beck could see it was a dead rat which the raccoon had scavenged. The combined impact of his pounding pulse and the disgusting sight of the mangy rat spawned a nauseating knot in his stomach. He leaned back on the headrest and exhaled strongly.

He observed the raccoon amble along the dirt shoulder about fifty feet, then scurry quickly across the roadway. It disappeared into the jungle of trees on the Spartan property.

"Let's call it in," Beck heard Carter announce after a period of time. "All units back to regular patrol."

Beck knew that Carter was crestfallen, but he was even more frustrated himself. He had never mastered Carter's trick of swallowing an unsuccessful chase or a soured investigation. Tonight's failure would vex him for the next week. He would have to recount the entire event to Rusie and talk it out with her; she was his only effective psychological outlet.

"Dr. Czar to Watch Commander."

"Watch Commander," came the reply.

"I'm abandoning my post at Spartan and heading for home. I'll be at the office by four tomorrow."

"Roger, see you then. Don't feel bad about these goofballs getting away. Time's on our side."

Beck appreciated Carter's consolation. It was true. They had always managed to collar criminals who were stupid enough to return to the Patrol's territory. It might take a few more robberies, but Beck felt certain that Hashem would help them sooner or later. And once the ECCP got its hands on the fiends . . .

Beck started his motor and angled out onto the pavement. He was physically and psychologically drained. Even the car seemed sluggish to him as he made his way home.

He pulled into the driveway and turned off the motor and headlights. Exhaustion overcame him, and he made no move to get out of the car. He leaned his head back once more, as the trying events of the evening flashed through his mind in fast replay.

"Who knows what Hashem has in mind for us?" he consoled himself. "*Gam zu letovah.* This, too, is for the good."

A movement in the rear view mirror caught his eye. He swung around and looked out the back window.

"Well, isn't that curious?" he muttered. "Another raccoon. This little fellow's carrying his dinner in his mouth, too. He couldn't possibly be the same critter I just left at Spartan. I wonder how many other ring-tailed cousins are roaming this neighborhood tonight. And to think that Hashem must feed them all! What a job!"

Beck watched the animal make its way along a fence and disappear through the brush.

"Just like Dovid Hamelech said," Beck observed. *"Pose'ach es yadech umasbiah lechal chai ratzon.* Hashem provides daily sustenance to billions and billions of creatures. It's the ultimate K.P. duty!

"Imagine the jillions of photons streaming down with the sunlight each day, captured by plants, converted into tons upon tons of organic material and consumed by armies of animals of every imaginable species. The world is one colossal, miraculous food factory.

"Only humans have the capacity to comprehend the vastness of this miracle, or even to recognize its existence. That naive raccoon envisions nothing but its one little sliver of meat that it will carry back to its lair. It has no inkling of the workings of the immense world of food, nor does it lend an instant's thought to how this particular meal fell to its lot.

"Of course, most humans are no better. How many hordes of people sit down to their meals every day, oblivious to the ten billion miracles Hashem orchestrated in order to produce this day's food? In what way are such people different from the unthinking raccoon? *People* should eat like *people*, and recognize the incredibly complex geosystem that produces their daily meals."

The raccoon and thoughts of Hashem's beneficence were a salve for Beck's frazzled nerves. Gathering his energy to climb out of the car, he realized how very tired he really felt. It had been an interminably long day . . .

The sun shone brightly on the back of Beck's shoulders the next morning as he emerged from the downtown subway terminal. He was still groggy from lack of sleep, having stayed up most of the night to prepare for his talk today. He was scheduled to deliver a summary of the research their lab had been doing on an oceanic warm core eddy about three hundred miles off the coast of New Jersey. The mid-Atlantic states had organized a week-long conference on ocean-atmosphere exchange processes and chosen Cahill's Centerplex Convention Center as the conference venue. It was the only work-related activity Beck had acceded to during his three weeks of leave following his North Pacific research cruise.

As Beck crossed Bloomington Street, he could see Police Headquarters four blocks away. The infamous crane was still perched atop the Long Office Building, but it was as still as death. What secrets did that long-armed beast harbor? What dark mysteries had it witnessed? Beck doubted that anyone in the throng of pedestrians swarming about him knew the crane's recent history. The story had appeared in a corner article on page fourteen of last night's paper.

"Of course, if Lowery had been killed," Beck hissed to himself, "they would have plastered it across the front page, with a full color photo of all the blood and guts. The newspapers fester with inverted morals. When a man gets killed, he's thrust into the limelight, but when a life is saved, it's hardly worth taking note. No wonder mankind has become insensitive to that most precious of all commodities—human life. As Jews, we must protest against this desecration of Hashem's order. A person must especially protest against *himself*, and battle against the insidious influence of the corrupt, ungodly world around him. I say, 'Let all the newspapers go up in flames!'"

Beck had dealt with the media quite frequently, and he considered them one of modern society's plenary forces for evil. In his opinion, they were a flock of vicious, nefarious vultures.

As bad as the papers were in Beck's estimation, however, he regarded television as infinitely more crooked, a manifestation of Satan incarnate, a source of the most unspeakable depths of depraved wickedness. He avoided looking at a television screen as though it were a poisonous viper. When he inadvertently chanced upon a television in someone's home, he shrank from it like a genteel nobleman might recoil from an open, stinking sewer line. Indeed, Beck often equated television with a bilge pipe teeming with putrefied manure.

On the subway ride home that afternoon, Beck relaxed into a bench by himself, tired from the day's conference proceedings. Across the aisle, a young woman was using a McDonald's paper cup to peel a wet piece of gum from the rail in front of her.

"Honey, yuh see what sumuhn done?" the woman addressed a child sitting next to her. Beck presumed it was her daughter. She could not have been more than five years old. "Ain't it selfish t'mess up sumuhn els's popurty?" the woman instructed.

The youngster looked at Beck and he beamed a smile at her, but she just stared back. They were strangers, he knew, but he felt obliged to encourage her. He was refreshed to discover that decency was still alive and well among some folks.

He leaned his head against the window and watched the streets and houses fly by. His paper had been well received at the conference. The audience had not probed too deeply, else they would have uncovered all the problems that plague every piece of scientific research. Working in the oceans is difficult, he mused, when the bottom is four thousand meters down. Atmospheric chemistry is a fascinating science, especially when it is allied so intimately with the equally fascinating scientific discipline of oceanography.

Nevertheless, Beck reflected, scientists too often lose sight of man's puny knowledge *vis-a-vis* the prodigious complexity that the Creator invested in the world. The ignorant public, of course, is deceived even further by bogus "oceanographers" gadding about in their private submarines, snapping pretty pictures of reef fish. One of these years, Beck pondered, he would write a book about the impotence of modern science.

"Hi, Benny," Carter called cheerfully as Beck stepped into the ECCP office. "How was your conference today?"

"Wonderful," Beck answered. "Hashem put all the right words in my mouth."

Beck chastised himself for not expressing his gratitude to Hashem earlier, and he was chagrined that Carter had been the emissary to remind him. At least Hashem had been merciful, and chosen a benign method to arouse him to his duty. This display of divine mercy in itself evoked another thank you from Beck's heart.

The rich aroma of fresh coffee suffused Beck's nostrils. The pleasant olfactory sensation, together with the sunlight flooding through the wide window by Carter's desk, invigorated Beck. He was happy to have dispatched his *parnassah* duties and now to be free to devote his energies to the recent crimes disturbing the *kehillah*.

"Well, let me bring you up to date," Carter said as soon as Beck was settled. "The lady who got hit on Blake Road last night was Elaine Bernstein, and I visited both her and her husband this morning. She was knocked down and banged an elbow, but she's all right. She's fifty-two years old, lives at 2301 Bonnet Court. She described the suspect as a short man, twenty to twenty-five years old, with short hair. Just on a hunch, I showed her a line-up card with Puppy's photo on it, and she picked him out right away. I'm writing an arrest warrant for him this afternoon, but the problem is he has no current address, so we're going to have trouble picking him up."

"Wonderful," Beck observed sarcastically. "We've got a nut roaming the streets and no way to apprehend him."

"Well," Carter continued, "I've been mulling over this case, and I've got a mind not to arrest him anyway."

"Why not?" Beck challenged.

"Because I think he's just a pawn, and I don't want to tip our hand yet. It's pretty certain that he was the hit man on both of Mrs. Stein's robberies and now Mrs. Bernstein's, and my gut reaction is that he pulled most of the other robberies also. But remember there was a getaway car in most of those incidents. I have a feeling there's a bigwig somewhere pulling all the strings."

"You win," Beck conceded. "I'll defer to your judgment."

Beck had long ago recognized the soundness of Carter's sleuthing instincts, and he gave him free reign to run their investigations as he saw fit. Carter had not failed him.

"By the way, Benny, before I forget, Carla Jones's office phoned to say that your call was traced to a pay phone. What's that all about?"

"Nuts!" Beck said in disgust. "I should've known. This gang is street-wise, for sure."

He informed Carter of the threatening phone call he had received the afternoon before.

Carter was silent a moment, then remarked, "To be honest with you, Benny, I don't think that farmer fellow was up to any trouble. Just from his reaction, I would say he was really expecting to walk into a doctor's office and was caught by surprise when he found himself face to face with a police officer. He looked almost disoriented. I've seen that type of reaction before."

"Well, maybe we'll find him one of these days," Beck

returned, "and put the question to him directly."

Carter finished entering some data in the computer and hit the ESC key. He swung his chair around and raised a finger. "I think your other statement is right on target, though—we're facing a street-wise outfit. Did you think about what happened last night?"

Beck was confused. "Not really. What was I supposed to think about?"

"I knew you were tired. Remember Dovid told us the plate on the red Camaro was XNC422, right? But last night it was carrying a tag that spelled DAISY. They're pulling a switcheroo just long enough to jack up a victim. Probably, they stop a mile down the road and switch the plate back to the regular one."

"Whew!" Beck whistled. "You're right. That trick passed right over my head."

"What's more," Carter added, "there *is* no DAISY registered with DOT."

"You're kidding," Beck said incredulously. "So how did they get the plate?"

"There are a hundred ways to do it, if you know how. Register an old clunker, get a plate for it, then report it junked. Or manufacture the plate yourself. It's not hard, but it does take some planning, and that's why I say these meatheads are playing with a full deck."

"I see what you mean," Beck replied. "Incidentally, did I tell you about my invitation to speak at the Wicomb Center tomorrow night?"

Carter instantly jumped out of his chair and rushed over to Beck.

"What!" he thundered, shoving his face in Beck's. "You're going to the Wicomb Center? Where is your common sense? I hope you're taking an armed escort."

"That bad, huh?" Beck said, taken aback by Carter's

vehemence. "A colleague of mine on the Citizens Advisory Council invited me to tell the Wicomb community about the ECCP."

"I'm serious, Benny," Carter replied. "That's a really mean area. Why don't you ask Major Toffat if an officer can drive you?"

Beck turned away from Carter and gazed out the open window, absently stroking his beard. He was startled as a jagged bolt of white lightning flashed across the sky. Large drops of rain began to fall from dark gray clouds.

"I'll be okay, Chet," he finally said reassuringly.

But Carter's reaction had abruptly stirred trepidations in a corner of his mind. He had not realized that Wicomb was so nasty. He hoped he was doing the right thing.

Carter shrugged his shoulders in resignation. He sat down again and inspected several sheets of paper on his desk.

"I've entered all the crime data you wanted put in the computer," he informed Beck.

"Good. Did you get my note about the blue Ford Escort? I left you the tag number."

"Yeah, I ran it in the computer last night. Belongs to Damon Hughes, 1139 Monk Street in the Western Precinct. We'll tuck that tidbit away for future reference. Listen, do you still want me to deliver those letters to DePaul?"

"If you can," Beck said appreciatively. "By the way, I won't be in the office at all tomorrow, and Thursday morning I'm driving to Martinsburg to talk to a Caterpillar dealer about construction cranes."

"Sounds like an exciting itinerary," Carter retorted as he clipped his police radio to his belt and stepped over to the door. He stood looking at the knob, hesitating, as though undecided whether to leave or not. Without warning, he turned around and addressed Beck.

"Benny, I'm asking you as one friend to another. How about if the Watch Commander and I take you down to Wicomb tomorrow evening? The Deputy Commander can take charge while we're gone. Believe me, I don't mean to worry you, but . . ."

Beck swung around and peered at the cop across the room. A distant roll of thunder penetrated Beck's head. For a long moment, neither one of them spoke.

"Thanks, Chet," Beck finally said in a subdued voice. "I'll be okay."

As Carter closed the door, the snap of the lock resounded in Beck's ears like a gunshot. He winced with an ominous foreboding.

8

"BOY, CHET WAS RIGHT!" BECK MUMBLED TO HIMSELF AS HE scanned the curbs for a parking spot. He had located the Wicomb Center, in the heart of a blighted, seamy neighborhood teeming with rowdy drunks, bands of tough youths, mounds of trash and block upon block of dilapidated shacks. Although the Wicomb Center parking lot had appeared full, Beck had decided to enter it anyway, on the chance he might find a corner to slip into. It was a grievous error, because the lot was full not only of cars, but of idle teenagers, mostly boys, clustered in small knots. Two youngsters in the corner were exchanging fisticuffs, but he could not discern whether it was horseplay. Several groups turned around to glare at him, and one belligerent show-off slapped a palm squarely on his car roof. Beck remained stoic as a dozen onlookers guffawed. He began slowly backing out of the lot, as though retreating gingerly from a hornet's nest.

He searched for a place to park on the street. It was close to dusk, and the corners were already dark. If he had not promised Farringdon the favor, he would have turned tail for home without further ado. He soon chanced upon a tight opening in the line of parked cars, one long block east of the Multi-Purpose Center.

A mean-looking gang of five older adolescents stood on

the sidewalk, leaning against the wall of a bank no more than ten feet from his car. They inspected him intently as he squeezed his vehicle into the opening. One gigantic fellow grasped a leash, the other end of which restrained a black and white pit bull terrier. Beck considered once again the advisability of fleeing for the safety and refuge of home.

He swung out of his car and surreptitiously flipped the external alarm switch, but it afforded him little comfort. He wondered what condition his car would be in when he returned, or if it would even be there at all. As he stepped onto the curb, the pit bull spied him for the first time and lunged forward, emitting a ferocious volley of barks. The other end of the leash held fast, to Beck's immense relief. He walked by the curb, giving wide berth to both the dog and the gang, nodding ever so slightly to them as he passed. They glared back. As he continued further, with his back to the enemy, each step was sheer suspense.

"Jew! Hey, Jew!"

The taunt pierced his ears like a poisoned arrow, but he displayed no reaction. The words themselves meant nothing to him. If an aristocrat bridles at the insults of a serf, it only demonstrates a lack of self-esteem. He was so much more noble and elevated than they.

"Hey, Rabbi Jew!"

He did not change his pace. Now he was thirty feet beyond them, with a glimmer of hope that he might survive. Just then, a stone whistled past his legs and pinged forcefully off the glass door of the Wicomb Center. He quickly ducked inside to safety, like a high-wire artist who had just teetered across Niagara Falls. He collapsed momentarily against a pay phone by the entrance.

"Thank You, Hashem. I was a fool for agreeing to come here, and I want to do *teshuvah*. Thank You for saving me from my own *aveiros*."

He added another fervent petition that the wild animals should disappear before he had to walk that same gauntlet back to his car.

The security guard by the information desk directed Beck to the conference room. He entered and immediately eyed Farringdon in the far corner. The room was configured auditorium style, with about fifty folding chairs assembled in seven neat rows. Most of the seats were already occupied.

He surveyed the audience in a glance. "All women, from youth to elderly. Same old story. Decent folks who are prisoners in their own homes, frustrated, not knowing where to turn for help."

Farringdon greeted Beck warmly and introduced him to Sergeant Jim Brennan, the Community Relations sergeant in Western Precinct. Beck conversed politely with the policeman, while Farringdon herded stragglers to their seats.

After preliminary comments, Farringdon introduced Beck with a glowing encomium for the East Cahill Citizens Patrol, and he expressed hope that the Wicomb community would coalesce to launch a similar effort. Listening to Farringdon, Beck almost felt depressed. Their chances of forming *any* type of effective community organization were virtually nil. The beasts on the street would devour them alive. Wicomb had to wrestle with more fundamental exigencies, such as engendering a decent value system in their children and resisting the onslaught of destruction and ethical decay bombarding them from every doorway and lamppost.

Beck pondered what he might say to help them. What was the best advice he could proffer? He would only have one shot, and he would likely not reach most of the audience. But if he could help one human being pull himself out of the abyss, his visit would be justified.

Beck went through the motions of relating how the East Cahill Citizens Patrol was formed, how it operated and why it became so effective in reducing crime. He had given the same dog-and-pony show to dozens of communities, but his heart was not in it this time. If this was all he could contribute, he thought despairingly, his evening would be wasted.

He wanted to give them a simple, pragmatic piece of advice, something which did not depend on other people or help from the government. Something that would heal the core of rot in their lives. He knew what he wanted to suggest—if he dared.

He stopped and took a deep breath. "My friends, let's forget about citizens patrols for a minute. I want to propose one step you can take that will pay huge dividends in the long run. This is something I would advise any family living in any neighborhood in the country—from the wealthiest to the poorest.

"My recommendation is for each one of you to go straight home after this meeting, pick up your television sets . . . and set them outside by the garbage."

He paused, not only for effect, but to assess their reaction. They seemed dumbfounded, as though he had proposed they relocate to the moon. He needed to assure them of his sanity.

"My wife and I pitched out our television more than ten years ago, and we've never regretted it. Television glorifies violence, materialism and immorality—all of the decadent ills underlying that jungle on your streets."

"Amen," several women chorused. Beck knew he was on safe ground now. No one had ever denied to him that television was a monstrous purveyor of evil, yet few gathered the strength to drive the plague out of their homes.

Beck proceeded to press the issue. "By the time your son or daughter turns eighteen, he or she will have seen about sixteen thousand murders, according to national averages. He will be so hardened to the loss of human life that he will hardly react when he witnesses it for real. He will also know how to aim a handgun, manufacture a pipe bomb and fence stolen goods. I don't say my own children are paragons of virtue, but I'll tell you one thing—my children are naive, and I'm *proud* of it!"

"Amen," came a growing chorus of voices. Beck felt like a preacher, and it energized him. Finally, he was speaking to them on a common plane.

"But that's not half the story," he expounded. "Look at these young boys shoplifting hundred dollar L.A. Gear tennis shoes. Who taught them that L.A. Gear is a symbol of success? *Television!*"

"Amen."

"It's ironic that television commercials portray London as the supreme vacation experience, as though you can't possibly be happy relaxing with your family in your own living room. And in England, don't you know that the commercials flash the glitter of Broadway and the monuments of Washington as the ultimate diversion? From where do you and your children absorb all these lies? *Television!*"

"Amen."

"Were your children born with the belief that gold chains and Mercedes Benzes are the goals of life? Where did they pick up these corrupt notions? From *television!*"

"Amen."

"You know, my friends, try a little experiment the next time your teenager looks out the window and sees his buddies driving by in a big, fancy Thunderbird or a sharp-looking Jeep with the top open. Say to him, 'Son, isn't it a shame that they only think of their own pleasures? What a pity they don't recognize the truly important things in life.' He'll probably look at you like you're some kind of nut, but maybe you will have planted a seed. *And keep watering that seed!"*

"Right! Amen!"

Beck was on a roll. "Right now—before your common sense is muted by the snickering of your neighbors—swear to yourselves that you will carry your televisions out to the garbage the instant you arrive home. Don't listen to anyone and don't speak to anyone until the deed is done."

A woman dressed in turquoise blue pants and a plain sweater raised her hand.

Beck thought to himself, Uh-oh. Here comes the barrage of rationalizations.

"You're right, suh," the woman said, "but I wuk all day, and television's mah only baby sittuh."

"Ma'am, I'll make a deal with you," Beck responded. "I'll hire five criminals, and send them to your house to watch your children while you're at work. They can act out all kinds of devilish skits to entertain your children. In fact, I'll ask them to put on the same skits your children would have seen on television that day. Is it a deal?"

There was no need for the woman to answer Beck's rhetorical question, and the audience knew it. Beck acknowledged an older woman in the third row, whose hand was raised.

"Doctuh Beck, ah bin sayin' yuh wuds fuh yeahs. Yuh see, ahm a widduh, an' ah luvta read. T'on'y thin' ah watch on television's thu weathuh evuh naht."

"The weather!" Beck motioned animatedly with his arms to create an effect. "The weather's one of the worst things on television! At least the violence and immorality in the other programs you can recognize as evil right away. But what does it do to your outlook on life when the weatherman says,

'It's going to be a gloomy day tomorrow. Rain, rain, rain. Expect the weather to improve by afternoon.' Ma'am, that's a corruption of the mind. Rain is a *blessing*! Let the weatherman live in the Sahara for ten years, and then we'll see if he still thinks rain is gloomy. I *love* the rain. I love the sunshine, too. They're both miracles from G-d!"

"Amen," half the audience chimed in together. Beck had discovered that there were few atheists among the poor. It was something they could be proud of, something they could teach the upper classes of society.

"I'm sorry, ma'am," he added in apology. "I didn't mean to jump on you so strongly. I was just exaggerating to make a point. Naturally, the weather report is not nearly as bad as the immorality and filth of other programs. But the truth is, there is hardly *anything* of redeeming value on television. And even if one could ferret out one microscopic kernel of virtue and truth in a day's programming, it is accompanied by such a mountain of lies and obscenity that one should *never* tolerate it within one's own four walls."

Beck was eager to go further, but he reminded himself of Will Rogers's sage advice, "The time to quit is when the audience still wants more." He brought the discussion to a graceful landing, thanked the women for attending and wished them the best.

"I certainly did not expect that performance," Farringdon said to Beck after most of the people had left. "You have an enormous advantage over these people, however."

"What's that?" Beck said inquisitively.

"You used the word 'obscenity,'" Farringdon explained. "Obscenity tends to breed obscenity, just as virtue breeds virtue. You don't understand how hard it is to break out of the cycle. You're on a different wavelength."

Beck admitted to himself that he knew little about how "the other side" lived, but was it not human nature to want to break away from evil, to better oneself? He said nothing to Farringdon.

"Benny, let me take you for a visit. Do you have an extra ten minutes?"

"Sure."

Beck wondered what he was getting into, but Farringdon's words, "You don't understand," still echoed in his ears. His pride was hurt, and he felt duty-bound to refute that accusation.

The two men exited a rear door of the Multi-Purpose Center. Beck glanced around nervously, but his former tormentors were nowhere in sight. Indeed, Beck noted, the streets were eerily empty, except for occasional deadbeats and a few toughs at the corners.

"I'm taking you to a family that I've been helping for the last three months," Farringdon explained. "A single mother with six children. Just this week a friend moved in with them, a seventeen-year-old boy who ran away from home."

They halted in front of a dingy, dark brown tenement, and climbed a set of crumbling concrete steps. Beck sidestepped as many cigarette butts and as much food litter as he could. Farringdon led the way, circumventing the torn shoes of a sordid tramp asleep in the corner. They ascended two flights of stairs before Farringdon stopped and rapped on a heavily scratched wooden door.

A scrawny child with a dirty face opened the door. Beck estimated she was eight or nine years old.

"Mistuh Donny!" she exclaimed with delight. "Mama, Mistuh Donny's heah."

Farringdon swept an open arm in front of Beck, inviting him to enter first. As Beck stepped across the threshold, a putrid aroma invaded his nose. He beheld a scene that made him reel with nausea.

A small table with a filthy and badly bruised formica

surface stood in the corner next to him, laden with dirty dishes and encrusted with the vestiges of past meals. A haggard-looking woman was playing solitaire at the table, oblivious both to her visitors' entrance and to the grease spots dotting her cards. An ugly cockroach scurried across the deck, but she paid it no more attention than an elephant notices a beetle. Another roach flailed in vain to rescue itself from a bowl of watery soup.

Two listless young boys lay on a threadbare couch in the middle of the room, glancing occasionally at a mangy dog moping at their feet, but mostly just shifting aimless stares between the bare walls and the ceiling. A smashed tomato oozed from under the pants of one of the boys, and three more cockroaches were huddled around the pool of juice.

A toddler dressed in nothing but a diaper waddled toward Beck. The youngster's kinky hair looked like a thousand miniature springs, each one bouncing with every step. Beck discerned two enormous, disgusting cockroaches entangled in the curls, but he could not tell whether they were dead or alive.

Beck spied the back of an older teenager slouched in a broken armchair in the far corner of the room, facing a television screen in front of him. Beck could not see the boy's face, but he appeared to be intent on the movie he was watching. Of all the players in this haunting scene, he and the little girl who had opened the door were the only two who seemed to have any existence in the real world. The teenager watching the television must be the friend who had run away from home, surmised Beck, as he struggled valiantly to ignore the knot gripping his stomach.

Just then, a loud commercial appeared on the television screen. The young man rose from his armchair, flipped the channel knob and swung around toward Beck and Farringdon. Beck clutched the doorknob and gasped in disbelief. It was Mark Lowery! The gold tooth was unmistakable.

"Are you all right?" Farringdon supported Beck's right arm.

"Yes, it's just . . . well . . ." Beck stammered.

"Come, let's leave." Farringdon gently coaxed Beck out into the hall and shut the door behind them. "You've had enough for one night."

Beck was grateful that Farringdon had rescued him. He felt like he had blundered into Act Twenty-Seven of an endless horror movie, and had been snatched back to the safety of reality just before the murder scene.

"Baruch Hashem, shelo asani goy!" he recited to himself with intensity. "Blessed is Hashem, who has not made me a gentile." Beck's mind was indelibly etched with the image of that abominably squalid room, and he knew that the *brachah* of *"shelo asani goy"* would forever evoke its grisliness.

As they emerged onto the street and headed back toward the Wicomb Multi-Purpose Center, Farringdon softly broke the silence. "You've never seen that side of life, have you, Benny?"

More than ever, Beck respected Farringdon's intelligence. He wondered what other treats Farringdon had in store for him.

"Don," Beck said honestly, "I've worked side-by-side with many people of all races, religions and economic levels, and I've met a lot of fine people wherever I've been. But I've never encountered a scene of such purposelessness and hopelessness. Those people are human beings, and I don't mean to discard them, but in my opinion they are beyond reach. You don't really believe you can help them, do you?"

"Benny, I think you're beginning to understand," Farringdon commented sympathetically.

Beck's neat world of right and wrong, good and evil,

open and shut, had just suffered a blow. The clean lines in his mental picture of life had taken on a fuzzy cast.

Neither man uttered a word as they strode silently down the block. Beck grappled inwardly with his emotions, fists tightly clenched. He began sorting priorities. No, he reminded himself, nothing within his *tafkid* required him to labor for the salvation of Wicomb. Come what may, his commitment was to *Yiddishkeit* and the *kehillah* in East Cahill. He filed his brush with the Dark Ages in a back cranny of his mind for future contemplation.

By the time they stood in the parking lot of the Multi-Purpose Center, Beck had regained his composure and his grip on reality. He *must* find out what Farringdon knew about Mark Lowery.

"Who was that young man who stood up just before we left the room?"

Beck's voice shattered the silence and echoed against the tranquility of the night.

"I really have no idea," Farringdon responded quietly. "I presume he's their new boarder, but I've never met him."

Beck wondered if Farringdon was lying. Probably not. If he himself had not used MacDougal's binoculars Monday morning, he also would not have recognized Lowery.

Farringdon politely thanked Beck for attending their meeting and expressed hope that there would be follow-ups. He got into his car and raised his hand in a terse wave as he drove off, leaving Beck in the still darkness.

It was at that moment that Beck realized his stupidity. Why had he not asked Farringdon to drive him to his car? Farringdon probably assumed that Beck had also parked in the lot. Surely, Farringdon had not abandoned him on purpose. Or had he? And to what fate? Beck conjured up Farringdon's parting smile and tried to decide whether it appeared sinister in any respect.

Beck turned quickly toward the sidewalk, hoping he would not meet anything alive for the next sixty seconds. Each click of his shoes on the sidewalk made him grimace, as though they proclaimed his presence to a hushed audience. He shriveled inwardly, as he fancied hidden eyes scrutinizing him from every window and doorway.

As he crossed an alley between the next two buildings, his heart jumped to his throat. There were his nemeses! The same gang of villains, the same leather leash extending downward, harnessed to the same vicious pit bull squatting on the pavement. All of them, including the bellicose canine, were facing away from him, and he sent up the most intense prayer of his life that none would turn around.

He passed the alley unnoticed, or so he thought. Unless . . . had they seen him coming and ducked into the alley ahead of his arrival? Were they merely playing tricks on him, pretending to be unaware of his passage? Why was his brain exploding with tension?

He continued walking softly, listening for the slightest rustle. His mind began to imagine the shuffling of footsteps and the patter of paws emanating from the alley behind him. He was desperately tempted to glance over his shoulder. He felt like breaking into a full sprint, but he decided instead to control himself. In another half block he would be safe.

All of a sudden, he heard a rushing whoosh, accompanied by a savage, bloodcurdling snarl hurtling toward him from behind. He whirled in time to glimpse the beast in midair, gums drawn tight and fangs bared, rocketing straight for his jugular. Simultaneously, the roar of a gunshot rent his ears, as a violent, bone-splitting pressure struck his upper chest. He was propelled backwards, his head cracking hard against the concrete building. The world went black.

9

"HE'S GOT A MEAN KNOT, BUT THAT'S ALL. YOU'RE SURE HIS head didn't hit the sidewalk?"

"Uh-uh. The dog knocked him purty hard, and he was off balance anyways, so he hit the wall, and then I seen his hat go flyin'. But he kinda slump downta the sidewalk, sorta slow. I think he got knocked out when he hit the wall. Hey, I see he's comin' to."

The world began to come into focus in front of Beck. Bright red and white flashes bounced from the sky to the building at the top of his vision. A rugged countenance framed by a fireman's hat was peering at him from five or six feet up. Another man was crouched over him, holding a rubber hose attached to a metal cylinder. He sensed the weight of a blanket draped across his chest, pulling at his loosened tie. The cement felt cool under his back.

A third human form slid into Beck's field of vision.

"Bobby!" Beck barely squeaked. "What're you doing here?" He recognized an undercover cop who worked in Eastern Precinct, a strong, masculine chap who, despite his lack of education, was a keen detective who had used his knowledge of the street to effect numerous arrests. It was a coincidence to encounter him in Wicomb, so far from his assigned precinct.

"Lay still, Docta Beck." Bobby laid a firm hand on Beck's shoulder. "Yer head jus' took a clobberin', but I'm glad t'see ya din't lose all yer brains."

Beck smiled wanly. "I never had much to begin with. What happened? Last thing I remember I was staring at a saber-toothed monster and thinking that the Day of Judgment had arrived."

"Hah!" Bobby laughed. "He's okay, doc. He's still got his humor."

Bobby slipped his powerful arms under Beck's back while the medic lifted his shoulders, and they sat him upright. He winced and shut his eyes tightly as a sharp pain stabbed the back of his brain. Bright stars splashed inside his eyelids.

"You okay?" the medic asked.

"Yeah, just give me a minute," Beck lied, opening his eyes again. He could see a number of other policemen restraining a mob of onlookers.

"Ya kin thank Chet fer thisun, Docta Beck," Bobby drawled. "If it han't been fer him, you'd've been made into mincemeat by that pit bull. Chet tole me ya was comin' here tonight and asked me to keep an eye out fer ya. I'm s'prised ya din't see me sittin' in m'car by the curb. Good thing I brought m' twenty-two. I'd've never picked off that dog with m' handgun. I seen 'im comin' an' turned 'im into a flyin' corpse jus' before he rammed ya. Othawise, we'd've had to find a dentist to remove his teeth from yer neck."

Beck shuddered at the grisly picture Bobby had painted. So it was the force of the dog's dead body that had propelled him into the wall and smashed his head against the building. Bobby must have made an incredibly lucky shot, Beck thought, to have killed the brute midair, sailing at top speed, an instant before it would have clamped a stranglehold on his neck.

No, there was no luck involved at all, Beck corrected himself. It was Hashem who had saved him for the second time tonight. He must ask Rav Feinman whether he should *bentch Gomel*. He felt an uncontrollable outpouring of love for the *Ribono Shel Olam*. He would try to evoke this emotion again when he recited *Shema* tonight.

He was also grateful to Bobby—and Chet, of course. He thanked Bobby with all his heart, and contemplated what he might do to demonstrate how sincerely he meant it.

He finally felt sufficiently recovered to stand up, and he pulled his knees to his chest to rise. They lifted him to his feet and steadied him a moment.

"Thanks, fellows," Beck said. "I'm fine. Maybe you can just help me to my car."

"Oh, no, ya don't," Bobby announced emphatically. "I'm takin' ya home. I already got a man to drive yer car, so don't worry 'bout it. Ya need some rest, an' tha's where yer headed."

Beck did not need a second invitation. He collapsed into Bobby's car and relaxed comfortably.

"Did you see the hoodlums who sicked that dog on me?" Beck asked when they had driven a few blocks.

"Yeah, I seen 'em, but m' first job was t' bag th' poochie and make sure ya was all right. They musta scrammed when they seen the cops. Too bad th' dog din't have no tags."

Beck had recuperated by the time they reached his house, but the officer accompanied him to the doorstep anyway. Beck reached up and rested his palm on the big man's shoulder.

"Bobby, I know I'm repeating myself, but I can't thank you enough. You can bet I'll recommend that the Chief award you a Silver Star, but the truth is, you deserve a lot more than any mortal will ever be able to give you."

Beck saw that the genuine emotion in his words had

penetrated Bobby's macho shell. He did not want to embarrass the cop further, so he added, "By the way, where'd you learn to shoot like that?"

"Huntin' geese with Pa since I was a boy," Bobby answered with a crack in his voice. "Ain't no good shootin' at nuthin', unless it's movin'. Faster the better." He winked impishly and extended his hand to Beck.

Beck wrapped both of his hands tightly around Bobby's big paw. The two men stood facing each other awkwardly in the doorway, each one unable to produce the right words to express his emotions. Finally, Beck whispered intently, "Thanks, my friend. Thanks for saving my life."

Beck noticed glistening tears gathering in Bobby's eyes, and he stepped quickly inside the house before the brawny cop was forced to wipe them away.

Beck was relieved that Rusie was not home. He had decided not to tell her about his mishap until after the trip to Martinsburg the next day. With a full night's sleep, he would be able to manage the drive, but if Rusie knew about the blow his head had just suffered, she would fret incessantly until he returned. Personally, he was more annoyed about missing his *Gemara shiur* than he was worried about the upcoming journey to Martinsburg.

The sun crowned the eastern horizon, its brilliant rays chasing the westbound ECCP Command Car. Earlier, Beck had roused Miriam when he went to *shul*, and she had popped out of bed with excitement. By the time he returned home to pick her up, she had long since dressed, eaten breakfast and *davened*. Now the two of them were zipping through the verdant, rolling hills of the state's western piedmont.

Beck gingerly fingered the sore lump on the back of his head. For once, he appreciated the hard skull that Hashem had engineered to cradle the fragile human brain and the fluid-filled interstices to absorb shocks such as he had sustained.

"Look, Abba! A herd of pure white horses. Aren't they beautiful? Especially against the dark green grass." Miriam was ebullient, excited by her sense of adventure.

"They are pretty," Beck agreed. "In fact, the whole countryside looks like a picture that belongs on a post card. It's so peaceful. Even the air smells fresh, doesn't it?"

On his cue, Miriam took a deep breath. A smile of contentment passed across her face.

"But you know, Abba, I was thinking," she said after a minute. "It's a shame the horses themselves don't appreciate the beautiful countryside. They're just dumb animals."

She looked at Beck for approval.

"Of course, you're right," he said. "Hashem didn't give them the *seichel* to distinguish between beauty and ugliness. To be sure, they instinctively recognize things which are beneficial for them and things which are dangerous or harmful. But abstract concepts like beauty and truth are not within their grasp. That's something which Hashem implanted in the human mind alone. Do you know why?"

She had a sharp intellect and accepted the challenge.

"Let me guess . . . I would say that since Hashem gave animals fewer abilities than us, He didn't want to tease them, so He didn't allow them to recognize beauty."

"What do you mean?" Beck asked.

"Well, if they could appreciate beauty, they might want to paint beautiful pictures or sing songs. But Hashem didn't give them the ability to paint or sing, so He couldn't let them appreciate beauty either, or else they would be frustrated."

"Oh, I understand," Beck replied haltingly.

He really was unsure if he understood, but he would not discourage her. She deserved credit for her effort, although she had not furnished the answer he wanted. He would try to lead her.

"Miriam, have you ever wondered why Hashem put us in this world? What's our main purpose in life?"

"Well, I suppose it's to serve Hashem and to keep the Torah," she ventured.

"Those are certainly among our main obligations," he replied. "But maybe you can regard those functions as part of a larger, ultimate *tachlis*, a final goal, and that is to make ourselves more and more aware of Hashem. '*Raishis chachmah yiras Hashem,*' we can translate as 'The beginning of all wisdom is awareness of Hashem.' The word '*yirah*' comes from the root *raish-alef-hay*, meaning 'to see,' 'to be aware.' Observing the 613 *mitzvos* strengthens our awareness of Hashem, of course, but so does contemplating the beauty of white horses lolling in green meadows. Do you understand how?"

"Sure, Abba. If we keep a commandment, it increases our awareness that there is a Commander, and in the same way, if we see the beauty of a horse, it increases our awareness that there is Someone who created that beautiful horse."

"Outstanding!" Beck exulted. "You phrased it much more succinctly than I could have. We can also add the corollary that the *more* you comprehend the beauty of the horse—its complexity, its behavior, its myriad perfect interactions with its environment, its ability to produce offspring, etcetera—the *more* you will become aware of the horse's Creator. So learning and observing the Torah is one route to *yiras Hashem*, while scrutinizing the beauty and perfection of the world is another route. Praising Hashem for both the Torah and the world is yet a third method. But the purpose of all paths is to draw yourself closer and closer to Hashem, and *that's* why He deposited us in the world—to gain the maximum possible awareness of Him before we arrive in *Olam Haba*. Now do you understand why horses have no appreciation of beauty?"

"Sure—they don't need it, because they don't have any *Olam Haba*."

Beck loved to discuss *hashkafah* with his daughters. They were born with such pure, sterling *neshamos*. Rusie and he *davened* constantly that those *neshamos* would remain unsullied by the sordid, decadent, *goyishe* environment swirling around them. Besides, it was invigorating to engage the girls intellectually. They were so bright and eager. They caught on immediately and often raced three steps ahead of him.

Miriam peeked at him, and half in jest, she remarked, "But if we are supposed to use the beauty of the world to become more aware of Hashem, why don't we move to the country, where we'll be surrounded by beauty all the time? I know that Torah life is not so strong out here, but maybe the other paths to Hashem will make up for it."

"Don't be fooled," Beck responded. "Six months of rising at four in the morning to milk the cows and pasture the horses will have you inspecting a horse's beauty with more critical eyes. Besides, you don't need to go to the country. You can spend an entire lifetime studying the beauty and perfection of the maple tree right in front of our house. Every one of Hashem's creations is awesome, and He made them all just for *you*. Do you realize how many things you have to thank Him for?"

Miriam was silent a moment. Beck glanced at the mirror and saw a truck gaining on them rapidly. It was the only other vehicle on the highway.

"Well, of course, I should thank Hashem for the food I eat. Let's see, what else . . ."

Beck knew that if he offered even one example, she

would get the idea immediately. He wanted her to evoke the concept from within herself, so he let her struggle. He checked the mirror once more.

"Oh, no!" he cried.

"What's the matter?" Miriam jumped.

"That truck nearly rammed our back bumper before he pulled into the passing lane. He should have moved over a long time ago. What a blasted fool! He could have sent us flying right off the road!"

By now the truck was abreast of them and had slowed down, but it was still passing them gradually. It was a heavy dump truck hauling a long, low-slung trailer bearing a gigantic bulldozer. Beck peered into the truck's oversized, west coast style mirror projecting from the right door. He could observe the driver, a tall, powerful looking man with sandy colored hair.

With the two vehicles side by side, barreling forward at high speed, the ECCP car appeared next to the mammoth rig like an inept dog absurdly racing beside a charging locomotive. The truck advanced slightly further, so that the midpoint of the long trailer was opposite the ECCP car. With the bulldozer towering above them, Beck felt like a defenseless midget. He noticed the truck driver turn his head and stare directly at them in the mirror.

Suddenly, without warning, the truck moved sharply to the right, straight toward Beck's left side.

"You imbecile!" Beck screamed, as he slammed on the brake and careened strongly to the right. The shoulder was narrow, and his right tires slipped onto the dirt beside the pavement, nearly causing him to lose control. He jerked the wheel back to the left and returned the car to the roadway just as the end of the big rig slid in front of him.

Emblazoned across the tailgate of the trailer, in bright red, block letters, were the words, "Tip-Top Roofing Co."

Beck braked the car and pulled to a stop well off the road surface.

"Are you okay, Miriam?" he addressed her worriedly.

"I'll be fine, Abba. My head just banged against the window. That truck could have killed us."

Beck suspected that that was precisely what the driver had in mind, but he revealed nothing to her. Still shaking, he hopped out onto the dirt and circled the car to inspect it for damage.

"*Baruch Hashem*, we're safe and the car is undamaged," he reported as he slipped back into the driver's seat.

By the time he angled back onto the highway and resumed speed, the mammoth truck had disappeared. Neither of them spoke a word for several miles. Beck listened to the steady hum of the engine and the smooth whine of the tires, all the while checking his mirror for any sign of their antagonist. Next time, he would be prepared.

Miriam broke the silence. "You asked me what I have to thank Hashem for. Today, we both have to thank Hashem for our lives."

Beck glanced at her and smiled weakly. "Thank You, Hashem, for saving our lives," he said.

They both fell silent again. Beck's thoughts focused on the Tip-Top Roofing Company. He was now firmly convinced that they were the masterminds that Chet had theorized—kingpins operating a robbery ring under their very noses. He decided to push Chet to obtain a search warrant for the Tip-Top premises, the sooner the better. He was infuriated that nothing could be pinned on them yet.

He was also frightened. What were the odds that his path would cross that of a Tip-Top truck in the middle of nowhere? Quite obviously, they had been tailing him, and they were out for blood. He wondered if they had also orchestrated the pit bull attack the previous night. He nervously glanced in the mirror again and breathed yet another sigh of relief to discover no trace of the enemy.

State Line Equipment and Supply Company was situated immediately outside the city limits of Martinsburg. As he swung into the parking lot, Beck glanced around and was impressed with the expansiveness of the premises. A modest brick building housed the sales and administrative offices, but it was dwarfed by four soaring pavilions sheltering a variety of cranes, graders, front loaders, combines and other mechanical monsters whose functions Beck could only guess. Beck surmised that State Line dealt in all kinds of heavy equipment, both for construction and agriculture.

Michael Devone was a ruddy, middle-aged man of medium build, with rough features. He wore a blue and gray plaid shirt, with a clashing red cravat around his neck, fastened in front by an opal colored clasp. He spoke in a soft voice that exuded experience and common sense.

"I'm real sorry," Devone was saying, "but insurance rules don't allow no children in the yards. We got a lotta magazines in the waitin' room that your little 'un might enjoy." He looked from Beck to Miriam.

Beck noted Miriam's crestfallen face. The big machines appeared so fantastic and chimerical from a distance, like dragons in a fairy tale, and now she would be unable to see them up close. On the other hand, he certainly did not want her perusing Devone's magazines, corrupting herself with all sorts of *sheker*.

"Miriam, we'll stop for a treat on the way home," he offered as feeble consolation. "Why don't you sit on those benches by the fence? You can see many of the machines from there. Maybe you can even borrow a paper and pencil and sketch some of them to show the kids when we get home."

He was appealing to her budding artistic abilities.

"Oh, by the way," he added, drawing a smudged paper from his inside jacket pocket. "You can look at this also. I make up a different list each week and carry it with me all the time, just for occasions when I have nothing else to do. It usually takes me about a half hour to do each item. Try not to lose it, okay?"

Her curiosity was piqued as she unfolded the paper and saw three extended columns of tiny print, under a bold heading:

THINGS TO THANK HASHEM FOR
(BESIDES THE TORAH AND THE MITZVOS)

For each item, contemplate its miraculously complicated nature, as well as the numerous benefits it confers on me. Then thank Hashem with a full appreciation of His gift.

my skin	*my teeth*	*my tie*
the hair on my head	*my larynx*	*my shirt*
my skull	*my tongue*	*my buttons*
my brain	*my saliva*	*my slacks*
my two arms and hands	*my blood*	*my belt loops*
my two legs and feet	*my blood vessels*	*my belt and buckle*
my fingers and toes	*my two lungs*	*my pager*
my fingernails and toenails	*my diaphragm*	*my shoes and laces*
my muscles	*my heart*	*my glasses*
my spine and spinal cord	*my stomach*	*Rusie*
my nerves	*my pancreas*	*Sara and Moshe*
my two eyes	*my gall bladder*	*Esther and Chaim*
my eyebrows	*my intestine*	*Naomi*
my eyelids	*my colon*	*Rochel*
my eyelashes	*my two kidneys*	*Avigayil*
my two ears	*my hat*	*Miriam*
my two nostrils	*my jacket*	*Basheva*

Brachah	clouds	clothing stores
Yossi	wind	office buildings
my parents	trees	hospitals
Rusie's parents	flowers	doctors
my friends	grass	policemen
the dining room	earthworms	firemen
the kitchen	bees	health inspectors
the bathroom	birds	engineers
the furnace	ants	auto mechanics
the plumbing	paper	rivers
the air conditioners	pens	lakes
doors	pencils	oceans
windows	erasers	mountains
floors	paper clips	forests
the roof	rubber bands	deserts
the sidewalks	plastic	glaciers
the swing sets	rocks	the polar ice caps
the shul	aluminum	rain forests
the yeshivah	iron	soil
Beis Yaakov	steel	farms
teachers	copper	farmers
electricity	rubber	fertilizers
the telephone	gold	livestock
my computer	silver	poultry
my camera	diamonds	wheat
my job	pearls	barley
the atmosphere	airplanes	rye
my food	cars and trucks	soy beans
water	trains	vegetables
rain	bicycles	fruits
sunshine	the U.S.A.	milk
light	cities	salt
darkness	factories	sugar
stars	supermarkets	bread

"My goodness, Abba," Miriam declared, "how did you ever get such small letters?"

She was intrigued by the layout more than the contents. She had tackled more than enough intellectual exercise for the morning, Beck realized, and he did not really expect her to invest much time in this new endeavor, but she would benefit simply from knowing that such an exercise is possible to undertake.

"And I don't see how you can cover *this* topic in just a half hour," she added with a grin, pointing to the word "atmosphere."

"Hah!" Beck laughed. "You're a hundred percent right. Myself and hundreds of other scientists have occupied a century trying to fathom the complexity of the atmosphere, and we all admit that we have barely begun to scale the height of the subject."

"Very punny," Miriam retorted.

"Actually, each item on the list is a lifetime of study by itself," Beck commented. "Hashem vested His infinite wisdom in every detail of the world. Even these big construction machines are saturated with infinite divine wisdom."

He swept his left hand grandly toward the sprawling pavilions, as he reached his right arm around her and gave her a gentle hug.

Devone stood open-mouthed, listening to the enigmatic exchange between father and daughter.

Beck chuckled. "Mr. Devone, you must think I'm some kind of kook, huh? Well, there *is* infinite wisdom in your equipment, whether you realize it or not."

"Mister," Devone replied, "I seen all types come in here, but you take the cake. Now, I don't mean no sass, but I thought you was comin' here to *learn* about this gear, not to *teach* me about it. I been sellin' this stuff for twenty-eight years just about, and ain't no one needs no divine wisdom to make 'em run, neither. All's you gotta do is put in the key and mash the starter. 'Course, you gotta know whatcher doin' so's no one gets hurt, but shucks, that don't take no college brains."

Knowing smiles passed between Beck and his daughter as he trudged off with Devone.

They entered the second pavilion along the roadway and threaded their way past a half dozen massive vehicles. Devone finally stopped in front of a yellowish orange crane with a lofty arm that nearly touched the roof.

He set his hands on his hips and tilted his head back as he looked up. "This here crane's the one you was askin' about on the phone. It's specially designed for close-in work, where you ain't got much room for maneuverin'. Caterpillar sells a lot of 'em to contractors doin' work on skyscrapers and that kinda stuff. Now, we was talkin' safety before. This crane's got a tonna safety features, 'cause you cain't afford to have no accidents when the sidewalk's three hundred feet down."

Beck examined the big machine. It was identical to the one he had seen on the Long Office Building three days ago.

"Mr. Devone, I'm particularly interested in how the cable is spooled in and out. Can you describe the controls?"

"Here, mister, let's hop up in the cab. Ain't no point in jawin' about it when I kin show you. Put your hoof on this here step and h'ist yourself up." He patted a metal plate projecting from the side of the cab.

There was ample room on the cushioned seat for the two men. Beck was surprised at the spaciousness and comfort of the cab. He estimated that they were sitting fourteen or fifteen feet off the ground. The commanding view and the novelty of the experience exhilarated him; it made him feel like a general ordering vast armies around on a battlefield.

"See this here lever," Devone proceeded with his instruction. "It's the cable brake. Keeps the cable from payin' out when you got a load. A man's always gotta have his hand near the brake. Now, this here lever on the right runs the cable take-up motor. The further you pull down on the lever, the faster she goes up."

Beck gripped the handle that Devone had just indicated. "Is there a spring to keep the handle from just dropping down on its own?"

"'Course, mister." Devone peered at Beck from under furrowed brows, as though a simpleton had just tossed him a childish question. "All the controls is sprung to keep 'em in neutral when they ain't bein' used. Also, see this here button on top of the lever? You gotta push it before you kin lower it. Just a gimmick, if y'ask me, 'cause anyways the cable motor don't engage 'til the lever's about three inches down."

"I see," said Beck. He combed his fingers through his beard and thought a minute. Leaning forward and inspecting the floor of the cab, he noticed two small vents on the angled section in front of the foot pedals.

"Mr. Devone, let me give you a hypothetical situation. Do you think it would be possible to depress the safety button on the cable lever, lower it just an inch or so and then run a string from the lever through those vents to the outside? That way you could stand on the ground and start the cable up just by pulling on the cord."

"Now why in tarnation would you do that?" Devone shot back. "You ain't gonna have no brake neither, so what happens when you let off the string? The cable lever pops up, the motor breaks off, and zoom! Down comes your load, and ain't no way to stop it. Listen, mister, ain't no man I know as pulls stunts on these here rigs. They's too dangerous. Why, you could kill a fella with them shenanigans!"

"But you do agree it's feasible?" Beck pressed his question again.

"Sure, I s'pose so. But mister, you gotta understan', they ain't no hot dogs in this business, if you know what I mean."

Beck had discovered what he had come for. "Well, Mr. Devone, you have certainly been helpful. Our investigation was stalled because none of us knew anything about the operation of big cranes. With the education you've given me today, I think our case is much clearer. I can't reveal the details now, but when it's all over, I'll send you a description of the incident we're dealing with. I think you'll be surprised."

They made their way back to the brick office building. Cool air from a bank of ceiling fans greeted Beck as they stepped inside. The cerulean hues of the walls and the spacious windows projecting their bright sunbeams inside further enhanced the natural, unpretentious ambience, and made Beck feel quite at home. Only a double row of modular cubicles set in a far corner, each occupied by an officious clerk, disrupted the cozy atmosphere.

Devone led Beck to a glass-paneled area sequestering several large mahogany desks. Reaching up to the top shelf of a long wooden bookcase, he produced a hefty stack of Caterpillar catalogs from previous years.

"Now you sit down right here, mister," he directed. "Ain't nobody gonna bother you here. If I ain't around when you're done, just have the gal up front page me. Would you like a cup of coffee or soda?"

"No, thanks. I appreciate the offer, though."

"How 'bout your little 'un? Want me to tell her where you are?"

"That would be nice, if you don't mind," Beck answered gratefully. "Tell her she can stay outside if she wishes, or she can join me in here. Thanks."

Beck pored over the catalogs for nearly an hour. As best he could discern, all Caterpillar cranes had sported the same array of safety precautions for many years.

There was no longer a doubt in Beck's mind that Lowery's close scrape with death was no accident on that fateful morning. With the binoculars, Beck had been able to observe a thin strand attached to the far right handle, and now he knew that was the control for the cable motor. He believed it was Robert Eberhart who had tried to murder Lowery. The only remaining question was the motive.

The realization that he was dealing with attempted homicide made Beck shiver. He closed the thick catalogs and replaced them on the shelf they had come from. Leaving the cubby, he quickly found Devone and thanked him warmly, promising once again to apprise him when the investigation was completed.

Stepping outside, Beck spied Miriam with her face pressed to the fence, fingers interlocked in the chain links. She was mesmerized by a gargantuan earth mover rumbling around the yard like a tank on maneuvers. He was delighted that she had been part of the excitement after all, and he regretted having to rend her from her fascination. But he was anxious to leave.

Beck guided the car along the street that passed for downtown Martinsburg. It was nearly noon, and even though they had packed a lunch, he wanted to buy Miriam something special before they headed home. He noticed a corner grocery store and glided to the curb. He was thrilled not to have to dodge "No Standing" signs or jostle for an open parking meter. It was a far cry from Cahill's downtown madhouse.

"Oh, look, Miriam," Beck pointed when they stepped onto the sidewalk. "Do you see the window in that drug store? It's an opportunity we can't pass up."

"What?" Miriam replied. "What are you talking about?"

"I'm talking about the sign in the window, listing all the medical products they stock. Do you see it?"

They walked past a bank, a dingy-looking antiques store, an open-air deli emitting savory odors, and finally stopped in front of the big storefront window of a pharmacy. They regarded a five-foot-tall poster suspended from two thin wires.

"I don't see anything special about this sign," Miriam commented.

"That's because you have to change glasses and view it through the eyes of the Torah."

"Oh," she began to realize the track he was on. "Why, how would Torah glasses see it?"

"Well just consider one of the items on the poster. It says Insulin Supplies," Beck proclaimed. "Have you ever watched anyone inject themselves with insulin? What a pleasure that my pancreas is producing insulin at just the proper rate. Let's rejoice over the miraculous gifts that Hashem gives us every minute and every hour!"

A young man wearing a ten-gallon cowboy hat, a pink shirt with mother-of-pearl snaps, crisp denim jeans and polished, high-top boots was passing them at that second. He caught Beck's declaration and turned his head to ogle them as he continued walking. "Wackos," the cowboy muttered to himself. "Absolute wackos."

His head was swiveled nearly a hundred and eighty degrees. He was hypnotized by these bizarre strangers and had abandoned all interest in where his feet were carrying him.

"They're also advertising crutches, walkers and wheelchairs," Miriam interjected, responding to her father's lead. "Remember when I broke a leg and had to use crutches? My arms were so sore, I couldn't wait to get rid of those things.

I still don't understand how broken bones heal, though."

"I doubt if anyone understands it too well, but certainly it is a wondrous *ness*," Beck answered. "Look at the other health aids they carry—supplies for dialysis, incontinence, intravenous feeding . . . We could remain here for hours celebrating the hundreds of *chassadim* that Hashem performs for us every day of our lives. *Thank You, Hakadosh Baruch Hu!*"

CRASH! Beck wheeled around in time to see the cowboy sprawled over an open pickle barrel, his right arm thrust into the brine, which had splashed up to soak his entire shirt front. His foppish sombrero had sailed into the expansive girth of the irate shopkeeper, who was now storming toward the hapless invader.

Beck stared at the prostrate cowboy. "Must be some kind of wacko," he muttered under his breath. He turned to Miriam and said, "C'mon, let's go."

10

SHABBOS WAS ALREADY IN THE AIR WHEN BECK EMERGED from *shul*. The sun had barely set, but *Kabbalas Shabbos* always had an immediate, reposeful effect on him, like halcyon oil becalming ocean-tossed waves. Rusie and he often joked that they were so *machmir* that they began preparing for *Shabbos* at the beginning of each week, by limiting their sleep and squeezing the most out of each day. Come Friday night, the crumbling foundations of their bodies and minds were fully primed for the revivifying elixir of *Shabbos*. They could never fathom how the *goyim* survived life without *Shabbos*. It seemed impossible.

Walking ahead of him on the sidewalk was Avraham Glick, flanked by his two teenage boys. The Glicks were a well respected family with fine children. Beck's thoughts shifted to his own children, who were always busy helping Rusie on Friday nights.

Ah, Rusie! Occasionally, his heart would well up with thanksgiving for that divine gift, but in the press of daily life, he too often failed to appreciate her true value. She was a golden *eishes chayil* and had subordinated her own life to the ideal of building their home. He sometimes wished he could achieve her level of selflessness.

He pondered with distaste the modern fad of women to

pursue professional careers. They were merely inflating bubbles of self-gratification, he mused, that would burst and vanish into nothingness when they died, if not before. Rusie, on the other hand, along with tens of thousands of other righteous Jewish mothers, was preoccupied full time, pouring her lifeblood into the futures of her children, grandchildren and all the generations to come. These glorious matriarchs were transfusing themselves into skyscrapers that will exist and expand permanently into the future, long after their worn out bodies are lowered into holes in the ground.

Yes, Beck considered, the impact of women's professional careers will have been forgotten within a few years or a decade, and certainly within a century, even for the most famous. By then, Rusie's sweat and tears will have crystallized into the cornerstone underpinning a towering Torah nation. In the final analysis, energies sidetracked into building careers are evanescent ghosts, while efforts invested in building one's family are the crescent seedlings of reality.

Judging from American Jewish demographics, the task of rebuilding the Jewish nation was being left to the Torah camp, and they were doing an admirable job. It was an ancient ideal that dated back to the *Avos* and *Imahos*.

From a practical standpoint, Beck conceded to himself, some mothers work to help the family make ends meet. But it is the career *attitude* that is so misplaced, the unfounded notion that women's greatest service to humankind, and most genuine self-fulfillment, resides in the workplace.

I don't know why I'm picking on the ladies, when the same holds true for men, Beck reflected. My professional career is also a fleeting endeavor. Just as Rusie can achieve permanence only through her accomplishments in the home, so I can achieve permanence only through accomplishments in Torah—learning it, observing it and teaching it to others. All other pursuits are vanity, both for men and for women. *Havail havalim, hakol hevel!* Vanity of vanities, all is vanity.

"Ab-ba! Ab-ba!" Beck heard the delightful syllables that represented Yossi's entire vocabulary. He saw the baby on the sidewalk, stumping his one-year-old legs toward him, his chubby left hand reaching up to Rochel's, who was quick to catch the toddler with each stumble. Rochel was wonderful with little children.

"Ima wanted me to remind you that Devorah will be with us for dinner," Rochel said when they approached.

"I know," Beck replied. "Is she already at the house?"

"Yes."

Beck felt a tinge of uneasiness. Rusie had informed him yesterday that she had again visited the new dry cleaning establishment on Benbrook Road, the one she mistrusted so much. The owner had not been present at the time. She had engaged the young female worker in a conversation, discovered that she was Jewish, and invited her for *Shabbos* dinner. At first, the girl had refused, stating that her stepfather would never permit it, but she finally yielded to Rusie's persuasions. The girl had given her name as Devorah Dickman.

Beck lowered himself into the Lazy Boy recliner in the living room, waiting for the children to line up for their *brachos*. He savored the relaxed sensation of *Shabbos*, as he rocked gently and stared ahead thoughtfully.

The delicate yellow of the plaster walls pleasantly balanced the deeper hues of the stained wood shelving he had built for their *sefarim*. Along with most Orthodox Jewish homes in Cahill, theirs sported older, and rather plain, furniture. The blue-green couch harmonized with neither the walnut veneer coffee table nor the well worn, rust colored carpet. He smiled perceptibly as he realized that the recliner he was currently occupying was the only piece of new furniture they had ever bought in their lives. True, they were blessed with a large and spacious abode, but it was not decorated to display materialism, at least not by American standards.

The Becks, however, had never been bothered by the mix and match decor. They enjoyed their home to the hilt. The girls worked very hard with Rusie each week to make it clean and neat for *Shabbos*. During the week, their home was a veritable refuge from the secular, materialistic, workaday world—and all the more so on *Shabbos*. Now, as he settled further into his cushioned chair, the *Shabbos* odors saturated his consciousness, and a deep contentment settled over his *neshamah*.

"*Hakadosh Baruch Hu*, thank You for *Shabbos*," he whispered, as a wave of unvarnished emotion swept over him.

Beck distributed the wine cups after *Kiddush*, saving the glass with grape juice for Yossi.

"Please forgive my ignorance," Devorah said after everyone drank. "I didn't realize I wasn't supposed to talk."

Beck looked up at her. He estimated she was eighteen or nineteen years old. Her long blonde hair, high cheek bones and delicate chin framed a countenance that appeared mature beyond its years. Beck imagined that her deep, blue eyes enshrouded a sea of sadness, but the enthusiasm in her voice intimated an inner spirit of youth yearning for freedom.

Avigayil, who was sitting next to Devorah, said, "Don't worry, sometimes we forget and talk, too." She bent over and added in an undertone, "I'll stay backstage and prompt you, okay?"

Avigayil excelled in defusing people's tensions.

A full hour passed before Beck leaned back, sated by the royal *Shabbos* dinner. The children had taken to Devorah immediately, and she to them. They had sung a number of inspiring *zemiros*. She had loosened up considerably, and they discovered that she had a sweet, generous disposition.

Devorah told them that the owner of the dry cleaner's was really her guardian, not her stepfather, although she referred to him as the latter. His name was Charles Henley. He was the only one who had defended her father when he was blackballed from an anti-Semitic business club in Philadelphia, and Henley had remained a lifelong friend of her parents.

Devorah displayed no self-consciousness as the children probed her history in the straightforward manner that only children possess. In 1944 and '45, both of Devorah's parents had suffered two terrifying years in Buchenwald, miraculously escaping death, while every relative in their respective families was murdered in one camp or another. They were the lone survivors.

In the winter of 1950, they emigrated to America and settled in Cahill, where Devorah's father opened a small hardware store. They had been totally secular Jews in Europe and made no efforts to build Jewish associations in Cahill. In fact, Charles Henley was their closest, and one of their only, friends.

Devorah was born late in their lives. Almost obsessively, they had repeated many stories about the concentration camp and the war to Devorah. Despite their ignorance of religious practice, they harbored an open pride in their Jewishness, an adamant identity forged in Hitler's crucible, where every other form of personal identity had been stripped from them. Devorah knew almost nothing about Judaism, but she knew with a vehemence that she was Jewish.

Then, in an ironic twist of fate, Devorah's parents died together in a fire when Devorah was only ten. Charles Henley, named as executor in their wills, had unofficially adopted Devorah, and for the past eight years, she had lodged with him. Although they lived just south of Bucknell Parkway, about a half mile from the Jewish neighborhood, she knew virtually no Jews by name, and none knew her. Her Hebrew name—the name her parents had always used for her—was her only link to the Jewish people, and she clung to it like a skydiver clutches the thin cords of his chute.

"He's always provided for me," Devorah remarked in reference to Henley, "although he's more like a prison warden supplying an inmate than a father nourishing a daughter. I get more companionship out of Schnapps—that's our darling little cocker spaniel puppy. Not that Charlie and I don't get along with each other. I don't mean to complain. It's just that within the last year or so he has become super-nervous and short-tempered and protective of his own privacy. Sometimes, I'm afraid of him."

"Did you tell him you were coming here tonight?" Rusie asked.

"Heavens, no!" she exclaimed with deadly seriousness. A flash of fear crossed her countenance. "He'd *never* tolerate that. An Orthodox Jewish house? No way! I think he'd kill me if he knew."

Beck raised his eyebrows, slightly shocked by the strength of her declaration. He suspected that Henley rarely allowed her to go *anywhere*. He also guessed that Devorah was not revealing all of the skeletons in Henley's closet. Or maybe she was unaware of how many skeletons were brooding there. She must long for the company of other girls her age, he thought.

"Look!" Rochel said in a hushed whisper, as she pointed to the high chair.

Yossi's head had been nodding inexorably downward for the last five minutes, as his full belly and heavy eyes overpowered his futile struggle to remain awake. Now, his forehead was mashed down on a pile of yellow squash. Everyone shook with suppressed laughter as Rusie gently lifted the baby, cleaned him and bundled him upstairs to the crib.

When Rusie returned, they *bentched* and cleared the table. While the older children readied the younger ones for bed, Devorah retired with the two adults to the front porch glider and chairs. The clear weather complemented the cheerful mood created by the fluorescent lights Beck had installed to illuminate the entire porch.

The night air was pleasantly cool. The feeble puff of a breeze wafted a sylvan evergreen odor from the stately pines standing in the yard beyond either end of the porch.

As they settled down comfortably, Devorah remarked, "You have wonderful children, you know."

"Why, thank you," Rusie replied with a touch of pride.

The silence which followed seemed to make Devorah uncomfortable.

"Nice weather, huh?" she said after a minute.

"Beautiful," Rusie answered.

Beck wondered if Devorah felt awkward, unexpectedly alone with the two adults, and deprived of the children's engaging chatter. His eyes met Rusie's for an instant, and an unspoken communication passed between them that something was on Devorah's mind. They held their peace.

"You know, we were discussing the Holocaust at dinner," Devorah finally broke the silence. "Can I ask you a question?"

"Sure," Beck and his wife chimed together.

"I hope you won't be offended, but you're going to think I'm questioning the existence of G-d," she noted carefully.

"Oh, Devorah!" Rusie said in a mock scold, as she laid a gentle hand on the young woman's arm. "You don't ever have to be afraid of what you say to us."

"Of course not," Beck agreed.

He understood that Devorah was closer to the Holocaust than most Jewish youngsters of the late twentieth century. She had undoubtedly suffered vicariously from her parents' lingering pain. She had more reason than most young adults to question the seeming contradiction between Hitler's ghastly success and G-d's omnipotence. There were many logical and powerful answers, but the appropriate response would depend on how she presented the question. It was important that she feel at ease.

"By the way," Beck interrupted her, "didn't you tell us that you took a philosophy course last year?"

"Yes. Why do you ask?"

"Well, you know then that philosophy is a type of science, right?"

Beck gave her time to think. He had already discovered that she possessed a sharp intellect and an inquisitive, rational mind. She'll make an outstanding homemaker for some lucky fellow, he thought. She's bright, she's organized, and she's not mentally lazy.

"In what sense is philosophy a science?" she pursued Beck's statement.

"In the sense that the logical processes of deduction and induction are the tools of philosophical investigations. That's how philosophy pursues Truth, and as you know, that's also how science investigates Truth. Am I making sense to you?"

Beck was not sure if he was even making sense to himself. He knew what he wanted to say, but he feared that he was aiming above her head.

"Sure, I understand," Devorah responded. "Philosophical analyses are based on logic, as opposed to being based on blind faith."

Beck was embarrassed that she had formulated his idea

so much more succinctly than he had himself. Clearly, she was no pushover, and for an instant, he was flustered. Inwardly, he tried to force himself to thank Hashem for this healthy blow to his ego, this salubrious, humbling experience. It was never an easy pill to swallow, though.

After a pause, he continued. "Well, the more you learn about Judaism, the more you will discover that it is a theology based on logic rather than blind faith, as you put it so precisely."

Besides being the truth, Beck supposed that this notion would appeal to her rationality.

"In fact," he added, "we have a tradition that Abraham kept all of the commandments of the Torah. Now G-d never gave him those commandments, but he figured them out on his own. Of course, we can't compare ourselves to Abraham, and I doubt that we would be able to deduce all of the Torah's specific commandments like he did, but certainly we could deduce most of the tenets and philosophies of Judaism just by making inferences from what we observe in nature and in history.

"What I am saying is that Judaism's basic metaphysical understanding of the world can be derived *a priori* simply by observing the world itself. There is a *Midrash* that G-d created the Torah first, and later He used it as the blueprint for building the world. Is it any surprise, then, that we can deduce the blueprint by examining the building?"

"Aha!" Devorah exclaimed, hunching forward on her chair. "If Judaism is so logical, then let me ask my Holocaust question." She was obviously excited.

"This girl is no dummy," Beck thought to himself. "She was letting me prattle until I set myself up for her kill. Let's see what she's going to back me into."

He and Rusie exchanged looks of consternation, mixed with the delight of an intellectual challenge.

"According to most history books," Devorah asserted, "Hitler killed himself by taking poison in April of 1945, seventeen days after the American army liberated my parents from Buchenwald. I know only too well what Hitler accomplished in his diabolical life. My mother told me one gruesome story that gives me goose pimples every time I think of it—about a friend of hers who came into the camp with twin infants. The Nazis told her that they were going to kill one of the twins right on the spot, but they forced her to make the decision which one it would be. She fainted. When she woke up, she discovered that they had killed both babies—by throwing them into the air and shooting at them like hunters shoot at geese overhead."

The Becks' attention was riveted on Devorah. The choking in her throat brought tears to their eyes.

"I fail to see any shred of logic," Devorah concluded defiantly. "Where is justice? How was it possible for a satanic figure like Hitler to rise to power, murder millions of innocent human beings without mercy and then take poison and escape to a peaceful grave? What kind of logic will Judaism make out of Hitler?"

Silence reigned on the Beck's front porch. They stared absently as the Rosensteins, an elderly couple who lived on the next block, strolled past. Beck smiled mechanically and returned Mr. Rosenstein's *Shabbos* greetings, but his mind was elsewhere.

Beck was somewhat befuddled. Obviously, Hitler was the central element in Devorah's view of the Holocaust. Other questions did not seem to bother her.

"Hey! It's Chet," Rusie announced, as a car stopped in front of the house.

Officer Chester Carter ascended the five steps to the Beck's front porch.

"Hi, folks. *Gut Shabbos.*" Carter spilled out the Yiddish

colloquialism he had learned through long years of association with the Jewish community.

Beck almost returned the salutation reflexively, but checked himself.

"Chet," Beck said cheerfully, "you arrived just in time. We're discussing the apparent injustice of Hitler's going to a peaceful death with so much blood on his hands. You care to join us?"

An instantaneous cloud of desperation settled over Carter's face, as though to say, "Oh, no, what did I stumble into now?"

He took a seat next to Beck and remarked, "I only stopped by for a second, Benny. I've got some important info for you." But he didn't seem to believe that Beck would take the hint.

"By the way," Rusie interjected, "this is Devorah Dickman, a friend of ours. And this is Chet. He's the police officer who works with the East Cahill Citizens Patrol," she explained to Devorah.

"Now where were we?" Beck resumed the colloquy, ignoring Carter's fidgeting. "Oh, yes. Devorah, you have presented a question that has a number of parts to it, so I think we should concentrate on just one or two of them. First of all, you are right—the existence of Hitler refutes the existence of G-d."

"Wha-at!" yelped Chet. He was uninterested in the debate, but Beck's declaration was extremely uncharacteristic. Rusie, knowing her husband's ways, remained quiet.

Disregarding Carter's outburst, Beck addressed Devorah. "Do you know what *Yersinia pestis* is?"

"Why yes, I do," she answered. "It so happens I did a term paper on it last year. It's the bacterium that causes bubonic plague."

"Very good." Beck was impressed. "The black death. It

killed a third of Europe in the years 1347 to 1350. Over history, it has destroyed at least ten million lives. Now where is G-d's justice? All those unfortunate human beings. And note that the bacteria themselves actually *benefited* from those destroyed lives—derived bodily pleasure from their acts of murder, if you care to look at it that way. That's even worse than Hitler, isn't it?"

"Wait a minute," Devorah responded, sensing a trap. "How can you compare a thinking organism like Hitler to some primitive bacteria?"

"It's easy to compare them, if you're an evolutionist. Both of them are nothing more than the end result of a series of random genetic mutations in their respective ancestors. In a million years, after *Homo sapiens* evolves into a super species, possessing intelligence and logic powers vastly superior to today's most advanced computers, they will look back and scorn our thinking capacity exactly the same way we now belittle bacteria. Therefore, Hitler is no more accountable for six million human deaths than *Y. pestis* is accountable for ten million human deaths."

Carter's thumb began bleeding under the nail, where he had been biting it in frustration. He drew out a handkerchief and dabbed the blood.

"*Unless,*" Beck emphasized the next thought, "Hitler was not created by the blind, sterile process of evolution, but rather by a higher Power—and it is that Power, therefore, who will hold him accountable.

"Which leads to the inescapable conclusion that Hitler received his just punishment *after* he died, since he evidently did not receive it before he died. In fact, Hitler is one of the best proofs of the World to Come—of existence after death, otherwise known as *Olam Haba.*"

"Why yes, it does make sense," Devorah conceded honestly. Beck had plucked the chords of logic in her brain.

Enthusiasm suffused her voice as she continued. "In fact, what you're saying *must* be the truth, and I'll tell you why. Hitler snuffed out six million lives, whereas he himself had only one life that mankind could have taken in retribution. Even if he were horribly tortured to death, it would have fallen very far short of true justice. It would have been impossible in this earthly world to punish Hitler for his crimes. Only in some higher, permanent world is it possible for him to be repaid in due measure. I assume there is a permanent type of existence in the World to Come—what did you call it?"

"*Olam Haba*," Beck said, full of respect for her acumen. "And yes, it is permanent. In fact, it is eternal."

Carter loudly cracked his knuckles one by one. He was sitting on the edge of his chair, nervously tapping his right foot on the porch's wooden floor.

"Come to think of it," Devorah ventured, "Hitler's diametrical opposite must also enter *Olam Haba*, and for the same reason. I'm referring to the righteous. How can a very righteous person be justly rewarded in this transient world? Take Moses, for example. Any pleasure or reward he received could have lasted only the hundred and twenty years that he was alive—hardly just compensation for the timeless and boundless good that he contributed to the world. Justice absolutely demands that virtuous people also go to *Olam Haba* to receive their full reward."

"Devorah, you have unearthed one of Judaism's great verities," Beck said praisingly. "Reward and punishment in this world are ephemeral and inadequate to the point of absurdity. *Olam Haba* is the world of true justice."

At that moment, the older three Beck sisters stepped out onto the porch.

Rusie glanced at them and inquired, "The kids are in bed?"

"Yes," Rochel responded. "The baby woke up, but he's going back to sleep."

Carter seized the break in the erudite discourse to announce, "Listen, Benny, I have to go soon, but you're going to want to hear the news I have for you." He made a move to stand up.

Beck laid a restraining hand on him, and said, "Just one more minute, Chet. Why are you so anxious? It's *Shabbos*, you know."

Carter had repeatedly encountered the Jewish attitude of serenity and quiescence on *Shabbos*. He had often told Beck that he envied the Jews' weekly hibernation, but tonight he displayed nothing but extreme irritation. He plopped down again, with a grimace of resignation.

"Kids," Beck addressed the three girls who had joined them. "We were just discussing *Olam Haba* with Devorah. Would any of you like to paint a picture of what *Olam Haba* might be like?"

"Sure," Avigayil piped up immediately, sitting down on the glider next to Rusie. "*Olam Haba* is like the Thunderbolts' stadium."

A smile sparkled in Devorah's blue eyes when she heard Avigayil's colorful and ear-catching analogy to the home of Cahill's major league baseball team.

"What do you mean, Avigayil?" Devorah asked. "I've been to many ball games, and they don't seem very heavenly to me."

"Devorah, you know that huge video screen behind center field?" Avigayil began describing the metaphorical image of *Olam Haba* that Beck had trained them to envisage.

"You mean the one they show the replays on?" Devorah asked.

"Right. It's about a hundred feet tall and maybe two hundred feet wide."

Beck recognized the exaggeration, but Avigayil's main point was that the screen could be seen even in the far upper reaches of the expansive stadium, and the players' movements could be scrutinized in slow motion and in great detail.

"When you get to *Olam Haba*," Avigayil continued, "they're going to put you on a platform on the pitcher's mound, and then everyone will turn their eyes to watch the big video screen. They'll be playing a rerun of your entire life. Whether you know it or not, there's a video camera focused on you in this world, twenty-four hours a day, until the day you die. Even on *Shabbos*. Abba says it's the only camera that's *mutar* on *Shabbos*.

"But you know who will be sitting in the front row watching the film? The *Avos* and *Imahos*, Avraham, Yitzchak, Yaakov, Sarah, Rivkah, Rachel and Leah. And of course, Moshe Rabbeinu and Aharon, Yehoshua, the *neviim* and all the *gedolim* through the ages. And your parents and grandparents, too."

"Oh!" Devorah gasped. The vividness of Avigayil's verbal picture, and the prospect of seeing her parents again, struck her heart. Her eyes became moist.

Miriam raised her hands excitedly and jumped into the conversation. "But you'll never guess who's sitting in a big throne by home plate."

"Who?" Devorah played her role. She enjoyed the girls' friendship immensely.

"Hashem!" Miriam cried.

As though on cue, Rochel now joined the fun. "Imagine, Devorah, that huge stadium filled with 100,000 *gedolim*, examining every one of your life's moves in slow motion. They'll first watch the way you ate supper tonight. The way you treated others at the table. How you spoke to them, how considerate you were, how thankful you were and, of course, how much you praised Hashem for the great *Shabbos* meal. Each one of your deeds during supper will be minutely inspected and studied by that glorious audience for a full day, and then they will conclude with an enormous roar of applause—a standing ovation that will rock the bleachers!"

"And Hashem will be roaring the loudest of all!" Miriam enthused.

"Then," Rochel went on, "they will advance the film to the next scene of your life and begin scrutinizing it. Your whole life will be put under the microscope. Are you sitting up straight for the camera right now? Remember, this picture is for eternity."

Devorah instinctively snapped herself erect.

"Wow!" she exclaimed. "That's awesome. How can a person go through life that way? It doesn't seem humanly possible."

"It's not, for most people," Beck said.

He was proud of the way his daughters had presented the case. It was not their first performance, and it showed.

"But if you can accomplish that attitude," he continued, "and respond accordingly for just thirty seconds every day, you will be infinitely greater than the person who knows nothing about that ubiquitous camera. Some pundit once said, 'It is better to have tried and failed, than not to have tried and succeeded.'"

Carter rose to his feet. "Well I've been trying and not succeeding for the last twenty minutes to get your attention, Benny. Do I have to handcuff and gag you? Or can we walk down the block and talk like civilized people? I *must* discuss something with you. It's about Mrs. Stein."

"Mrs. Stein!" Beck startled. "Why didn't you say so, Chet? Excuse me, folks, I'll be back in a few minutes."

"Mind if I come?" Rusie said.

"Oh, I'm sorry," Beck addressed her. If no one had been

present, he would have kicked himself hard for not thinking to include her. Too often, he overlooked her foremost role in the Patrol, as well as in his life in general. It was a selfishness, a rotten *midah* that he wished he could uproot. He resolved to try harder.

"Of course, I'd like you to come," he told her with conviction. He feared, however, that the damage had been done. It was a minor slight by secular criteria, but a flagrant act of gross negligence by Torah standards. To be married, to live closely with another human being, and still to behave considerately toward one's spouse at all times and in every detail—that was the great test of marriage, the unparalleled opportunity for perfection.

When the threesome reached the sidewalk, Beck remarked stridently, "Chet, why didn't you speak up? If I had known you were bringing information about the robberies, I would have broken off our discussion immediately."

"Why, you . . ." Chet sputtered, unable to find a word from Webster's to complete the sentence and unwilling to utter an apt descriptor from his "working" vocabulary in the presence of Beck and his wife.

"Binyamin, that's not fair," Rusie lectured. "Chet told you as soon as he arrived that he had some important news. Don't mind him, Chet."

They continued down the block and stood by the light at the next intersection. Beck noticed for the first time that Carter appeared haggard. He had discovered Carter's uncontrollable habit of chewing on his tongue when he endured long periods without sleep. Right now, he was chomping so hard that Beck feared he might draw blood.

"What time did you start work today?" Beck asked.

"Five-thirty this morning," Carter answered. "I was supposed to be gone by two this afternoon to take Renee out for our anniversary."

"Then what are you doing here?" Rusie squeaked.

"I'll get to that part in a minute," the officer replied. "First, let me tell you that I spent the entire day on the phone with credit card companies and retail stores. Thank G-d, they were all very cooperative. Now, are you ready for this one?"

"Shoot," Beck barked.

"Every one of the credit cards that have been stolen in the last ten days was used between seven-thirty and ten p.m. on the same night as the robberies. All of them were used to purchase expensive jewelry. You see what the game is?"

"Sure," Beck responded. "These crooks are not stupid. They pull off a robbery an hour or two before the stores close, then use the credit cards before the owners have the presence of mind to report them stolen. Have any of the cards been used after the evening they were stolen?"

"Just once. And that's the big news I came to tell you. Mitch called me from the County Police just as I was leaving today. They arrested a girl for using a stolen credit card, and they noticed she was wearing a *menorah* necklace set with nine little rubies. She wasn't very Jewish looking, so they suspected foul play, and they called me to help out. I called Mrs. Holland, and sure enough, Mrs. Stein had worn that necklace the evening they met for dinner. The robber must have ripped it off her."

"Beast!" Beck snarled.

"My words exactly," Carter quipped. "Mitch asked me to come out for the interrogation, so I phoned Renee and put off our dinner. She wasn't too thrilled, but I'll make it up to her."

"You better!" Rusie threatened.

"When I got out to the County, Mitch was already grilling her. She started singing when she saw there were two of us working her over. She said her fiance had given her both the necklace and the credit card the day before yesterday—Wednesday. Now, my fine feathered friends, I'll give you one guess who her fiance is."

"Spill it out, Chet," Beck demanded.

"None other than one Mark Lowery!"

"Wowee!" Beck howled.

"I said the same thing to Mitch in somewhat more colorful terms," Carter said. "Now I'm headed to get an arrest warrant for Lowery. I'll serve it after his VOP hearing on Monday. Boy, will he ever be surprised!"

"You're nasty," Rusie said with feigned seriousness.

"I love it," Beck commented gleefully.

"How about if you pick me up at eight-thirty Monday morning?" Carter suggested. "You can drive, because I'll be tied up with the arrest afterwards."

"It's a deal. Dovid's coming, too. And listen, thanks for stopping by. I'm really sorry I delayed you," Beck extended in truce.

"Tell Renee we're *all* sorry," Rusie added. "Treat her nicely. She puts up with a lot from us."

Beck turned to his wife after Carter left. "He's a gem, isn't he?"

"Not too many policemen like him," Rusie agreed. "Hashem has blessed our *kehillah*. Let's walk around the block before we go back home. I hardly ever get to talk to you alone."

They directed their feet toward the side street. Before they took three steps, Rusie gasped and clapped both her hands to her mouth.

"Binyamin!" she said in a hush. "See that man by the lightpost?"

Beck observed a man on the opposite sidewalk striding toward them. A black puppy with floppy ears was scampering around him.

"Yeah, what about him?"

"That's the owner of the dry cleaners on Benbrook Road! That must be Devorah's stepfather, Charles Henley!"

"Are you sure? What's he doing in this neighborhood?"

"Quiet!" Rusie shushed her husband. "He's coming this way. Just take a look at him as we walk by."

Beck noted the man's long, straight, dark brown hair. He looked to be about forty-five years old and was dressed in a starched white shirt with gold cufflinks adorning each sleeve. He wore a scowl on his face and looked at the ground as he passed them by.

They walked another few paces and glanced backward.

"Binyamin!" Rusie clamored, a look of fear gripping her countenance. "He's turning down our block. He'll see Devorah with the kids on the porch!"

11

"OH NO!" BECK CRIED. "I'M GOING TO RACE AROUND THE other way and try to get Devorah inside before he arrives."

Beck was panting when he reached his property. Glancing down the street, he sighted Henley still half a block away. He slowed to a brisk walk, so as not to attract the man's attention. He took the stairs to his porch two at a time.

"Quick! Get inside!" he motioned to Devorah. "No questions. Kids, you stay here."

Once they were safely indoors, he informed Devorah, "Rusie and I just saw your stepfather walking down the street." He was still breathing hard.

"What!" she cried, her face blanching.

Her instantaneous agitation frightened Beck and made him wonder what fearful secrets she was withholding about her stepfather.

"Stay here, Devorah. I'm going back onto the porch."

The little puppy had just scrambled away from Henley and was now bounding up the steps to the Beck's porch.

"Schnapps!" Henley called sharply, but when the dog ignored him, he started up the walkway to their house.

"Yip! Yip!" the animal barked, excitedly poking its nose around the floor like a robotic vacuum cleaner gone berserk. Two of the girls bent down to grasp the puppy.

"*Shabbos!*" Beck reminded.

They retracted their hands.

By now, Henley had climbed the stairs, but neither looked at nor spoke to anyone. Beck observed the nasty scratch on Henley's jaw that Rusie had mentioned earlier. Pointedly avoiding Beck's eyes, Henley reached out to fetch the dog, but it abruptly leaped away from him and vaulted onto the glider.

"Devorah's sweater!" Beck whooped to himself, as he spied the pink cardigan their guest had been wearing. The dog sniffed the sweater and began yelping, its tail wagging vigorously. Beck's heart was pounding.

"Dumb dog," Henley grumbled, as he gathered the puppy in his arms. Without a word to Beck, he descended the steps and brushed past Rusie, who was now coming up the walk. She joined Beck on the porch, and they both watched as Henley disappeared into the darkness.

"What a strange fellow," Beck commented.

"Didn't I tell you so?" Rusie said.

The family moved indoors and stood in the living room with Devorah.

"*Baruch Hashem*, he didn't notice your sweater, Devorah," Beck said with relief.

"Her sweater?" Rusie inquired. "Oh, Binyamin," she addressed her husband, "don't you know that men never notice clothing?"

"Well, *baruch Hashem* that He created men with that blind spot," he responded. "You see, all of Hashem's creations have a useful purpose!"

"Ha!" Devorah chuckled. "You're both wrong. I borrowed that sweater yesterday from a friend of mine. I don't think Charlie has ever seen it on me."

Devorah's repartee provided the comic relief they needed, and they all enjoyed a hearty laugh.

"When is he expecting you home tonight?" Rusie asked.

"Oh, he's not. He thinks I'm spending the weekend with my friend. The one who loaned me the sweater. She agreed to cover for me tonight in case Charlie calls her house."

"Wonderful!" Rusie said. "So why don't you stay the rest of *Shabbos* with us?"

"Right! Oh, please do!" the three girls chorused, hopping up and down.

Devorah, still shaken by the nearly disastrous encounter with Henley, required little arm twisting to accept their invitation. The buttressing effect of their open hospitality provided the warm support she required at that moment.

It was not long before linens were spread in the guest room and Devorah wriggled into the covers like a butterfly in its protective cocoon. The comforting serenity of a *Shabbos* evening snuggled around the Beck's home.

Crack! The sharp rap of a gavel echoed across the expanse of Judge O'Brien's courtroom.

Beck, Carter and Dovid Berg had arrived at nine-thirty and had waited patiently while several Violations of Probation were heard. Only one more remained before Lowery's case was called.

Judge O'Brien's court was in the old, north section of the courthouse. Beck preferred it over the renovated, modern wing to the south, which was more utilitarian but too impersonal for his tastes. The turn-of-the-century north facility admitted its visitors through the Joseph Randall Great Hall, a spacious, soaring, red marble chamber topped by a vaulted ceiling bearing a detailed mural of pastoral life. Leading off the Great Hall, white marble Ionian columns marched down the wide hallways like sentries on parade.

Judge O'Brien's courtroom was the first one along the middle hallway. The rich oak panels enveloped the spacious room, imparting a sense of strength and endurance. Visitors were limited to the ten double rows of filigreed oak benches filling the rear half of the room. Immediately in front of the first row was a sturdy, molded railing supported by a picket of upright columns arabesqued with leafy carvings. This rail separated the visitors' gallery from two heavy tables, one for the prosecution and one for the defense, facing the judge's imposing bench across an open space of at least fifteen feet. The bench itself, highlighted by thin, delicate gold strands, conferred an aspect of authority on its occupant.

Judge Samuel O'Brien was a salty Scot who had grown up in Texas and had never relinquished his colorful Texas spunk. "I'm a Texan by nature, and I never took an interest in being rehabilitated," was the way he liked to describe himself. He was one of Beck's favorite judges.

Beck would have liked to catch O'Brien's eye and nod a greeting to him, but an unwritten courtroom code precluded any hint of familiarity. It was all a facade, Beck knew, a charade of impartiality meant to impress the public and to mollify their own consciences. In truth, many of the lawyers and judges were well acquainted with each other and often enjoyed warm friendships, having acted out their respective roles for years in one courtroom performance after the next.

"Don't tell me Lowery is not going to show," Beck whispered to Carter. He scanned the courtroom again, but still saw no sign of the young man about whom they had come to court.

"He'll show, don't worry," Carter said. "Even if he's late, O'Brien will hear the case."

They turned their attention to O'Brien's conduct of the hearing in progress.

"Your Honor," the defense counsel was saying, "I have represented Mr. Edwards since he was released two months ago, and I can attest that he is a new man. His heart discovered his real calling in religion, and he is born again. Your Honor, at this point, the Lord has his soul, and I ask you to forgive this violation."

"What!" O'Brien thundered. "Well, the Lord may have his soul, but I've got his hide—and I aim to keep it!"

Beck glanced at Dovid, as they barely smothered their snickers.

"Oh, no!" Beck suddenly groaned, his good humor evaporating as his gaze extended past Dovid to the door of the courtroom. He turned around to Carter and whispered, "Here comes Lowery. And look who his attorney is, Mr. Righteous himself!"

Lowery wore a grim, worried countenance. His gold tooth peeked from between barely parted lips. Holding the door for Lowery and waddling in behind him was a round tub of a man with white hair.

"Oh, I forgot to tell you, Benny," Carter whispered back. "Cunningham told me that Horace Grimm convinced the ACLU to pay for Lowery's defense."

"Figures," Beck sputtered in disdain. "That deceiver would do anything to extort another buck."

He felt sorry for Grimm's client. The sight of Mark Lowery stirred Beck's memories of his evening in Wicomb and his shocking introduction to the pathetic hopelessness of Lowery's environment. Now, Beck thought, Lowery was being subjected to yet another episode of abuse, and to another impostor taking advantage of his helplessness.

Beck fortified himself with thoughts of duty to his *kehillah*. In a different place and time, he ruminated, he might press the court for leniency, but not now. Fair or not, Mark Lowery would have to be sacrificed. In an obscure back corner of his mind, he tucked away the faint hope that he might make it up to Lowery one day.

Lowery and Grimm sidestepped their way into the front aisle. As he plumped down heavily onto the bench, Grimm caught sight of Beck and cast a smirk toward him, his bulbous nose crinkled in a sardonic smugness that had become his trademark. Beck stared back stonily, refusing to display any sign of response.

"By the way, Chet," Beck whispered to the officer, "did you tell Cunningham what we want to do with Lowery?"

"Yeah, I had a meeting with him earlier this morning. The plan is to wait for Grimm to make the first move. Cunningham thinks he'll ask for a postponement. If he does, Cunningham will immediately inform the judge that the State is also in favor of the postponement."

"Great!" Beck said approvingly. "Dependable Chet, that's what we ought to call you."

"And how about your half of the job?" Carter asked. "Does O'Brien know we want to interrogate Lowery about the robberies?"

"Believe me, Chet, he's on board. He understands we want this postponement today, so we'll have both the VOP *plus* the robberies to hold over Lowery's head."

"By the way, how did you get the word to O'Brien?" Chet asked with curiosity. "I hope you didn't do anything underhanded. If it gets out, it'll ruin the whole plan."

"Now why are you assuming that I'm the one who said anything?" Beck retorted. "All I told you was, 'Leave it to me.'" The twinkle in his eye elicited a frown from Carter.

"Shh!" Dovid hissed at the two men. "We're not in this courtroom alone, you know."

"He's right," Carter said. "Grimm may not have as much lard in his ears as he has on his torso."

They fell silent and listened as O'Brien sentenced Mr. Edwards to the remainder of his fifteen-year term for violating probation.

"State versus Mark Antonio Lowery," announced the clerk.

Grimm rolled his rotund shape next to Lowery, behind the defense's table, while Owen Cunningham, an experienced District Attorney, stood to the left behind the prosecutor's table. Lowery was seated, but both lawyers stood facing the judge's bench.

As expected, Grimm made a move to have the hearing postponed. He picked up a gold fountain pen from the table and pointed it high in the air, like a preacher waxing to his sermon.

"I know my colleague, counsel for the State, will disagree, Your Honor," he intoned, "but I hope Your Honor will understand that the defendant had no counsel until Wednesday of last week, when I was retained by the American Civil Liberties Union to protect the defendant's civil rights, which have been severely breached. I believe there is compelling evidence to convince Your Honor to dismiss the charge of alleged violation of probation, but I require a reasonable amount of time to prepare that evidence so that it can be presented properly. My colleague, counsel for the State, will undoubtedly argue that I have had sufficient time to prepare this case, but Your Honor is wise enough to understand that attorneys in private practice do not enjoy the luxury of light case loads and the relaxed schedules that are often the privilege of those in the public employ."

"What an egotistical peacock," Beck hissed. "Hogwash!"

"Shh!" Dovid cautioned. He knew that his boss could be carried away by his opinionated outbursts.

The judge turned to Cunningham and said, "Mr. Cunningham, counsel for the defense seems to have spoken for you already, but I would prefer to hear the State's position directly from your own mouth."

It was a pointed reprimand, but it slid far below the

clouds where Grimm's high-held nose was parked. He did not so much as flinch.

Cunningham was fulminating, and had he not known what was in store for Mr. Grimm and his client, he would have launched an explosive counterattack.

Instead, Cunningham calmly replied, "The State has no objection to a postponement, Your Honor."

"Wha—!" Grimm started. In his surprise, he stumbled backwards, falling heavily against the polished oak railing. As though on cue, Carter rose and headed for the back of the courtroom, and as he exited, Beck caught a glimpse of a blue uniform in the anteroom.

"Bobby's here to help Chet with the arrest," Beck whispered to Dovid. "He's a good man."

Grimm quickly regained his equanimity and pressed a corpulent hand on Lowery, who had grinned broadly and attempted to rise upon hearing Cunningham's concurrence. Suppressing a smile of victory, Grimm scribbled down the new date O'Brien set for the hearing.

"Come on," Grimm said in an elated undertone to his client. "Let's go to my office."

Grimm squeezed his bulky waistline through the opening in the railing. As he passed Beck, he wrinkled his nose again, buoyed by what he considered a masterful courtroom strategy.

Lowery, in tow behind his attorney, caught sight of Beck for the first time. His eyebrows rose in a flash of recognition, but he said nothing. They were so close that they could have touched hands. Beck was again nagged by a feeling of pity for the unfortunate young man. In a sense, Beck pondered, Lowery was merely a pawn in their real war with Horace Grimm, their war against the fashionable focus on civil rights to the neglect of civil duties and the emphasis on personal freedom to the exclusion of personal decency.

"Dovid," Beck said pointedly, "this hearing was a *mussar haskel*. Do you see how pride blinds a person to the existence of Hashem? Mr. Do-Good has just managed to flip Lowery from the frying pan to the fire, but his arrogance has prevented him from realizing it yet. When a man thinks that he fashions his own success, he grows bigger and bigger in his own eyes until he's so bloated with conceit that there's no room left for Hashem. Finally he says, 'Look, G-d, there's not enough space for both of us, so You're going to have to leave.' Come on, Dovid, let's follow them out and watch the fun."

As he rose, Beck's eyes met Judge O'Brien's for an instant. Beck could not repress the slender curl adorning the corners of his mouth. He cocked his head in an almost imperceptible nod, but O'Brien only stared back.

"You're under arrest!" Carter barked as he snapped a handcuff on Lowery's right wrist, simultaneously twisting it clockwise and backwards until it met its mate, which Bobby had just seized in a crushing grip. The maneuver was accomplished so smoothly that Lowery was cuffed even before he had time to react.

"Wha-at!" spluttered Grimm, his eyes flaring and his throat working up and down. "What are you doing to my client! This is flagrant police brutality and an unconscionable breach of my client's civil rights. I demand his immediate release." Saliva collected on his puffy lips.

"Tell it to the judge, chump," Carter snapped coldly, a smile playing at the edges of his mouth as he thrust the arrest warrant in Grimm's face. "Here's the man you want to speak to."

He pointed to Judge O'Brien's signature at the bottom.

"Why, that double cr—" Grimm stopped himself midsentence, aware at last that the whole morning had been orchestrated for this embarrassing trap. The mushy fat on his clenched fists turned white as he boiled, "You'll regret this!"

Just then, Grimm caught sight of Cunningham emerging from the courtroom, and he snarled as he fired a poisonous look at the prosecutor. In response, the latter attempted to mimic Grimm's crinkled smug nose, but the result more closely resembled the ungainly snout of a cow contorted with pain.

Grimm turned around and stormed out of the anteroom into the wide hallway.

"Wait," Bobby called out to Grimm's receding silhouette. "How 'bout yer client?"

Grimm continued down the hall as though he had not heard. His obese form disappeared among the red marble appointments of the Great Hall.

"I guess the ACLU's not paying for this half," Beck joked. He and Dovid had watched the whole show from a corner of the anteroom. Beck's remark elicited chuckles from the two cops.

"Can I meet you tomorrow, Benny?" Carter proposed as the two officers led their ward into the hall.

"Good idea," Beck answered. "Four o'clock at the office?"

"Gotcha, boss."

"Come on, Dovid," Beck addressed the young man next to him. "We've got our own work to attend to."

The warmth of the bright sun struck the two figures as they descended the marble courthouse steps. Beck stopped and glanced around nervously.

"Expecting someone?" Dovid asked.

"No, but I don't want to meet up with Eberhart or any of the others who may be interested in this case. I've had more than my quota of close calls for this month. One more, and Rusie won't let me out of the house." He turned to the right toward Dorchester Street. "Let's get the car and head home."

The Dorchester Street traffic zipped by as Beck again glanced over his shoulder, still anxious about being followed. He saw two men in khakis behind them, but neither appeared to be interested in them. They stopped at the crosswalk. Across the intersection, a yellow sign read, "DANGER. HEAVY TRAFFIC. WAIT FOR WALK LIGHT." A television truck from a major network was stopped at the red light.

"Television!" Beck sputtered. "Dovid, do you understand why television is such a frightful instrument? In the course of a year, it fills the viewer's mind with millions of portraits of *gashmius, tumah*, violence, disrespect and hardheartedness—all made vastly more impressionable by today's technology of brilliant colors, realistic action and penetrating audio. Each one of those vivid images will require an antidote of hundreds of encounters with *kedushah*. Each second of television viewing will need a year's worth of *tzeddakah* and *chessed* to offset it. The truth is, you'll *never* catch up. That's why we must react with the most extreme fear and trembling when we accidentally see a television screen. It's like being exposed to hepatitis, *chas veshalom*, and having to anticipate the months of convalescence that will be required to heal the disease and the possibility of permanent liver damage."

They remained on the curb, deep in thought. Beck hoped he had ignited Dovid's philosophical machinery. The light changed to WALK, but neither of them noticed. The two men in khakis glared with annoyance as they skirted around them.

"You know, Benny," Dovid remarked, "I've been thinking about the discussion we had the other day on *bechirah*. It seems to fit in perfectly with what you just said."

"How so?"

Beck derived genuine pleasure from Dovid's mental peregrinations. The young man had a logical mind and never hesitated to exercise it, and he always steered it down lanes bordered by common sense, guaranteeing his arrival at solid conclusions.

"Well, Benny, we concluded before that one has *bechirah* to choose right and wrong. What you are saying with regard to the television, is that a person *must* limit his options. The inference is that the consummate use of one's *bechirah* is to employ it in ways that *limit* one's *bechirah*."

"*Voila, mon cher!*" Beck enthused. Dovid's perspicacity excited Beck.

"Let me continue," Dovid replied impatiently. "This conclusion explains an enigma that has bothered me ever since our *bechirah* discussion. Here's the problem.

"Suppose a person trains himself to enjoy helping others. As he refines this self-training more and more, he begins deriving immense joy from each *chessed* he does. He soon arrives at the stage where he no longer uses his *bechirah*, his conscious free choice, to do a *chessed*. Rather he is *driven* to do the *chessed* by his expectation of the extreme pleasure it will provide him. In a sense, he has lost his *bechirah*.

"But are we to conclude, therefore, that his reward will be diminished, since his *chessed* is now motivated primarily by the sensation of pleasure? Can we say that a man who has scaled a towering mountain, and need not expend further energy, should be denied the reward of surveying the beautiful vista? Surely that contradicts intuitive truth.

"Following what you said about television, however, this seeming contradiction is resolved. Simply put, when you use your *bechirah* to *limit* your *bechirah*, your reward comes for the conscious steps you took to school yourself and to narrow your options.

"Just as an example, Benny, we will get *s'char* twenty-four hours a day, for the rest of our lives, for not owning televisions, even though we have already advanced to the level where we despise television.

"It's almost too good to imagine, Benny," Dovid's voice rose with excitement. "With enough self-training, a person can actually be rewarded for engaging in activities that delight him and refraining from activities that pain him. When it comes to immorality, ignorance *is* bliss, while *knowledge* is the source of the greatest suffering."

Beck was hypnotized by Dovid's soliloquy, his line of reasoning that penetrated one of the great verities of Jewish *hashkafah*. He had not fleshed out the full body of implications and caveats, but he had at least dissected the skeleton.

Beck *kvelled* with pride over Dovid's mental triumph. Here was a young man with a bright mind and an open heart, who could speak unpretentiously about the joys of performing *chessed*, concerned that such pleasures might be held against him. For over a year, he had observed Dovid, admiring the inspirational gratification the young man derived from helping other people. It was the uppermost factor that had driven Dovid to join the ECCP, whose entire *raison d'etre* was *gemilas chessed*.

Rusie and I *must* find him a *shidduch*, Beck thought. That will afford him the ultimate venue for heightening his delight in *chessed*.

All at once, Beck was distracted by an anxious foreboding, as though he sensed someone spying on them. He visually relocated the khakis, who had turned down Dorchester and proceeded down the opposite sidewalk. No, he quickly decided, they were not suspicious. He surveyed the scene behind them but discovered no one out of the ordinary. He rubbed his sleeves to force down the goose bumps on his arms.

It's just nerves, he thought to himself. He turned back to Dovid and said out loud, "Dovid, it's late. I think we should get back to the office."

"Hey, buddy, move it, 'foh I dumps ya off da co'nah!" a gruff voice snarled at Beck from behind, catching him completely off guard.

Startled, he turned around to face a short, muscular man with a splotchy face, set with round eyes and a flat nose. A tiny diamond drop pierced his right earlobe.

Beck's adrenalin squirted. He recognized the man as one of the spectators in Judge O'Brien's courtroom.

"Don't jes' stare," the man roared. "Ya 'ready bin hoggin' da sidewahk ten minutes. Lemme by." The bellicose words were unmistakably reflected in a hateful scowl.

Beck parted from Dovid to allow the stranger passageway. He estimated the man to be in his early twenties. Beck took note of his green baseball cap with a pirate caricature affixed to the crown. A white patch with the name Damon was sewn to the breast of his dark blue workshirt. It stirred a faint memory in Beck's subconscious.

"Ya little cussin' Jew!" the man bellowed.

He angled his right elbow outward as he charged through, catching Beck's right forearm. The blow knocked Beck backwards, and he stumbled as he tripped off the curb into the busy street. He felt a stabbing pain of asphalt tearing his flesh as his right palm skidded along the street surface.

Instantly, Beck scrambled to his knees to rise. The words "DANGER! TRAFFIC!" seared his brain.

Suddenly, terror seized his face as he caught sight of a gigantic, gleaming white car bearing down on him. He met the driver's gaze, eye to eye. It was Horace Grimm!

12

"SCREE-EECH!" THE SCREAM OF RUBBER ON PAVEMENT pierced the air. The white Cadillac came to a stop, its chrome bumper barely six inches from Beck's nose.

"Benny!" Dovid roared, as he dashed into the street. He grabbed Beck roughly by the left arm and fairly dragged him to the curb, as a dozen onlookers rushed to help.

"Dovid!" Beck yelled over the babble. "Where did that guy go? The one that knocked me down."

Dovid craned and dodged his head about, but he could not see past the gathering huddle of curious thrill seekers. All he glimpsed through the throng of elbows was a span of white sheet metal receding into the distance as Grimm drove off.

"Here! You come my store!" a high-pitched accent issued from the center of the circle. A short, oriental man reached down and slipped his hands under Beck's armpits. Beck felt himself lifted by the man's wiry strength.

"Back! Arr gen'reman back!" ordered the little man.

The authority in his voice seemed to drive an opening wedge through the throng. Dovid supported Beck's left arm as the Oriental took Beck's bloodied right shirt cuff and led him into an import-export store three doors down Dorchester from the courthouse.

"You come my store," the man repeated. "Fix you up."

As he led them into the store, the pungent odor of incense filled their nostrils, while plush *tatami* cushioned their feet.

"I Mikiachi Goto," the man added.

"Thanks a million, Mr. Goto," Beck said as the man washed the blood from his hand into a basin.

Beck judged that Mr. Goto was about fifty years old, although his fingers moved with the dexterity of someone half that age. He wore a multi-colored embroidered cap atop his straight black hair, but was otherwise dressed as an American businessman in a double-breasted, navy blue suit and burgundy leather dress shoes.

Beck surveyed the image of the store's interior reflected in the mirror above the sink. Dark wooden shelves laden with abacuses, dragons and other oriental gifts were bracketed to a wall, while wicker containers of various sizes and shapes were suspended from overhead rafters. On a small table in one corner, brightly decorated rice paper scrolls were drying under a brass lamp. An intriguing collage of colored rice and various-sized chopsticks festooned most of the back wall and seemed to emphasize the diminutive size of the store. A string of colorful paper lanterns cascaded from a plant hanger near the window.

He must not do much business, Beck thought to himself. This place can't be more than twenty feet square.

The possibility flashed through his mind that Hashem had sustained Mr. Goto for the sole purpose of providing refuge to a Jew in his time of need.

"You rucky," Goto commented. "In Japan is ohd saying, 'When kamikaze miss, he just die to try again.' Ha! Ha!"

"Believe me, Mr. Goto," Dovid spoke up, "he was not trying to be a kamikaze. Someone bumped into him."

"Oh, not nice! In Japan is more ohd saying, 'Sword that

fry from hand by mistake is also deadry.'"

"Well put, Mr. Goto," Beck said. "The only difference here, I'm afraid, is that this may not have been a mistake."

"Sk, sk, sk," Goto clucked mysteriously.

"I do appreciate your help, Mr. Goto," Beck added, extending his hand. "Here's my card. There should be more caring people in this world like you."

Dovid abruptly reached out to restrain Beck's outstretched arm, but he was too late to prevent Beck from handing over an ECCP business card. Beck cast a bewildered look at Dovid, who shot a stern gaze back at him.

Beck thanked the Japanese man again as they departed. Once they stepped out and turned to the right on Dorchester, Beck surveyed the scene, but saw no sign of their protagonist.

When they reached the next intersection, Beck demanded, "Okay, Dovid, what was that all about?"

"Benny, I wish you hadn't given him our card. It may have been a mistake."

"Why, Dovid? I doubt if our friend can even read it."

"Maybe so," Dovid replied, "but guess what I saw in the corner under one of those shelves."

"*Nu?*" Beck did not like to be strung along.

"A cardboard box," Dovid revealed.

"Now *there's* a frightful sight," Beck teased. "You must have been shut in a box when you were a child, and the subliminal fright is returning to haunt you. Listen, I know a good therapist who deals with—"

"Oh, yeah?" Dovid shot back. "Well, Mr. Know-It-All, it so happens I spied a shipping label addressed to the Tip-Top Roofing Company pasted on the box's flap."

"Oh, no!" Beck's humor instantly vanished.

"Oh, yes!" Dovid returned emphatically.

"Well, this has *got* to be pure coincidence," Beck said.

"Goto is too nice a man to be involved in anything shady. If he were guilty of something, why would he have drawn attention to himself by volunteering to bring us into his store?"

"Look, Benny, I'm just reporting the facts," Dovid replied. "Personally, I agree with you that it's just coincidence. Goto may have pulled the box out of the rubble at the construction site by the Long Office Building. It's only two blocks away."

"That sounds like a reasonable possibility," Beck said hopefully. He was not totally convinced, however, and remained disquieted by Dovid's discovery.

"By the way," Dovid added, "the car that almost turned you into a pancake . . . I assume you got a look at the driver."

"Yes, Dovid. A *very good* look. Like a drowning man looks at the luxuriant dentition of a shark headed in for the kill."

"Wait a minute, Benny, that was coincidence for sure. There's no way Grimm could have known we would walk down Dorchester, or that we would talk at the light for five minutes before crossing."

"True. But don't you think we've had our quota of coincidences lately? Makes me wonder . . ."

The two men said nothing more as they proceeded to the Police Headquarters garage and collected the ECCP Command Car.

"Have a nice day, Major," Beck sang out to the sentry as they exited.

The guard was well known not only for his jolly disposition, but also because his last name was Major. It was something of a departmental joke, since he saluted so many men of higher rank each morning. Beck had exchanged cordial greetings with Officer Major on numerous occasions. He was an older, slightly overweight gentleman, with a puffy face. Beck made a mental note to bring him a bag of

Rusie's irresistible chocolate chip cookies the next time he came to Headquarters. The man deserved a proper thanks for the many times he had reserved a privileged parking spot for the Command Car.

It would not be the first time Rusie's culinary arts worked their magic, Beck mused. Her creations were part of the wide-ranging arsenal he employed to cement and re-cement good relationships with people at all levels.

As he guided the car onto the freeway, Beck reflected to himself, *In his own way, the garage sentry is as vital to the ECCP's smooth operation as Chief Vincent himself. Every ounce of respect the ECCP has accorded to hundreds of officials has been returned with double and triple interest. Besides, each human being, regardless of his station in life, is so precious in the eyes of Hashem. The Ribono Shel Olam brought countless legions of stars and vast galaxies into existence, but the affairs of man on the planet Earth are the sole focus of His kindness and concern. How can I think anything less of my fellow man than does the One who created them?*

The Command Car hummed quietly on cruise control. Beck's thoughts wandered loosely from the twinkling galaxies of the heavens to the pastel lights of Japanese lanterns. From there, his mind shifted to rice paper hanging out to dry, rice paddies sprouting under the sun, solar radiation streaming through the layers of the atmosphere and finally back to the stars dotting the expanse of space. Beck silently laughed at his own circumvolution.

"Benny, can I ask your advice on something?" Dovid finally broke the peace.

"Sure," Beck responded. "What's up?"

From the reticence in Dovid's voice, Beck guessed that he wanted to discuss a personal matter.

"You're going to laugh, Benny. I've been thinking a little

more about what you and your wife have said to me in the last few months, and I think I might be ready to think about *shidduchim*."

Beck took his gaze off the road for an instant to look at Dovid's eyes. It was a serious topic and it had to be discussed in a serious vein. He read in Dovid's expression that the young man had given the topic some heavy consideration.

"Dovid, if you're ready, you know that Rusie and I would do anything to help."

He tried to speak from his heart, to ease the young man's embarrassment. Inwardly, he was thrilled that Dovid was undertaking this most essential life step.

"The truth is," Dovid said, "I really don't know where to begin. I don't even know the type of girl I'm looking for. Obviously, she must be a *shomeres mitzvos*, but what other criteria should I have? Should she be a seminary graduate? Should she know anything about homemaking or raising children?"

"Now, wait a minute, Dovid. Don't get bogged down in technicalities. Let's back up to square one. First of all, as you said, she must be an observant Jew. Without that, there's nothing to discuss.

"The next most fundamental qualification is that the girl be a *mentch* and have a lot of common sense. For instance, does she treat people with decency, and does she have a pleasant demeanor? Does she display intelligence and responsibility and a modicum of maturity in the way she responds to various situations? Or, perhaps, does she have some really odd habits or unnatural behaviors? Does she have a temper? Is she lazy?"

"Well!" Dovid marveled. "I'll need to hire a private eye to discover all that!"

"Who said you're supposed to discover it?" Beck answered.

"What do you mean, Benny? Am I just supposed to draw straws and hope for the best?"

As he exited the freeway, Beck braked the Command Car at a red light.

"Dovid, there's one thing I can guarantee you in this business. You are the *least* qualified person to make any judgment about a prospective *shidduch*. Especially since you're on the *chassan's* side. Do you know how many men have been duped by a little curl and a dab of perfume? Once you're married, it's too late to discover what her *natural* odor is or that she spent two hours to make that curl stay in place."

Dovid laughed half-heartedly. "Benny, now you're really scaring me. What am I getting myself into?"

"I'm sorry," Beck apologized. "There's no cause to be frightened. I'm just saying you're not the right person to render judgment. You're too close to the situation, and being a man, you're too easy to rope in. Sometimes, women have much more *seichel*. They're not impressed by a little rouge on the cheeks."

"So what do I do?" Dovid asked in consternation. "My mother's not around to inspect the girl. Besides, our lives are on entirely different wavelengths."

"Tell you what. If someone suggests a possible *shidduch* to you, I'll run her name by Rusie. If Rusie doesn't know her, I'll try to arrange for them to meet. If she passes muster, then you can meet her."

"Thanks, Benny," Dovid said. "I appreciate your help. I just hope the girl doesn't have *too* much *seichel*, though. Otherwise, she may see right through *me* and nix it from the start."

Beck laughed. With sincere feeling in his voice, he turned to Dovid and spoke gently, "Good merchandise is never hard to sell."

A touch of red flushed Dovid's ears as he looked down at the gray carpet on the floor.

To ameliorate Dovid's awkwardness, Beck monopolized the conversation. "Dovid, I know it's a big step in your life, but I want you to know that Rusie and I firmly believe you are doing the right thing. And we promise not to rush you.

"You have much to consider. So far I only mentioned the basic attributes you should search for in a girl—*mentchlichkeit* and common sense. But that's merely step one, to sift out the riffraff. However, there must be additional screenings. Do the girl and her family enjoy good physical and mental health? Does she have the same basic outlook on *Yiddishkeit* as you? There's a lot we still have to talk about. Maybe you'll stop by this *Shabbos*, and we can discuss it more leisurely."

"Wonderful!" Dovid said. "There is so much to consider, and I truly value your advice. I only wish there were some foolproof way to know that a certain girl is the right *shidduch*."

Beck reached over and squeezed Dovid's forearm. "Dovid, my friend, don't worry about finding the right *shidduch*. Concentrate instead on *being* the right *shidduch*. And once you're married, concentrate for the next hundred years on being the best husband you can possibly be."

Beck stepped on the accelerator as the light changed to green. Neither of them said a word as they made their way home.

It rained cats and dogs through the entire night. A howling wind had heralded the storm around midnight, and it raged for an hour or more before the bucketloads began falling. It was a violent, concentrated weather front, followed by steady precipitation until noon the next day. It left the streets littered with twigs and branches.

By afternoon, when Beck made his way to meet Carter

at the ECCP office, neighbors had cleared most of the boughs that hindered traffic. Nevertheless, Beck was still obliged to step over numerous sprigs scattered along the sidewalks.

"It's Hashem's way of pruning the weak and dying limbs," Beck thought. "With thousands of trees lining our streets, it's a job we could not possibly do ourselves. Hashem, thank You so much for Your *chessed*."

Just then, he heard a sizzling noise overhead. He looked up and spied a small, wet branch that had fallen on a power line. A ribbon of smoke was rising from the limb. He pumped his legs faster to get to the office.

"'Bout time you showed up," Carter ribbed, as Beck walked in.

"I'll feed you my alibi in a minute," Beck answered. "But first get on your radio and report a limb lying on a high-tension wire in the middle of the 1400 block of Manchester. It's smoldering right now, and it'll probably ignite as soon as the wood dries out."

Carter radioed the report, then turned to Beck. "I see you've been on storm patrol. No wonder you're late."

"Well, to be honest with you," Beck said sheepishly, "I was actually helping Basheva learn to ride a bike. She had wanted to learn last year, but I kept procrastinating. Now I could kick myself. Each year makes it harder to get these old bones to move. I don't know how I'll ever manage when Brachah comes of age. *Baruch Hashem*, Yossi's a boy. He'll learn on his own."

"Come on, you old man," Carter teased. "The way you're talking, it's nearly time to salt you away in a cemetery."

"Over my dead body!" Beck retorted, drawing a laugh from the cop.

"Well, Benny," Carter suggested, "I've got a truckload of info for you, so let's get going."

Beck tossed his hat onto the closet shelf and took out the coffee can. As he scooped grounds into the filter cup, he glanced at Carter and noticed him chewing hard on his tongue.

"Before you tell me anything, Chet," Beck said, "I first want to know how much sleep you've had in the last twenty-four hours."

He knew how much paperwork went into each arrest. A lot of it was a preposterous waste of officers' precious time, but it had become essential to thwart the unscrupulous lawyers looking to get every criminal off the hook.

"Listen, boss," Carter replied, "I'm going to crack these robberies if it kills me, so don't worry about how much sleep I got. It was nothing."

"Oh, no you don't!" Beck declared with conviction. "We're not doing anything until you tell me."

"But I *did* just tell you," Carter said.

"You did?" Beck was perplexed. Then Carter's last words, "It was nothing," flashed in his mind, and he understood. His heartstrings pulsed with gratitude for this indefatigable *shaliach* from Heaven, and he sent up a heartfelt "Thank You, Hashem."

"Care for some?" Beck offered, as he held out the carafe of fresh brew. "You might need it."

"Thanks," Carter replied, extending his mug. "You know, I feel sorry for Lowery in a way. He's one of the few we've dealt with who seems to have a little speck of decency in him. Too bad he keeps such bad company. The truth is, he's lucky he's still alive."

"Now you've fired my curiosity, Chet. I assume you grilled him yesterday."

"Actually, I did even better. I got a writ from Judge Scalia and pulled Lowery's fiancee out of Women's Detention. Remember, she's the one that got arrested in the County with the stolen credit card and started this whole ball rolling."

"Oh, I remember, Chet. My bones may be getting creaky, but the old noodle is as good as new."

"Anyway, I pulled her up to Eastern yesterday afternoon. Her name is Dawn Jackson. She just turned eighteen—old enough to make her a legal adult. So I put her in one room and Lowery in another room and started playing one of them off against the other. It's been a long time since I've enjoyed a good game of cat and mouse, and I forgot how much fun it is. I wished you were there."

"Me, too," Beck interjected.

"The scoop is like this. You remember Puppy, the guy who did Mrs. Stein's first robbery? It turns out that Puppy is Lowery's half-brother. They've got the same mother, but their fathers have never gotten along. Lowery and Puppy have always had a rocky relationship, too.

"Lowery says he took the *menorah* necklace and credit card from Puppy's car a week ago Sunday, which was the day after Mrs. Stein was robbed for the second time and stabbed. Lowery saved the necklace and credit card to give to Dawn for her birthday on Wednesday. And by the way, Dawn corroborated all this.

"Both Lowery and Dawn fingered Puppy as the one who had robbed Mrs. Stein the first time, but they claim they don't know anything about the second robbery and stabbing. I tend to believe them, especially Lowery. Dawn is something of a sneak, so I take her with a grain of salt.

"Now here's where it gets interesting. Lowery says that Puppy has definitely pulled a number of other robberies, but he doesn't know any specifics—except that Puppy has hurt many of his victims and that Puppy usually carries a knife.

"Several weeks ago, Lowery complained to Dawn that he

didn't like Puppy hurting people. The little snitch that she is, she ran and told this to Puppy, and that's why Lowery is on the outs with Puppy. Both Lowery and Dawn claim they don't know where Puppy is living right now, but I think they're both lying. I get the feeling that Lowery is running scared of Puppy."

Carter paused and sipped the coffee.

"Ouch! That's hot!" he yelped.

"Ooh!" Beck winced with sympathy. "You okay?"

"I'll manage," Carter said as he dismissed the matter.

Beck combed his fingers through his beard, trying to digest Carter's report. There were many details, and he took his time mentally sorting through them.

"You didn't quiz Lowery about the crane incident, did you?"

"Benny, you took the words out of my mouth. When I first mentioned the subject, he was as surprised as a rabbit stumbling on a fox's lair that I even knew about it. But he instantly clammed up tight and kept insisting that it was just an accident. Benny, I've been in this business long enough to know when a man is afraid for his life. I'm telling you straight, that crane affair was no accident. Someone tried to kill Mark Lowery!"

"And that means, of course," Beck added, "that they'll probably try again. I'd say Lowery is more like a rabbit tied to a spit—and the fox is stoking the fire already!"

"Something like that, I guess. If you ask me, Lowery didn't move to Wicomb to join his righteous friends. He was *hiding out* there."

Beck flicked away several long hairs that had fallen from his beard onto his shirt front.

"Let me get this straight, Chet. According to Lowery, Puppy robbed Mrs. Stein three weeks ago, and then again ten days ago when he stabbed her. A week ago Sunday,

Lowery stole Mrs. Stein's necklace and credit card out of Puppy's car, and on Wednesday he gave them to Dawn. Lowery denies doing any of the robberies himself, is that right?"

"Right. And I believe him. I think he's basically a good kid, but he's been abused and misused by everybody, from his father and mother to other family members to his fiancee to—"

"To Horace Grimm," Beck blurted. "By the way, he didn't show up for Lowery's interrogation, did he?"

"Are you kidding?"

"Figures!" Beck remarked scornfully.

Beck walked over to the window and raised the lower sash. A gentle breeze flowed in, bearing the lingering aromas of the morning's rain. He picked up several papers that blew off Dovid's desk and plunked down a tape dispenser as a paperweight.

Without warning, he turned around to face Carter. "Chet, I don't know how you feel, but I'm getting frustrated. This case is going too slowly. We don't know what part Eberhart is playing, we don't know who's driving the getaway cars, and we don't even know where we can find Puppy so you can put him on the rack. By the way, does Puppy have floppy ears and a tail, or does he have a real name, too?"

"Oh!" Carter jumped up. "I forgot to tell you. Lowery told me that Puppy's name is Damon Hughes. Remember, he's the owner of the blue Ford Escort."

Beck stared at Carter in stunned silence. A well of fear reawakened in his soul and shot a wave of tingles up his spine.

"Did you say Damon?"

"Right, Benny. Don't you recall I gave you his name before? I thought you said your memory was up to snuff."

"Chet, I haven't seen you since yesterday, so I didn't have a chance to tell you. A guy named Damon almost killed me yesterday!"

"Wha-at!" Carter blanched. "What are you talking about?"

Beck related the incident on Dorchester Street after he and Dovid left the courthouse, and their rescue by Mikiachi Goto. Carter listened closely, his alarm growing.

When Beck finished, Carter heaved his attache case up to his desk and opened it. Rummaging through the manila file folders in the pocket, he withdrew a police mug photo and flipped it onto the desk.

"Take a look at Puppy," he announced.

"That's him!" Beck shouted. The image of his erstwhile assailant made him shudder. He wished he could wring the man's neck.

"Look, Benny," Carter said sympathetically. "I know you're frustrated, but please give me another twenty-four hours. I've got a hunch that the case is going to break soon. I want to go home now and grab about four hours of shut-eye, and then I'll be back in the precinct. I've got something up my sleeve. Will you trust me?"

Beck peered closely into Carter's eyes. He chastised himself for being so impatient, failing in his *bitachon*. Certainly it was not Carter's fault. The cop was doing everything humanly possible.

"I'm sorry, Chet," Beck muttered. "Of course, I trust you. You've never let me down yet."

Beck arranged for phone calls to be forwarded and stuffed some papers into a folder to carry home, while Carter rinsed the coffee pot. They locked the door behind them and descended to the parking lot.

"I'll call you tomorrow morning if anything happens," Carter promised. "I'm sure it'll all come to a head soon. For your own sanity, Benny, put the robberies out of your mind and enjoy your evening. And for G-d's sake, stay home tonight!"

"Thanks, Chet," Beck answered, puzzling over the meaning of Carter's parting entreaty. "Regards to Renee."

Beck eased himself into his car and started the motor, but sat stroking his beard for several minutes. Finally, with a look of grim determination, he grabbed the seat belt buckle and jammed it into place.

"No, I can't leave it up to Chet entirely," he mumbled. "Let him do his *hishtadlus*, and I'll do mine."

He drove out of the lot and turned to the right. Several minutes later, he pulled into the main section of the Spartan Industrial Park and guided his vehicle past the long row of buildings.

"There it is," he noted. "That's the path Dovid must have discovered through the woods."

He turned off the engine and slowly coasted along the deserted end of the long asphalt lot, coming to a stop opposite a narrow break in the thick undergrowth. He listened to the cacophonous melody of the trees' myriad songbirds, accompanied by a thousand crickets rasping forth their staccato message. A steamy humidity seemed to rise like an evanescent ghost from the verdant forest.

Actually, the path doesn't look too muddy, even with the rain we had last night, he observed. As long as I don't slip off the trail like Dovid did!

Beck alighted from his car and strolled over to the path's entrance. He tried visually to penetrate the thick wilderness, but the trees seemed to stare back at him, their leafy appendages flapping in the wind as though mocking his impotence. Even the path was not visible for more than ten feet before it was swallowed by the choking vines and inviolable, tangled forest.

What forbidding secrets lay sequestered on the other

side of this jungle barrier? he pondered. What keys would that distant world offer to decipher *this* world of *sheker* and deception? Beck imagined himself before a darkened stage, waiting for the curtain to rise and the lights to shatter the black suspense. He was exploding with a madness to crash through that timber rampart, to rip off the veil and unearth the *emes*.

He faced around and returned slowly to his car. He inserted the key in the ignition and peered once more through the slender break in the bulwark of disheveled scrub, where the path led off into the inscrutable unknown.

As he drove away, he said, "I wonder if I'll be able to find this spot again tonight."

13

"OH, LOOK, BINYAMIN. THERE'S THE BIG DIPPER," RUSIE noted with delight, as she pointed skyward.

"Hey, you're right. Isn't it amazing how six autonomous stars can hurtle through space at enormous speeds for thousands of years and still maintain their constant relationship to each other and to Earth? Hashem is behind it all. Man has difficulty firing a rocket ship on a track accurate enough to hit a nearby planet two years later—and only then by dint of repeated engine blasts to correct the course. Our paltry abilities, by contrast to Hashem's, are solid proof of His majestic miracles."

Rusie, having put the younger children to bed, had suggested to her husband that they go for a walk. They enjoyed each other's company immensely, and even though ECCP activities often pre-empted Beck's evenings, they snatched brief opportunities to be together whenever possible.

As they passed from under a towering white oak, the sky became visible again.

"It's so clear tonight," Beck noted. "The stars look like midnight jewels sparkling in a curtain of black velvet. They're all the more brilliant because there's no moon. By the way, thanks again for the delicious *Rosh Chodesh* meal."

"You're welcome."

Years ago, Rusie had adopted the practice of preparing a fancy dinner each *Rosh Chodesh*. It was a treat the family had come to anticipate. The conversations at these repasts often centered around the meanings of *Rosh Chodesh*, and vignettes of what *Rosh Chodesh* must have been like in the times of the *Beis Hamikdash*. As Beck did with many topics, he often distilled these *Rosh Chodesh* discussions to glean other lessons on the greatness and glory of the Jewish people.

"Careful of the glass, Rusie," Beck cautioned as he pointed an index finger downward.

A thousand glass shards remained in a pile from a broken soda bottle on the sidewalk. They stepped on the grass around it.

"Why do people have to be so inconsiderate?" Rusie said. "The least they could do is clean up the mess so children won't be cut."

"You're assuming the bottle was broken by accident," Beck corrected. "Chances are that some kid threw it down on purpose."

"Someone ought to wring his neck, then," she replied. "That type of maliciousness is disgusting."

They walked another half block in silence. A black cat crouching under a parked car peered at them as they passed, a distant streetlight reflecting a neon glow off its eyes.

"Why is there evil in the world, Binyamin?" Rusie wondered aloud.

"Ah, the Problem of Evil," Beck answered. "I remember discussing the topic in a philosophy class I took twenty-five years ago. I don't recall what was said, but whatever it was, I'm sure it was wrong. The professor was an avowed atheist."

"Really!" Rusie declared. "It seems to me that an atheist would not be able to answer the Problem of Evil, as you call it. In fact, it ought to weigh like a ton of lead on his mind, to the point of abject depression."

"That's what I would think, too. Judaism, on the other hand, has many very rational explanations why evil exists in this world."

"Like what?" Rusie probed.

"Well, for one thing, evil is our entrance key to *Olam Haba*."

"It is?" Rusie said incredulously. "How so?"

"Reb Yisrael Salanter used to remark that any good undertaking is always opposed by a battery of obstacles. Actually, it's a principle enunciated in the *Gemara*. In fact, there's a correlation—the more good there is in a person, and the more righteous his intentions and desires, the more barriers Hashem erects to oppose him, the more evil temptations are marshaled to sidetrack him. The bigger a person is, the stronger is the *yetzer hara* Hashem throws against him.

"A person's station in *Olam Haba* is a direct reflection of his successful fight through life, his accomplishments in resisting these tests of his character. A Jew's admission ticket to Gan Eden is his conquest of the *nisyonos* of evil. The word *nisayon* comes from the word *ness*, meaning to elevate, because that is the result when one overcomes each *nisayon*. Gehinnom, on the other hand, awaits a person's surrender to life's *nisyonos, chas veshalom*."

"Binyamin, that's a dreadful prospect," Rusie interrupted. "It almost doesn't pay to be a Jew. The risks are too frightening, aren't they?"

"Listen, Rusie, it's possible to rid oneself of all the risks, all those *nisyonos*. Just *daven* that Hashem should make you grow some fur and a tail, and start walking around on four padded feet. You'll be able to trot through the park at midnight without fear of molestation, every trash can will proffer another scrumptious meal. You'll never receive another bill in the mail nor have to change another diaper nor run another carpool. All your unending responsibilities will be lifted from your shoulders, and you will be able finally to breathe a great sigh of relief. Of course, you'll finish your life as a dog, your sole future merely to fertilize the earth with your rotting body. But you will have escaped the risks of all *nisyonos*.

"The answer is, of course, that it pays to do *anything* to be a human. And if you're a human, it pays to do anything to be a *tzaddik*, to face any *nisayon*, to struggle for a lifetime through the most extreme adversity. The gold mine under the mountain promises us an indescribably pure reward and fully justifies the most painful toil to dig and dig and dig until we strike it."

They stopped at the crosswalk and waited patiently for traffic to clear. The black cat emerged from its shelter and sidled silently over to them. It purred contentedly and arched its back as it brushed Rusie's leg, first along its right side, and then turning around, along its left side. Rusie looked at her husband and smiled.

Crossing Larchmont Avenue, they continued down Bellwood, a quiet side street. A Cahill Water Department backhoe was parked by the curb, next to a gaping hole excavated in the pavement. They stepped off the curb into the street, over some rubble, and up to a barricade surrounding the opening. Flashing amber lights atop the barricade warned traffic away. Peering over the edge of the hole, they saw a half dozen jumbled pipes sprawled across the bottom like spaghetti dumped in a deep cauldron.

"Talk about digging until you strike something!" Beck remarked. "I doubt if they'll hit gold, though. Certainly not the gold of *Olam Haba*."

"You know, that's really a good point, Binyamin. I can

understand your contention that the infinite pleasure of reward in *Olam Haba* makes it worthwhile to stand up to every evil temptation and test that Hashem throws our way in *Olam Hazeh*. But if so—if the reward for success is so immense—then we ought to rejoice over *nisyonos*. In fact, we ought to *daven* to Hashem to send us even more *nisyonos*."

"On the face of it, you're right," Beck returned. "But do you know the best way to overcome a *nisayon*? It's virtually foolproof, if you can pull it off."

"How's that?"

"By running away from the *nisayon*. The first and foremost challenge presented by every *nisayon* is whether you will flee for your life. Or as Chazal say, 'Hevei borayach min haaveirah. Flee from sin.' That's why we don't watch television, *chas veshalom*, which dishes out the most tempting portions of *gashmius*, *pritzus* and *apikorsus*. Secularists accuse us of being sheltered, but we know that our job is to be sheltered, to remain naive and innocent our whole lives.

"The number one test we face every day is how hard we will *daven* to Hashem *not* to send us any more tests. We say it every morning right off the bat in *Birchas Hashachar*. We say, 'Al tevienu lidei nisayon. Don't put us to the test.' Unfortunately, most people just barrel through that *tefillah* without realizing how crucial it is to their success during the entire remainder of the day."

They fell silent as they stepped back onto the sidewalk. Making no move to walk on, they silently watched the amber strobe lights pop out their bright pulses. Beck noticed Rusie raise the palm of her hand to cover a wide yawn.

"Binyamin, do you mind if we head home?" Rusie asked gently. "I'm really tired, and I still have to wash the *milchig* dishes."

"Of course. I'll even dry them as you wash."

He smiled at her and silently thanked Hashem for the

umpteenth time for his precious, peerless mate.

They crossed Larchmont and proceeded toward Millbank.

"By the way, Rusie, do you mind if I make just one more addendum to our discussion on evil?"

"No, of course not."

"I just think it's important to realize that Hashem unleashes evil in this world for many different reasons. We only discussed one of those reasons. Maybe on *Shabbos* we can get the kids to join in, and we'll flesh out another one of *Yiddishkeit's* answers to the Problem of Evil."

"Sounds like fun. Speaking of evil, what's happening with the robberies?"

"That's what I wanted to mention to you now, Rusie. After we're done with the dishes, I'm going out for a little while." Beck spoke carefully.

"You are? What for?"

"Rusie, we know that the Tip-Top Roofing Company is mixed up in this robbery business. For some reason, Chet seems to be going slow, but I'm convinced they're the key. So tonight I'm going to visit their premises and see what I can see."

He held his breath, awaiting her reaction.

"Don't do it, Binyamin." Rusie was instantly wide awake.

"Please, Rusie. There's absolutely no danger. That's why I'm going at night, so there won't be anyone around."

"How do you know they don't have a watchman, or a dog, or some type of booby trap?"

"Well, of course, if I see there's anyone around, or any danger at all, I'll leave immediately. But they're so isolated, they probably assume no one would ever think of them, let alone go snooping around."

"Binyamin, I just sense something sinister about the whole affair. I'd rather you not play around with *tumah*."

"Look, I know you have good feminine intuition," Beck countered. "But it's not infallible." Immediately, he was sorry for the strident edge in his voice.

They paused as they reached the walk leading to their front porch. Beck looked into his wife's deep brown eyes.

"I promise you I'll make a beeline for home if I suspect any type of danger at all. Okay?"

She returned his gaze, but said nothing.

"Do you have your watch on?" he asked. "What time is it?"

Beck had never been able to tolerate a watch clinging to his wrist.

"Ten-thirty," she answered.

"*Oy vey!*" he declared. "Rusie, it's late. Do you mind putting the dishes in the drainboard, and I'll dry them when I get home? I really would like to make this a fast run over to Tip-Top."

In his mind, he doubted it would be either fast or easy. He only hoped it would not be as perilous as Rusie feared.

"Okay," she replied. He could tell her tongue acquiesced where her heart dissented.

"Go ahead," he urged. "I'll watch you into the house before I go around to the driveway."

She looked at him again forlornly. He was almost tempted to renege.

"I'll be okay, Rusie. I'll be home soon."

As she closed the front door to the house, he felt a cold isolation, a sense that he was now on his own, vulnerable, unprotected. He looked up and down the street, but he saw no one.

He walked briskly along the sidewalk leading to the rear of the house. Standing on the driveway, he again surveyed his surroundings, then jumped into the car, locked the door and craned his neck around to make sure no one was crouching in the back seat. He started the engine and checked under the seat for the flashlight he had commandeered from the ECCP cabinet earlier in the day.

He looked up again and caught sight of his wife's silhouette against the kitchen window. He flashed the headlights once. The kitchen light went off and on in response as he drove away.

While he parked his car adjacent to the clearing by Dovid's footpath, Beck mumbled, "*Baruch Hashem*, that was easy to find."

He stepped out of the car, locked the door and turned on the flashlight. Facing the dark shadows of the jumbled trees, he steeled himself.

Too bad the road from the west side of the tracks is so pitted, he thought. I'd much rather go through that way. On the other hand, if there's a watchman, he won't see me coming through the woods. Now, *there's* an advantage to wearing a black suit and black hat.

He tugged the brim of his felt hat. Then he amended, On the third hand, I wouldn't want to meet up with any four-legged creatures in this jungle either. And they won't care what kind of a clown suit I'm wearing!

He ducked past an overhanging branch and found himself on the trail.

"*Hakadosh Baruch Hu*, please extend Your *siyata dishmaya*. Help me safely through this woods, and if there is any information available at Tip-Top, please let me find it."

The path was fairly recognizable. It was obviously used frequently enough to remain clear of major obstructions. The ground surface was well-covered with grass and fallen leaves, and he made good progress. He was nervous, but only because it was so dark.

He soon noticed the trees thinning out.

"*Baruch Hashem. Baruch Hashem.* Thank You, Hashem,

for getting me through this wilderness unscathed. I think I can see Tip-Top's clapboard office building that Dovid described. Now what's this ahead?"

He shone the light forward and illuminated a dead tree that had fallen across the path where it emerged from the woods. He raised his right foot to step high over the log, but as it came down on the other side, he felt the ground move underneath.

"*Hiss-ss-ss.*"

Beck's adrenalin level jumped as he heard a muffled snarl. He instantly retracted his foot, but he was off balance and fell toward the right. As he threw out his hands to catch himself on the log, the flashlight shot out of his grip. He heard it strike hard against something in the distance.

A white furry object bounded three yards to a nearby tree and scampered up the trunk.

"Possum," Beck moaned. His heart was pounding.

The flashlight had been extinguished when it impacted. Beck traced the log to its end and groped around for the light with his shoes, but when he could not locate it after five minutes, he decided to go on.

Im yirtzeh Hashem, I'll remember the basic course of the trail on the way back, he consoled himself half heartedly.

He turned to face the Tip-Top building. He was still shaken by the encounter with the possum and desperately wished to avoid further surprises.

Beck saw no lights, nor any signs of life. The dim starlight was enough to discern scattered junk, old shingles and various rusted tools piled up near the foundation. A corrugated fiberglass awning rigged to the wall sheltered a red and black motorcycle. The building itself appeared ancient and badly in need of fresh paint. Vines crept up part of one wall. A trellis on a second wall extended from the earth to a second-story window and was completely overgrown with thick ivy. Bare areas dotted the cedar shingle roof.

Beck stood stock-still, about forty feet from the building, and listened intently. He heard nothing other than the ubiquitous crickets.

He took a few stealthy paces and stopped again to listen. Still hearing nothing, he crouched down and began creeping carefully around the left side of the building, attempting to avoid stepping on twigs. Finally, he spotted the door.

Halting once more, he strained his senses to detect any signs of life, but discovered none.

The wooden steps felt rotten underfoot and cracked loudly as he stepped onto them. To Beck, it sounded like gunshot, and he wished they were concrete rather than wood. He stopped mid-stride and listened once more.

He reached for the doorknob.

"I can't believe it," he muttered, as the knob turned in his hand. "It's unlocked."

The hinges creaked noisily. Again, he stood absolutely still, his hand grasping the half-opened door, his legs straddling the threshold. He concentrated with his whole being, struggling mightily to detect any movement inside. But it was pitch black.

He tiptoed in and closed the door behind him. He heard the lock automatically slide into the doorstrike, and he wondered again why he had not found the door locked.

He groped along the wall for a light switch but found none near the door. He decided to stand still a minute and allow his eyes to adjust to the nearly total darkness.

Suddenly, he heard a faint shuffle. He whipped around and saw a shadow moving barely three feet from his face!

14

AN INTENSE LIGHT PIERCED BECK'S EYES AS HE CAUGHT sight of the glint of steel. His heart exploded.

"*POLICE! FREEZE!*" The thunderous command crashed through Beck's eardrums.

"Benny! Is that you?"

"Chet?"

"What in . . . what . . . Benny! What are you doing here? Benny! I could've killed you! . . . I could've killed you, Benny! . . . Benny! What are you doing here? I can't believe it! . . . Benny! I could've killed you."

Beck had never heard Chester Carter on the verge of tears. He was babbling like a baby.

"Benny, I could've killed you. What are you doing here?" Carter was choked up.

Beck was speechless. At the same instant, he was relieved and frightened, ecstatic and dejected, invigorated and paralyzed, delirious with deliverance and abashed at his own exposure.

"Benny! In another second I was ready to pull the trigger. I was aiming at your chest. Thank G-d! Thank G-d! Thank G-d!" Carter was still beside himself.

"Chet," Beck finally found his tongue. "I'm terribly sorry. I don't know what to say. I figured no one would be here at night, and I might have a chance to get some clues to our robberies. I didn't even expect to come inside, but I found the door open."

"Of course," Carter replied. "I left it open when I stepped outside to see what all the racket was about."

"You mean the noise when I nearly squashed a possum?"

"Serves you right," Carter accused. "Didn't I tell you to stay home tonight?"

"Yeah, but I had no idea you would be over here, Chet."

"I got a search and seizure warrant from Judge O'Brien this afternoon. Didn't I tell you I'd have some information for you in the morning? Didn't I tell you to trust me? Didn't I tell you . . ."

Beck recognized Carter's rhetorical parries and thought it best to keep quiet. He had unwittingly placed Carter in a terrible position, and now the big cop needed time to salve his guilty conscience.

"I'm sorry," Beck repeated. "I take the blame."

Carter slipped a light filter on the end of his flashlight. It was a device Beck had invented for circumstances where they had to dim and diffuse the concentrated beam of the ECCP flashlights.

The two men stood like ghosts in the eerie half-light. Beck noticed that Carter was in plain clothes—dark blue sweatshirt, black jeans and black and white sneakers.

"How'd you get in?" Beck asked softly.

"Second-story window. There's an ivy trellis going up the outside of the building."

"I noticed."

"Well, it lets you into a storage room."

Beck perceived the lingering edge in Carter's voice. He decided not to speak again until Carter said something first. Another awkward minute passed.

"You see the loft up there?" Carter finally remarked

more calmly. "There are several small rooms built against the back wall."

Beck's eyes were finally adjusting to the low light. For the first time, he noticed that the interior of the building was essentially one large, open, two-story vault, perhaps seventy-five feet from side to side and fifty feet from front to back. Along the wall to the far right he could faintly discern several desks laden with papers and books. On the opposite side of the room, a variety of tools, canisters and materials were berthed on a series of wide, sturdy shelves stretching at least twelve feet up the wall. In the center of this scene, as one entered the front door, was a long, heavy looking table with several wooden folding chairs sitting at odd angles around it. A smell of tar pervaded the air.

"What loft?" Beck said, squinting toward the rear of the building where Carter was pointing. "Oh yeah, I see it."

Beck noticed along the entire face of the back wall a platform about fifteen feet off the ground, extending some twenty feet forward.

"How do you get up there?" Beck inquired.

"It all depends. If you're an employee, you climb up that staircase on the end," Carter replied, pointing toward the right. "If you're a cop, you shinny up the trellis, like I said before."

"Glad to see you've got your humor back," Beck noted.

"Well, don't try to rattle it again. And speaking of being rattled, I got the surprise of my life when I climbed in that window. I knocked over a pile of rain gutters coming in, and they made enough racket to wake the dead."

"Well, Chet, as long as I'm here, I may as well help out. What have you found so far?"

"Truth is, Benny, I just got here myself about twenty minutes ago. I took a quick look up in the storage room where I entered, and then I searched the little room next to it. That's when I heard the commotion you were making outside."

"*Nu?* Did you find anything?" Beck wanted to avoid further discussion of his grand entrance.

"Just this, Benny." He unfolded a piece of paper from his shirt pocket and shined the muted flashlight on it.

"Looks like Japanese, Chet, doesn't it? Or Chinese?"

"Greek, as far as I'm concerned, boss. You're the professor, not me. The only thing I can recognize on the whole page is the number up here . . . 1431. Didn't you tell me that was the address of that fellow Mickey Mantle on Dorchester Street?"

"You're right, Chet! By the way, it's Mikiachi Goto. Have a little respect. For all we know, it's one of the royal family names."

"Whatever. They all sound the same to me."

"Listen, Chet, let's go back upstairs and start combing the place. You finish the room where you found this Japanese note, and I'll take the room next to it. Afterwards, we'll look around downstairs."

Leading the way with his light, Carter threaded them past the trash cans, phone wires and other paraphernalia lining the floor and ascended the stairs.

"It's locked," Beck said, trying the knob of the first door in the loft area.

"Okay, we'll worry about it later," Carter responded, walking on. "The next room is the storage room. See the mess I made?"

Beck poked his head inside and immediately felt the cool night air on his face. Through the open window, he saw the trees swaying in the distance. Inside, a pile of aluminum rain gutters lay scattered on the floor like giant pickup sticks, while two others remained leaning against some glass hurricane lamps sitting atop a case of low, metal shelves. A pile of hemp rope was curled in a far corner, next to a closet door. The entire room seemed to be coated with dust.

"Ah-choo!" Beck sneezed.

"Sh-sh!" Carter shushed. "The whole world doesn't have to know we're here."

"Why, who's around?"

"No one, I hope. But you never know."

Beck hoped that Carter was only ribbing him. He closed the door to the storage room, and they proceeded to the next room.

"This is the room I was working on," Carter introduced Beck to the surroundings. "The Japanese letter was lying on this desk. I looked through some of the other papers, but they don't appear suspicious. Inventory of some sort, that's all."

"This room certainly appears more used than the storage room," Beck observed.

The chamber was only about ten feet square, but two wide, double-hung windows on the outer wall made it appear more spacious. The rich aroma of tongue-and-groove cedar paneling masked the tar odor of the rest of the premises. The plush carpet, mahogany roll-top desk, leather-covered executive chair, antique brass lamp and curios displayed on a cherrywood bookcase gave the room the ambience of a cozy hideaway.

"Hey, Chet, do that again," Beck said.

"Do what?" Carter had been playing the flashlight around the room.

"Shine your light on that picture hanging on the wall. The big one next to the desk."

Carter directed the beam toward the three-foot-tall, wood-framed oil canvas. It was a painting of a large daisy.

"That's strange, isn't it?" Beck commented.

"Looks sort of gimmicky to me," Carter answered. "Of

course, what passes for art today . . ."

"I don't know a thing about art," Beck continued, "but . . . here, let me see your light, Chet. The yellow center of the flower seemed to phosphoresce from the glow of your flashlight."

Beck stepped up to the painting and brought the beam close to the canvas.

"Ay-yai!" both men shouted, jumping back as the picture, and the paneling behind it, sprang open like the lid of a jack-in-the-box.

Carter grabbed both of Beck's shoulders from behind and wrenched him to the floor.

"Down!" he commanded.

They remained motionless, looking up at the inset cabinet that had been revealed.

"Stay down," Carter ordered. He crawled to the other side of the desk, unplugged the brass lamp and slid it over in front of Beck's prone figure. Still on his hands and knees, he picked it up and waved it in front of the opening in the wall.

"I guess it's safe. I was worried about a motion-triggered booby trap."

The two men stood up guardedly.

"Ingenious!" Beck exclaimed, examining the section of wall that had swung open. "The lock release mechanism is triggered by a photoelectric cell positioned in the center of the daisy. Feel how mushy the floorboards are next to the wall? There must be a safety lock underneath, so you have to step up to the wall before you illuminate the photocell. That prevents the sunlight or room light from springing it open."

"I'm more interested in those boxes," Carter said, indicating several metal cases stacked on shelves inside the hidden cabinet. They were just above Carter's eye level.

He took one of the boxes down and set it on the desk. Unhooking the snap lock, he cautiously raised the lid.

"Wowie zowie!" he exclaimed. He took the filter off his light and trained the beam inside the box.

"Oh, no!" Beck marveled. "There must be a million bucks worth of jewels in here."

The steel box, about ten by eighteen inches, and about four inches deep, was painted a drab, army green on the outside, but was lined on the inside with dark blue, downy velvet. A silk pillow covering the bottom filled up half of the box's four-inch depth. Resting on top of this pillow was the most astonishing array of gold, silver and platinum settings, encrusted with diamonds, pearls, rubies and other precious gems. There were rings, earrings, necklaces, bracelets, pins, brooches.

"Incredible, Chet! Look at this."

Beck daintily grasped a magnificent tiara between his thumb and index finger. He lifted it carefully out of the mound of other jewels. Scalloped bands of glimmering silver, beset with flashing diamonds flowing in whorls around a line of clear, deep-green emeralds, rose in a crescendo toward a resplendent ruby in the center. The ruby was rectangular in shape with angled corners, about an inch wide and one-and-a-half inches tall, and it sparkled with a brilliant, royal crimson hue.

"This stuff is priceless, Chet. Where do you suppose they got these jewels? I can't imagine they robbed them off ordinary citizens. Not in this neighborhood, at least."

"You're forgetting their M.O.," Carter lectured. "Remember, they're using the stolen credit cards to make high-priced purchases at jewelry stores. The question is, what are they doing with the goods once they collect them?"

"Well, Chet, there are three more metal boxes in the cabinet. What's your bet? Are they full or empty?"

"There's one way to find out," Carter replied. "Will you do the honors?"

Beck moved around Carter and stepped over to the hidden cabinet. Two of the remaining boxes were identical to the one they had just opened. The third one was a battleship-gray color and had a different style hasp. A small, brass padlock was hooked through the hasp.

Beck carefully lowered the gray box. On the top, painted in black lacquer, were a series of Japanese characters.

"I guess we'll need some pliers to get this one open. If we find another tiara, I call first dibs," Beck said with a laugh. "Hey, why'd you turn your light off?"

He slowly turned around with the box and glanced at Carter. Instantly, his smile vanished.

"What's the matter, Chet?"

Carter was standing motionless, his arms outstretched and his ears straining. He slapped a palm on Beck's arm, with an abrupt gesture to shut him up.

"Hear that?" Carter said in a whisper.

"No. What?"

"Quick! Benny, put this stuff away. We've got to get out of here! Someone's coming!"

Beck was in no position to argue. He had too often witnessed the accuracy of Carter's uncanny bloodhound instincts.

Beck still heard nothing, but he hurriedly returned the second box to the shelf where he had found it. Then he helped Carter finish replacing the jewels in the first box and returned it to the cabinet. As they snapped the wall back in place, Beck detected the rumble of an automobile exhaust.

"You've got good ears, Chet," he remarked.

They started out of the door.

"Hey!" Beck yelped as he ran into Carter. The cop had stopped short.

"The lamp, Benny! I unplugged it and moved it to the other side of the desk, remember?"

As Beck dashed back into the room, he saw lights reflecting off the distant trees. A car was pulling up to the building.

"Quick, Benny! Close the door on your way out. We'll duck into the storage room. And keep the noise down!"

Beck heard car doors slam and the rough voices of several men in front of the building. He pulled the door of the jewelry room closed and winced at the cracking sound it made. Then he scrambled after Carter, who was frantically motioning with his hand from the storage room.

"Hurry, Benny! And don't step on the gutters, for G-d's sake!"

As Beck piled into the storage room, he heard the front door lock clicking open. Rusie's urging him to stay home tonight unexpectedly loomed in his mind. He was ashamed of his naivete and stupidity in thinking there would be no danger.

"Am I ever glad you're here, Chet," Beck whispered. "I feel totally vulnerable. If you don't mind, keep your American Express handy, would you?"

"Wouldn't leave home without it," Carter returned with a silent wink, patting the leather holster on his hip.

Carter left the door to the storage room slightly ajar and stood peeking out. Beck noticed that the breeze outside had kicked up, and with the door open, fresh gusts began blowing into the room.

Beck did his best not to trample the rain gutters lying in the middle of the room. He wished he had picked them up earlier. Now it would be impossible to do so without giving themselves away.

"C'mon, ya nitwit! Hit th' light."

The deep-sounding, harsh voice from below was clearly

audible in the loft. Without warning, the entire interior of the building was flooded by light.

"Can you see them?" Beck whispered in Carter's ear.

Carter nodded his head and stepped back to let Beck look out through the crack of the door.

Eight banks of long fluorescent strip lights marched across the high ceiling. For the first time, Beck noticed stenciled patterns adorning the upper fringe of the ash wall paneling. A large, quartz wall clock was nailed above the front door. Long metal rods, used to open and close the sashes, extended from the second-level windows nearly to the floor. Along the edges of the hardwood floor itself there were still unsullied vestiges of its original beauty, but the closer Beck looked toward the center of the room, the more he discovered the floor splintered and pocked and coated with black streaks of tar. Incongruously, the heavy table in the center of the room was still in prime condition, accentuating the deterioration of the rest of the surroundings.

"Siddown, Sissy," the deep, sonorous voice barked again.

Beck spied the sandy colored hair of a muscular man already seated at the table, facing away from the loft. He was speaking in the direction of the desks along the far wall, to someone whom Beck could not see. Seated opposite the sandy haired man was a short fellow in his early twenties with curly, black hair, wearing a blue, long sleeved workshirt and a green baseball cap.

"Damon!" Beck hissed.

"Quiet!" Carter cautioned, squeezing Beck's arm. "You know him?"

"I sure do," Beck muttered. Although his whisper was barely audible, his expression was full of venom. "He's the knave that knocked me into Dorchester yesterday."

Beck unconsciously fingered the bandage on his right hand.

"Sissy! I said siddown 'fore I smacks ya. Puppy 'n I ain't got all night."

Beck winced as the sandy-haired man slapped the table loudly with his fist. He stood up and faced toward the left. Beck estimated he was in his early forties, much older than Damon. The sleeves of his blue and gray plaid shirt were rolled up past the elbows, revealing indigo tattoos on his thick arms.

"Chet!" Beck exclaimed in a hush, his lips next to Carter's ear. "That's the fiend that tried to run me off the road on the way to the Caterpillar dealer!"

"Gee, Benny," Carter ribbed in a faint voice. "Looks like a reunion. All your friends are here."

"I'm glad you think it's such a joke, Funny Boy," Beck murmured.

He looked down at the tall man who had swerved his big rig into the ECCP Command Car. Thinking of the danger his daughter had sustained made Beck boil.

"Easy, Jack," Beck heard Damon speak for the first time. "Sissy's mad 'cause we showed up late."

"'At's right, Ritondo," a sandpaper voice issued from the left side of the building. "Ya tole me 'leven. Here I'm hangin' by th' gate, waitin' fer ya to take yer fancy time, 'n what if a fuzz shows up to pop a few questions at me, huh? Next time I ain't waitin'."

"Ain't gonna be no next time," Jack answered. "I told ya before we was wrappin' up this operation tonight. That's what we're here fer. Now come siddown. Alright, I 'pologize fer bein' late. My old lady was givin' me a hard time."

"Figgers!" Just then, the sandpapery voice stepped into Beck's view.

"Robert Eberhart!" Beck breathed excitedly. "Hey, this really *is* a reunion."

The tall man's long black ponytail and hooked nose were

unmistakable. He was wearing a stained, orange shirt, tucked into a wide leather belt holding up his patched blue jeans.

"A guy what cain't run his ole woman, how's he 'sposed to run a outfit like this, huh?" Eberhart rasped.

"Look, Sissy," Jack shot back. "I'm tryin' ta sugar ya, but I'm fed up ta th' gills. One word from th' Tramp, an' yer purty ponytail's gonna be decoratin' a shrunken skull."

Eberhart's jibe about Jack's inability to manage his wife must have struck a sensitive nerve, Beck reflected. He watched as Eberhart finally took a seat next to Damon. From his perch in the loft, he now possessed a clear view of Eberhart's and Damon's faces, as well as Ritondo's back.

"I was ready to send ya ta th' cleaners anyway," Jack continued, still fuming, "when ya goofed up with Puppy's brother."

"How'd I know th' little punk was gonna monkey hisself onto th' crane?" Eberhart asserted defensively. "I done my best, di'n't I?"

"Lissen," Damon interceded. "How's about we don' cry over spilled milk. Wha's done is done. Anyways he's still gotta be bumped off. An' I wish you'd stop callin' him my brother, th' little cuss."

"Why, 'cause he stole that Jew necklace from yer car?" Eberhart said accusingly.

"'At's right," Damon replied. "Nobody messes with my stuff 'n gets away with it, hear?"

"You was disobeyin' orders yerself," Jack commented. "Ya shoulda handed me the loot as soon as ya got back from Macy's that night."

"I tried, Jack, but ya wasn't here."

"Then ya shoulda paged me. Ya wasn't plannin' ta keep that necklace yerself, was ya, Puppy?" Jack quizzed pointedly.

"'Course not, boss. I know th' rules. An' if Mark ha'n't broken th' rules 'n given that card to his girl, he wou'n't be in th' fix he's in now. It's jes' as well, 'cause it's easier to keep 'n eye on him in a jail cell than hidin' out who knows where."

"Well, this'll be a lesson fer ever'body. Rules is rules," Jack lectured sternly. "We get this shipment out, then it's Mexico 'til winter. But th' next round, ever'body sticks ta th' rules, unnerstan'? That means ya got two hours after th' stickup ta use th' card, then ya melts it. That was yer goofup, Puppy. An' all loot gets turned in ta me on th' double. It's too bad Lowery's such a mushmelon. He'd 'a made a good yoker. I tried ta warn him. Ain't got no sympathies fer him no more."

"Yeah, well, he may 'a already done us in, Ritondo." Eberhart spoke up. "I seen Scratch today."

"Ya did?" Jack sprang up as he raised his inflection. He instantly seemed very alert. "Wha'd he say?"

"The cops jerked Lowery in yesterday 'n rubbed him over good. Bet an ant's tail he blabbed."

"What!" Jack thundered, stomping around the table and over to an empty, wooden fruit crate resting under one of the front windows. He stood with his back to the others, gazing out the window into the black night.

Suddenly, he raised a shoe and rammed it into the crate, smashing one of the slats.

"Why, that sneakin' . . ." he snarled.

"Now you siddown, Ritondo," Eberhart continued. "There's more. They also pulled Dawn's chain fer two hours. But she won' sing, 'at's my guess."

"How'd they get ta her?" Jack demanded. He had swiveled around to face the other two, but made no move to return to the table.

"Ya 'member Scalia?" Eberhart answered. "Th' rat what's in cahoots with them Jews that likes to play cops 'n robbers?"

"Ha! Ha!" Damon interjected, pounding his fist on the table in mirth.

Eberhart glanced inquisitively at Damon.

"Puppy almost bumped one of 'em off yesterday," Jack explained, "but he blew it."

"Look who's talkin'," Damon retorted. "As big as th' trailer is, an' you still cou'n't broadside their fuzz car."

"He was lucky, that's all," Jack defended himself.

"Maybe his G-d was watchin' out fer 'im, Ritondo," Eberhart smirked.

"Yeah, Jack," Damon offered, "maybe th' Jews' G-d is gonna get ya. Maybe He's gonna get all 'a us."

"Would ya can the church talk?" Jack shot back, red-faced. "Ya knuckleheads shoulda been preachers."

He strode back to his place at the table, an expression of agitated anger outlining his rough face. Before sitting down, he stretched over the wide table to retrieve an ash tray. The untucked tail of his plaid shirt rose over his waistline, exposing a black leather belt.

From his roost in the loft, Beck silently elbowed Carter and pointed down to a silvery object protruding from the back of Jack's belt.

"It's a semi-automatic," Carter whispered. "A round from one of those would sure clear your sinuses."

Beck shuddered at the thought and inhaled sharply to check the status of his nasal passages.

"Oh no!" he gasped in terror. He was suddenly overcome by a violent urge to sneeze, to expel the dust he had sucked in. He turned from the door and pinched his nose hard, battling that irrepressible human reflex.

"Choo!" His ears popped painfully as he struggled to contain the noise.

"Benny!" Carter noiselessly mouthed the exclamation, a look of shock on his face.

Beck's heart jumped. He instantly looked out through the door again, desperately praying to Hashem that his disturbance had gone unnoticed.

"What was 'at?" Damon jumped to his feet.

"What was what?" Jack said. "Siddown."

"'At noise. Din't ya hear somethin', Sissy?" Damon addressed Eberhart.

"Nah, jes' Ritondo smackin' down th' ashtray."

"Puppy," Jack said, "what're ya so jittery fer? Siddown, 'fore I knocks ya down."

Damon slowly lowered himself into the chair, nervously scanning the corners of the room. His face bore a worried frown. He sat close-mouthed, waiting for Jack to proceed.

In the loft, Beck tried valiantly to calm himself. He stole a look at the big wall clock above the front door. It was five minutes before midnight.

"*Kachatzi halailah,* almost midnight," he intoned, his heart still racing. "Hashem, please protect us. And *please* prevent me from sneezing again!"

Jack remained silent, leaning back in his chair. Beck imagined he could hear the ticks of the clock's second hand, as though this evil room had a heartbeat of its own.

Damon was still glancing around nervously. Suddenly, he sprang up, but his chair snagged a crack in the floor and tipped backwards. As it struck, the resounding clap shattered the lull like a thunderbolt in the night.

"Siddown, Puppy!" Jack ordered. "Where ya goin'?"

"I don' care what ya say, Jack," Damon insisted, "I heared somethin'. Maybe it was jes' a animal in th' trees, 'n maybe it weren't."

He strode over to a metal cabinet holding a stack of about ten thin drawers and pulled on a handle in the middle of the stack. Beck glimpsed a pile of blueprints lying flat in the drawer.

"Wrong one," Damon grumbled as he closed the drawer and opened the one below it.

"Whew!" Beck breathed to Carter. "That's some persuader."

From their vantage in the loft, the two men watched wide-eyed as Damon withdrew a mean looking knife from the cabinet. The hilt was pure black, with a leather thong attached to a ring on the end. Beck guessed that the sinister, steel blade was at least eight inches long, but only about three-fourths of an inch wide. The two honed edges merged symmetrically to a highly sharpened point.

"That'll pierce body armor like butter," Chet muttered.

"Ribs, too," Beck added ominously.

Damon ran his finger along the flat side of the blade.

"Put that away!" Jack demanded. "I got my piece right here, ya nitwit. Any animal comes moseyin' in th' door, I'll blow his brains out."

He slapped the lump protruding from his belt.

"Save yer stick fer next winter, Puppy," he added.

"Aw, leave 'im alone, Ritondo," Eberhart said. "It's 'is s'cur'ty blanket."

Damon uprighted his chair and sat down, gently placing the knife on the table in front of him, his right palm caressing the hilt.

"Okay," Jack conceded. "If it makes ya feel better."

At that moment, a sharp rapping on the wooden door echoed loudly through the building. Damon sprang to his feet, upsetting his chair again and sending it crashing into the metal blueprint cabinet.

"I tole ya, Jack!" Damon's hushed cry was full of alarm. He seized the dagger.

"Siddown, ya goofball!" Jack ordered. He jerked a thumb up at the wall clock. "Din't I tell ya th' Tramp was comin' at midnight? Is a good thing I tolerates ya, Puppy, 'r else you'da been gone long ago. You's too jumpy fer this line 'a work."

Damon stood befuddled, gazing from Jack to the big clock. He lowered the knife, obviously shamed.

"Get th' door, Sissy," Jack said.

Beck contemplated the rudeness and coarseness of the sordid characters below him. The cruelty they practiced on the public citizenry, he thought, dominated their own interpersonal relationships as well. He wondered who the Tramp was and where he would fit into the pecking order. He strained to get a peek at the newcomer.

Eberhart stepped quickly to the door and swung it open. The fluorescent light illuminated a man in his mid-forties, with thick, dark brown hair, standing on the threshold. His immaculately pressed white shirt was starched from the collar to the tips of the long sleeves. A stony aura of absolute authority emanated from his bearing and was reinforced by his polished gold cufflinks, olive dress slacks and gleaming Corfam shoes. The only detail detracting from this picture of invincibility was a long, vicious scratch along his left jaw.

"Charles Henley!" Beck whispered in shock. A morbid dread shot up his spine.

Without a word, Henley moved into the room, the hard soles of his leather boots clomping on the wood floor. Looking straight ahead, he strode purposefully to the left end of the table. There was no chair at that end, and he remained standing.

"Puppy!" Jack bawled. "Don't jes' stand there! Get th' Tramp a chair, ya nitwit!"

Damon sprang up as if his life depended on it. Grabbing a swivel chair from one of the desks, he wheeled it noisily and barely slipped it under Henley as the latter sat down. Beck was afraid to consider Damon's fate had he missed.

"Now ya two knuckleheads siddown 'n le's geddown ta

business," Jack resumed. "Th' Tramp ain't got all night. He done give th' orders, 'n he's doin' us a favor ta show up and make sure I give 'em to ya jes' th' way he wants 'em, so lissen close, hear? 'Cause the Tramp don' want no mistakes, get it?"

Henley leaned back, staring at the wall. Without moving his eyes, he extended his left hand outward, palm up.

As if on cue, Eberhart quickly fumbled in his shirt pocket, withdrew a cigarette, lit it and gingerly placed it in Henley's grasp. Henley brought it to his lips and inhaled a deep puff. A billow of white smoke blossomed and gently rose like a ball of dirty cotton from his mouth. He abruptly expelled a sharp jet of air, forcefully puncturing the compact cloud and leaving it in disarray.

Immediately, Jack passed Henley the ashtray he had meant for himself.

In obsequious tones, he addressed Henley. "Before I tells 'em the plans, if ya doesn't mind, I think ya oughta know Lowery got worked over by th' cops yesterday."

Henley lowered his eyes to stare coldly at Jack. His look was an unspoken command for Jack to continue.

"Sissy says he sung," Jack noted in a subdued voice.

"Did not!" Eberhart spoke stridently, jumping to his feet. "I said I *thinks* he sung."

Eberhart seemed frightened to be the purveyor of such unwelcome news. The entire room appeared to freeze, as all eyes focused on Henley. He remained utterly motionless, a stoic expression on his face.

The ticking of the wall clock pealed in the atmosphere like a giant metronome meting out the seconds toward a condemned man's execution.

After a long silence, Henley transferred the cigarette to his left hand. Everyone else remained as still as statues, transfixed with suspense. Then Henley slowly raised his right hand to his neck and drew a stiffened forefinger sharply across his throat. Eberhart and Damon simultaneously gripped the edge of the table.

Another fifteen seconds passed.

Finally, Jack sucked in a deep breath and said solemnly, "Sissy, when we leave here, call Scratch. I don' care what time it is. If he balks, tell 'im it's an order from th' Tramp. Tell 'im ta get holda Calley right away. Calley knows what ta do. He's jes' waitin' fer th' go."

He paused again, his fingertips drumming on the table.

"Lowery'll be dead by mornin'," he intoned callously. "My heart bleeds peanut butter fer 'im."

Beck shivered. He would love to instruct Chet to put a bullet through Jack's skull on the spot.

"Now le's ferget 'bout Lowery 'n get crackin'," Jack added. "Sissy, yer job is th' loot. Go up to th' Tramp's nest 'n get th' boxes. There's four 'a them. I already give ya d'rections to th' Jap's house. Stay there 'n watch 'im check th' loot against th' inventory. An' make sure he signs it, hear? Ya can leave 'im a copy of th' inventory if'n he wants it. I got another copy hid away, so nobody pulls no shenanigans. All's fair 'n square, hear?"

"Yeah, well, when do we get paid?" Eberhart demanded.

Jack pounded his fist forcefully on the table, causing Damon's knife to rattle.

"Jes' do yer job right, 'n don' ask no questions, hear me, Sissy?" Jack bellowed, heaving himself up straight. "Ya got some nerve askin' 'bout gettin' paid with th' Tramp right here. Ya ain't been cheated yet!"

Eberhart seemed cowed by Jack's outburst.

With pique still in his voice, Jack continued, "The Tramp ain't givin' none 'a us nothin' fer sev'ral months, 'cause they gotta dump th' loot in Japan first. Dependin' what they rake in, tha's what we get."

"Long as that girl don' interfere," Damon pouted.

"Who? Daisy?" Jack asked. "Whatsa matter with Daisy?"

"Puppy's right," Eberhart interrupted, a serious tone gripping his voice. "Now don' get me wrong, Jack. I don' mean no lip to th' Tramp. Ya hear me, Tramp? I don' mean no lip. But sometimes ya's too soft on 'er. 'Sides, ain't no woman a man can trus'."

Henley stood motionless, as though made of granite.

"Daisy don't know nothin', Sissy. Ya ain't gotta worry 'bout her. Ain't that right? She don't know nothin', right?" Jack asked, turning to Henley.

The latter was still staring coldly at the far wall. Suddenly, he parted his lips.

"And she never will," he said grimly.

The words shocked Beck. He had forgotten that Henley was capable of human speech. His voice possessed a cruel, steel timbre that surprised and frightened Beck.

"Why, whatcha gonna do, huh?" Eberhart pressed. "'Course I don' mean no lip, ya hear? But ya brung her up since she was a kid and now ya's stuck, now she's like yer own kid. What if she finds out and goes blabbin', huh? 'Course, I unnerstan' yer feelin's, but ya ain't gonna do nuttin', is ya?"

Henley fixed an icy stare on Eberhart, as if in answer to the latter's pointed question.

"Yeah," Eberhart repeated, trying to justify his straightforwardness. "Whatcha gonna do if she blabs?"

Henley continued to glare at Eberhart. Then, while Beck watched in absolute horror, Henley once again raised his hand and flicked his forefinger across his throat.

"Ach!" Eberhart breathed in sharply. "Naw, ya wou'n't do it, Tramp."

"*Rasha gamur*, you evil man!" Beck fulminated inwardly. "If I get out alive, the first thing I'll do is snatch Devorah out of his clutches. She doesn't realize the *sakanah* she's in."

"Now look here, Sissy," Jack resumed control of the

conversation. "Jes' ferget 'bout Daisy. 'Sides, we's all gonna be in siesta land by t'morrow night, if ya jes' shet yer mouth and foller orders."

He tilted his chair onto its two rear legs and stretched his arm toward a narrow set of shelves behind him. He jerked a large envelope from under a stack of papers and dropped it on the table.

"Now here's th' inventory, Sissy," he said, handing Eberhart several pages stapled together. "Look it over 'fore ya go up ta get th' loot."

Beck stepped silently back from the door of the storage room and turned to Carter.

"Chet! Eberhart's coming up here in a minute. We better stand back."

He traded places with Carter, allowing the cop to peer out the door, while he stood behind. He surveyed the rain gutters scattered on the floor, trying to determine where he could step without risk of knocking into something. The chief obstacles were the two gutters resting against the hurricane lamps, extending diagonally down to the molding beside the open window. He decided it would be prudent to step over these hurdles, and not wiggle underneath them.

Beck swung around once more to check Carter's position, and in so doing, his right *tzitzis* flew out from his waistband. One of the strings caught underneath the pedestal of the largest hurricane lamp and wrenched it forward before Beck was able to check his motion.

The lamp slammed to the floor with a crash, exploding the silence and shooting glass fragments everywhere.

15

"WHAT WAS THAT?" BECK HEARD JACK SHOUT FROM BELOW.

"I told ya I heared somethin' before!" Damon yelled. "Come from upstairs!"

"Grab yer piece, Sissy!" Jack commanded.

Carter instantly closed the door to the storage room, making as little noise as he could.

"Benny! We've got to get out of here," he whispered frantically, as they heard chairs scraping downstairs. "I'll never be able to hold off all four of them. Quick! Follow me!"

Carter bounded for the window and swung his legs out.

"Keep quiet!" Carter urged in a hushed voice. "We don't want them to know which room we're in. And wait till I get to the bottom. This trellis won't hold both of us."

Beck heard shoes tramping on the stairs! He sent up a desperate prayer that their foes should stumble and break their necks.

"Hurry, Chet!"

Carter had already scrambled about half way down, abandoning all moderation. His rough treatment of the aging trellis finally took its toll, and the entire structure began separating from the building with a heavy creak.

"Oh, no!" Beck moaned, watching Carter plunge the last six feet to the ground. Carter leaped nimbly out of the way as the entire trellis and vines tumbled with a whoosh. Beck observed him whip a police radio from a back pocket.

It was then that the peril of his circumstances fully smote Beck's consciousness. He panicked.

"Hakadosh Baruch Hu!" he despaired, paralyzed with fear. "I promise I'll never again put my trust in a mortal. Oh, why did I ever think that Chet and his gun would save me?"

He felt like crying.

"This 'un's locked!" Jack's harsh voice came through the darkness. "Try th' next door, where we keep them gutters."

Jack's abrupt shouting, so close at hand, finally jolted Beck into action. He fairly flew on his tiptoes toward the door, nearly tripping over a large cinder block standing on its end. He flattened himself against the wall next to the door's hinges.

Crash! A boot landed with great force on the door. It flew wide open, stopping no more than two inches from Beck's nose and smashing hard against the upright cinder block by his feet. The door rebounded halfway closed as the brick landed forcibly on Beck's shin. He closed his eyes tight and clenched his fists in pain.

He opened his eyes again and watched in terror as the door slowly opened into the room once more, admitting a long window of fluorescent light that stretched over the floor. Several dark shadows were cast across the light, like black devils framed in white fire.

"Whatcha see?" he heard Damon say.

"Nuttin'."

The next five seconds seemed like an eternity to Beck. A dryness gripped his throat. He was certain that the pounding of his heart was audible a mile away, like the beat of a giant war drum summoning vengeful Indians to the final kill. He stopped breathing.

Then he saw it.

The silver tip of a revolver barrel advanced slowly into the room past the edge of the open door. A curled finger firmly encircling the trigger crept into sight, followed by a mammoth, hairy fist gripping the handle. Then a gold cufflink piercing a white sleeve appeared.

Beck felt himself about to faint.

All of a sudden, he saw the hand drop down quickly out of sight, and the shadow it was attached to jumped back out of the room.

"Imbeciles!" he heard Henley growl in disgust.

"Ha! Ha!" Jack's laughter sounded more like a squeak. "Jes' them gutters, 'at's all. Sam musta left th' winda open when he was cleanin', an' the wind blew 'em down. Stay outa there, Sissy, 'less ya wants yer feet ampitated by all th' glass."

Beck saw the door open further towards him, as Eberhart peered into the room.

"What a mess!" he declared.

"Hey, boss," Damon spoke up hesitantly. "Ya don' mind we check th' loot, do ya? This bus'ness is makin' me nervous."

"Good idea," Jack replied. "Now ya jes' calm down, hear me, Puppy? Ain't nobody 'round 'ceptin' us chickens."

Beck was delirious with relief as he saw the shadows disappear and heard footsteps shuffling away from the doorway.

"Thank You, Hashem," he uttered with intense *kavanah*. "I LOVE YOU!"

He listened for a second to the muffled voices coming from the next room. Then he moved swiftly and silently, stepped over the lifeless rain gutters that had saved his own life and found the hemp rope curled on the floor.

"It's ancient," he muttered. "Hope it holds."

He tied one end of the rope to the closet doorknob and flung the remaining coils out the window. Hoisting his right leg up, he draped himself backwards over the ledge, balancing his body on his stomach. He heard his jacket rip on a nailhead as he wriggled himself out and eased his full weight onto the timeworn rope.

"Please make it hold, Hashem!"

Wrapping his legs around the line, he steadily lowered himself hand over hand.

"Ah-h!" he gasped, as he felt a jerk on the rope. Glancing up, his stomach churned as he spied one of the three strands frayed in half where it rounded the window ledge.

He looked down.

"Fifteen feet to go," he mumbled as he continued to strain.

He managed to ease downward another five feet, when the rope snapped. He felt himself hurtling toward earth. Miraculously, both his shoes landed between crosspieces of the trellis and were cushioned by the thick vines piled on the ground.

He extricated himself quickly and ran behind the building toward the road. It was so dark he could barely follow the gravel surface.

He tried to run on tiptoes to minimize the noise. The walnut-sized cobblestones tested his equilibrium as his soles continued to slip on the loose roadbed.

"Oof!" he grunted, as his foot collapsed unexpectedly in one of the pits on the road. He went sprawling, his arms scraping the rough stones, dirt spraying his face and grit stinging his eyes.

He pushed himself up on his hands and sat upright.

My hat! he thought. Where'd it go? He stood up and brushed off his trousers, then scouted around the grass by the roadside until he located the wayward hat. He flopped it on his head and tugged it down tight, dust and all.

This must be one of the hairpin turns that Dovid drew on the map, he said to himself. I see the road heads off to the left from here. Boy, I sure wouldn't want to attempt this turn at night!

By now, Beck was about a hundred feet from the building. He considered himself out of immediate danger and thought it best to hide. He headed for the nearest tree, a large white oak, but he had not moved three paces when the toe of his right shoe rammed into an unyielding object.

"Blast it!" he yelled. "That hurt!"

He bent down and saw a shiny steel grate, about six feet long and two feet wide, that had been dumped in the grass. He picked it up and leaned it against the oak's broad trunk, then ducked behind the big tree.

"Bravo!" he sang out, as he heard the eggbeater rumble of a helicopter. "Chet must have reached Foxtrot."

He spied the blinking white light of the police helicopter in the distant sky and, simultaneously, a fusillade of blue flashes bouncing off the trees along the gravel roadway.

"Wow! Chet sure got some backup this time!" he cheered. "Must be seven or eight squad cars. Looks like an army!"

As the chopper droned to a hover position overhead, its spotlights burst into four penetrating beams, and three million candlepower of intense white light flooded the clapboard building.

"It's like the first redemption," Beck marveled to himself. "A night shining with the brilliance of day. *Hodu Lashem ki tov!* Give thanks to Hashem for he is good!"

Beck retreated another fifty feet into the woods and remained out of sight as the caravan of police cruisers negotiated the hairpin turn. He then dashed back up to the roadway. Within another twenty seconds, no fewer than ten high-powered rifles were trained on the Tip-Top building.

"POLICE! YOU'RE SURROUNDED! COME OUT WITH YOUR HANDS UP! . . . REPEAT! POLICE! COME OUT WITH YOUR HANDS UP!"

The booming loudspeaker fired shock waves through Beck's body. He noticed a large boulder on the other side of the road, opposite the hole he had fallen into. He ran to the boulder and slumped down behind it.

"REPEAT! THIS IS THE POLICE! COME OUT WITH YOUR HANDS UP!"

A deafening silence reigned over thirty seconds of motionless suspense. Then Beck watched as a tall figure with a ponytail stepped slowly from the front of the building. Robert Eberhart had his arms raised high in the air. He was followed immediately by Jack Ritondo. The two men stopped when they reached the gravel line of the parking lot. Six crouching officers rushed toward them and smothered them in a tight huddle. Beck spotted chrome flashes of handcuffs as the prisoners were bundled roughly toward a distant police wagon.

Suddenly, Beck spied a big man jumping out of a window along the rear of the building. Beck recognized Henley's gleaming white shirt, one long sleeve tucked around a gray box, as he dashed for the distant woods.

"Go get him, Chet!" Beck cheered silently as a figure in dark clothing sprinted from the far side of the building in pursuit of the tall man. Two uniformed officers gave chase as well.

Beck smacked his palms together as he saw Carter catch up to Henley and tackle him to the ground. A sharp crash reached his ears as the box went flying and struck a tree trunk. Henley was instantly pinned down by his three pursuers.

"Oh, no!" Beck exclaimed as he turned back to the

building. "It's Damon! And all the police are in front!"

The baseball-capped figure clambered out of the same window Henley had used and raced for the motorcycle parked under the fiberglass awning. The loud report of the exhaust blasted the air as Damon swung the big bike across the grass and onto the road. Two officers finally noticed him and dashed for their squad cars.

"They'll never catch him!" Beck shouted.

Without losing a second, Beck jumped up and hopped to the side of the boulder he had been using as a blind. He leaned down and placed his arms underneath the rock, straining with all his might to move it. It began to roll onto the gravel just as the roaring motorcycle barreled down upon it.

Beck observed Damon's eyes pop and terror grip his face as he careened to the right. A violent crunch ripped through the air when the machine slammed into the pit that had tripped Beck earlier. Damon was instantly separated from the bike and sailed twenty feet forward, his shoulder slamming hard into the steel grate that Beck had leaned against the oak trunk.

Beck stood speechless, watching Damon's unstoppable flight. His mind was consumed by a hideous vision of a white Cadillac and a chrome bumper screeching unrelentingly toward his own skull.

"Midah keneged midah!" he exclaimed.

Immediately, Beck dashed forward to where Damon had landed. The young man was writhing in pain, lying on his right side, his left arm sprawled limply across his abdomen. He was whining pathetically, totally unaware of Beck's presence.

"Docta Beck!"

Beck suddenly realized that a bank of headlights were bathing his figure. He whirled in time to see a large, powerful police officer braking his legs from a full sprint.

"Bobby! Wow! Am I ever glad to see you!"

"Docta Beck!" Bobby repeated. "What're ya doin' here? Ya look like ya been run over by a truck. Y'all right?"

"Sure I'm fine, Bobby. I just took a spill, that's all. This fine gentleman on the ground, however, is a different story. He was trying to play Superman without a cape. You got a medic?"

"On th' way," Bobby answered. "But ya ain't tole me what ya was doin' here?"

"It's a long story, Bobby. If you can spring yourself loose, I'll let you drive me around to my car. It's over on the other side of Spartan."

"Sure, go hop in my cruiser. It's th' first one in line. Lemme jus' tell th' sarge."

Beck traipsed onto the gravel and shielded his eyes from the bright headlights. The lead police car had skidded to a halt a scant foot from the boulder he had rolled out. Leaning over the massive ball once again, he shouldered it onto the grass, then dusted himself off as thoroughly as possible.

"This one's locked," he muttered, trying the passenger door on Bobby's cruiser.

Stepping around to the driver's side, he hopped in and climbed over a brown clipboard lying in the middle of the seat. As he swung around, his knee knocked the clipboard onto the floor.

"What's this?" he said, retrieving the clipboard. "Discharge of Service Firearm. Looks like Bobby's report on the incident last week when he shot the pit bull."

Beck glanced down the handwritten page.

"Wow! He doesn't even mention my name, or the danger I was in. Say, this isn't right. Somehow, I'll have to put in my two cents."

Beck sank into the passenger's seat and reclined the back

of his head on the headrest. He breathed deeply, savoring the unanticipated security and relaxation. An inordinate weariness overtook his senses. He closed his eyes.

"*Hakadosh Baruch Hu,* thank You so much. You have given us a major victory tonight. Please continue our victory in court, so we can put these guys away for a long time.

"And please forgive me for being so discouraged lately. I'm really sorry. I fell prey to a terrible *yetzer hara.* Discouragement and unhappiness are the antithesis—the very enemies—of my *bitachon.* My pessimism and dejection declared that I no longer believed You are in charge of the world, *chas veshalom.* Even in the worst of straits, I simply *must* understand that everything is happening at Your command and is therefore to my ultimate benefit. I see how You can bring the *geulah* instantly, and from the most unexpected quarter. You are wonderful! I LOVE YOU, HASHEM!"

"Ready, Docta Beck?" Bobby sang out cheerfully as he jumped behind the wheel. "Thanks fer movin' that rock. When I seen it before, I thought I was a goner fer sure. Wonder who put it there."

"I did, Bobby."

The officer whipped his head around to stare at Beck, a look of consternation fixed to his face.

"I told you it's a long story," Beck explained, "but now's not the time."

They rode in silence, bouncing along the gravel lane to the city street. Bobby turned right and crossed the railroad tracks.

"By the way, what are you doing Thursday morning?" Beck broke the tranquility.

"Day after t'morrow? Sleepin', prob'ly. I'm workin' th' night shift this month. Why?"

"Chet and I have an appointment downtown with Chief Vincent, to bring him up-to-date on the robbery situation.

Until half an hour ago, I didn't think we'd have much good news to tell him. I'd like you to be there, if you can, Bobby."

"Sure, Docta Beck. I'd love ta."

"Great. We'll pick you up at the station at eight-thirty. Go around that loading dock just ahead. You see my car parked at the far end?"

Bobby braked the cruiser next to the lone vehicle isolated near the woods. Beck hopped out and closed the door, then leaned his elbows on the open window.

"Thanks for the ride, Bobby. And listen, I'm going to need your help when we talk to the Chief."

"Why? Whatcha mean?"

"Well, you know how much work Chet has been putting into this case, don't you? And other officers, too. Sometimes, you cops are too modest. I want to make sure the Chief knows what I think of his men."

"Naw, that ain't fer me, Docta Beck," Bobby said with a wave of his big palm. "Ya wanna pat Chet on th' back, 's okay with me, but I'll jus' lissen."

"That's a deal, Bobby. Let me do the talking. Thanks again for the lift. I really mean it. Thanks for everything!"

He stepped back and watched as the police car pulled off into a wide arc through the empty parking lot. When he turned to face his vehicle, his eyes fell on the path angling into the woods.

He strode over to the edge of the asphalt and gazed into the deep darkness of the tangled trees. It seemed to him an eon since he had last stood there. A wave of strength and confidence flooded over him, invigorating him with the flush of knowledge and the surety of truth.

He looked Heavenward at the sparkling velvet sky.

"I mean it. Thanks for everything!" he repeated softly.

16

"THE SKY IS GORGEOUS, ISN'T IT?" DOVID GUSHED, HIS foot braking the ECCP Command Car to a stop at a red light.

"Certainly is," Beck replied. "I've witnessed many flaming sunrises at sea, but I've rarely observed one in the city. It's already long past dawn, of course, but those thick clouds on the horizon make it appear just like a glorious sunrise. Looks like Hashem is stoking a good fire to warm up the world today."

"Hey, Docta Beck," Bobby called from the back seat, "ya oughta been a poet, 'steada a science type, y'know."

"Listen, Dovid," Carter interrupted. He was sitting next to Bobby on the rear seat. "If you'll stay on Bucknell to the next freeway entrance, you'll cut out all that construction. The Chief's expecting us at nine, so we've only got twenty minutes. Benny, would you mind handing me a pen off the dash?"

Beck reached forward and lifted a ballpoint pen from a Plexiglas holder.

"You know, I was thinking," Beck said.

"Uh-oh!" Carter quipped from the rear.

Ignoring the dig, Beck continued his sentence. "Tuesday night was *Rosh Chodesh*, the beginning of the month. That's when the moon is new, when it ceases diminishing in size and begins its emerging period of growth. Our Sages compare the Jewish nation to the moon, so is it any surprise that our great victory came on the night of *Rosh Chodesh?*"

"That's an interesting point," Dovid said as he applied the accelerator.

"Say, Docta Beck," Bobby said, "I been meanin' to ask ya. How come th' Jewish days always starts with th' night, 'steada the normal way?"

Out of the corner of his eye, Beck saw Carter jab his right elbow hard into Bobby's ribs.

"Ow! Whatsa matter? Cain't I ask a simple question? I din't insult ya, did I, Docta Beck?"

"Sh! Can't you tell he's in a *mussar* mood?" Carter shushed.

Bobby appeared bewildered.

"No, of course you didn't insult me, Bobby. In fact, Dovid and I were pondering that same question yesterday, but the phones wouldn't leave us alone. Do you remember, Dovid?"

Beck swung around to hand the pen to Carter and was surprised to see him gritting his teeth, his right fist upraised toward Bobby. When Carter noticed Beck watching, he instantly relaxed and extended his hand to receive the pen.

"Listen, Bobby," Chet grumbled. "Let Benny and Dovid discuss philosophy, if they want. But I need your help writing up these four indictments. I'm going to the grand jury at eleven o'clock this morning, and I've only finished Eberhart's so far. I'm working on Ritondo right now, and I need to come up with a clearer statement in block number four . . ."

Carter always kept his mind on business, Beck thought to himself. He addressed Dovid again.

"*Nu*, Dovid, do you remember the discussion?"

"Sure, Benny, we drew an analogy between the events of

the world and the fact that the day is always preceded by the night."

"Right," Beck replied. "A person always starts from a position of ignorance, by definition, and only through the passage of time does he have the chance to become enlightened by knowledge of the truth."

"I'll give you an example, Benny," Dovid offered. "Just look how ignorant a baby is, and how he acquires more and more knowledge as he progresses through life."

"That's true, Dovid, but that example is too obvious. Unfortunately, most people go to their graves in old age hardly more enlightened than the baby you spoke of."

"What do you mean?" Dovid inquired.

"Look," Beck answered. "You're entering the freeway right now. *Im yirtzeh Hashem*, we'll be zipping along at fifty-five or sixty miles an hour, our thoughts far away, feeling perfectly snug in our cozy buggy. But do you realize the extreme danger we will be putting ourselves in?"

"We will?" Dovid said worriedly. "How do you figure?"

"Well, Dovid, imagine that a loaded tractor-trailer on the other side of the freeway suddenly jumps the median and starts sailing right toward us. It'll be curtains for all four of us, of course, and there's nothing we can do but pray for mercy and an instant death.

"Now suppose that just as the big truck's bumper kisses the front end of our car, the truck vanishes into thin air. Poof! Just like that. Of course, we'll laugh nervously, elated that it was all a mirage. But I'll guarantee you we'll zip down the next mile of highway with an entirely new appreciation of our continued safe passage. Until that experience, we were traipsing naively through life in total darkness.

"There is an infinite amount of knowledge to be accrued in this world, Dovid. The Jewish day starts with night to remind us that Hashem expects us to drink in as much of that knowledge as we can, to attempt to bring ourselves to the light of day."

"Docta Beck," Bobby spoke from the back. "You's makin' me nervous with talk about trucks smackin' us . . . Ouch! Hang it, Chet, would ya stop pokin' me! You's makin' me black 'n blue."

Beck exchanged smiles with Dovid. They continued on the freeway in silence, listening to Chet and Bobby argue over language for the indictments.

"Benny, isn't there a fallacy in your analogy?" Dovid contended suddenly.

"What analogy?"

"I mean, we're supposed to garner as much truth and knowledge as we can, yet by the time one dies, even the wisest person will have acquired virtually nothing compared to the infinite wisdom Hashem invested in this world. Hence, all of us are consigned to a permanent, deep, abject darkness. How can you compare that unending night to the Jewish day, which, after twelve hours of darkness, leads to light?"

"Dovid," replied Beck, "The twinkle in your eye tells me that you know the answer to your own question."

Dovid sneaked a sheepish glance at his mentor.

"*Olam Haba?*" he chanced.

"Explain," Beck said curtly.

"I'll give it a shot," Dovid ventured. "We can observe that nothing in *Olam Hazeh* is permanent. Eventually, the tallest mountains are ground to dust, august noblemen die and decompose to gases, great civilizations flounder, massive stars explode and disintegrate to nothing. Even matter itself is not permanent, as Einstein revealed, because it can be transformed into energy.

"Indeed, the only entity of permanence is Hashem. All *Olam Hazeh* is nothing more than a manifestation, a mere materialization, of Hashem's will and has no independent existence of its own. Of course, to our infantile eyes, these mere reflections of Hashem take on a true-to-life appearance, masking the One who gives them their reality. That is the deception of *Olam Hazeh*, the darkness of the Jewish night.

"In *Olam Haba*, on the other hand, all of the ephemeral, physical characteristics of existence are stripped away, and the *neshamah* now gains a clear view of Hashem, the unchanging Reality that produced the illusory phenomena of *Olam Hazeh*.

"It's like a spectator in a theater audience, who watches a well-performed, lifelike drama, and afterwards is granted an unexpected visit with the lead actor behind stage. Up to that point, the bright theater lights had been used solely to enhance the deception that the actor was plying on the spectator. Try as he might, the spectator could only scratch the surface of the famous actor beneath the makeup. Now, behind the scenes, the spectator is finally able to perceive the great man's true nature, stripped of his props and costumes and pretending behavior. That's *Olam Haba*; that's the light of the Jewish sunrise."

"Extremely well put," Beck beamed in approbation. "Our calendar is a daily reminder that we are in a world of blindness and superficiality, preparing ourselves for a world of light and true reality."

Beck paused and cast a furtive glance over his shoulder. When he was satisfied that the two officers were well-embroiled in their work, he continued.

"There's another lesson to be gleaned from the Jewish day, Dovid," Beck said, keeping his voice even to avoid attracting the attention of the rear seat occupants.

"Another lesson?" Dovid returned.

"Yes, the fact that day is always preceded by night is a

mashal that the *umos haolam* will flourish throughout history until *Yemos Hamashiach*. At that time, Klal Yisrael will rise like the sun to dominate Hashem's *briah*."

He hoped that he had thrown in enough Hebrew terms to render his statement unintelligible to any novices with big ears. Another quick glimpse backwards reassured him that Chet and Bobby were engrossed in their own *tete-a-tete*.

"Now, Dovid, we are not referring to chauvinistic nationalism, although throughout the ages, our enemies have foisted that distortion upon Chazal's intent. Rather, we are saying that the process which each person undergoes in *Olam Hazeh* is duplicated on a national scale."

"I don't understand," Dovid admitted frankly.

"Well, we just noted that the task of a person in *Olam Hazeh* is to strip away the facades that hide Hashem and to become aware of His actual presence as intently as possible, until one arrives in *Olam Haba*, where Hashem will manifest Himself without any facades at all, and His presence will be unmistakably clear. On a national scale, too, Klal Yisrael's function is to be an *ohr lagoyim*, a light unto the nations. It is our mission to peel off the screen behind which Hashem operates, to reveal to the world His existence, His mastery and His nature, as best we can. The nations of the world and our own *yetzer hara* will darken the road. But we must persist through the night, until *Mashiach* arrives at dawn. At that time, everything we endeavored to teach them will become unmistakably clear, illuminated by the brilliance of day."

As Dovid steered the car off the exit ramp, Beck turned around again.

"Excuse me, Chet, would you hand me that box on the back shelf? Rusie donated some of her famous chocolate chip cookies to the cause."

"Sure," Carter answered as he handed the box forward. "Can I steal a few?"

"*Chas veshalom,*" Beck retorted. "These are worth more than a box full of jewels."

"Ha! Ha!" Bobby laughed. "Don' tell Charles Henley, right, Docta Beck? And by th' way, ya still din't tell me why th' Jewish day starts at night . . . Ow! Hang it anyways, Chet, if ya jabs me once more, I'll slap ya upside th' head. A body cain't get eddicated anymore 'thout gettin' beat up!"

"Cut the horsing around back there," Beck ordered. "Dovid's pulling into Headquarters now, and they don't let children in unsupervised."

As Dovid swung the Command Car into the parking garage, he pulled to a stop by the sentry. Beck leaned over Dovid and thrust the box of cookies into the chubby guard's hands.

"Here, Major. Breakfast from my wife. It's low calorie."

"Hey! There's a friend," Officer Major replied with a wink. "Take the Colonel's spot, first one by the door. He's outa town this week, and besides, he ain't married, so I don't expect to get no breakfast outa *him!*"

"Thanks, Major," Beck said with a wide smile.

The elevators seemed particularly slow, Beck thought as the foursome stood in the mezzanine lobby. He had hoped they would arrive early, because the Police Academy graduation exercises would take place later in the morning, limiting the time Chief Vincent could spend with them.

"Hi, Major," Beck greeted MacDougal, extending his hand.

"Nice to see you again," MacDougal returned. "I'll tell the Chief you're here. I think he wants to meet with you in the conference room, so why don't you go in and make yourselves comfortable."

Beck slipped his hat onto the shelf above the conference room coat rack and tossed his notebook on the long table in front of the upholstered chair he usually occupied during the Advisory Council meetings. He felt comfortable in the carpeted surroundings, with Currier and Ives prints fixed to the paneled walls and fresh coffee perennially steaming on the walnut sideboard.

"Look here, guys," he remarked. "Come over to the windows."

He stepped next to the tall, plate glass windows looking out over downtown Cahill. The others followed suit.

"See the roof of the building next door? That's the Long Office Building. Looks as if the repairs are finished. It was only two weeks ago that I stood here stupefied, watching Mark Lowery on his journey to death. Seems more like two *years* ago, so much has happened since then."

He gazed absently at the black roof, in his mind's eye picturing the big crane thrusting its steel arm skyward, Lowery writhing at the end of the ascending cable like a doomed minnow being reeled in on an angler's line.

Beck harbored conflicting feelings about Lowery. True, Lowery had robbed Woody's two years ago and deserved every ounce of punishment they could squeeze out of the system. However, the indelible image of that hopeless abyss in Wicomb, which Lowery called home, still burned in Beck's mind.

Besides, Beck admitted to himself, one of his heartstrings had been plucked by what Dawn Jackson had told Chet—that Lowery was distraught when victims were hurt during the course of the robberies. It merely illustrated that human instincts are not easily overcome. Maybe, Beck meditated, Judge O'Brien had seen the same potential in Lowery and had therefore given him a light sentence for the Woody's incident.

"Gentlemen, good morning!" Chief Vincent strode through the door. "Doc, how are you?"

"Just fine, Chief," Beck replied, shaking hands. "You

certainly look crisp this morning, all that gold draped on your uniform."

"It's just for the image, Doc," Vincent replied with a twinkle. "Graduation and Commendation Exercises this morning. I've gotta look spiffy. Here, come sit down."

"Thanks," Beck said as they all took seats around one end of the sprawling conference table. "You know, Chief, when I originally called to set up this meeting it was for the purpose of bringing you up-to-date on our robbery situation, but I didn't expect to have much to tell you. As you know, however, the case was solved Tuesday night."

"Yes, I'm aware of it," Vincent remarked. "Mack got a lot of information from Charlie Toffat, but I wouldn't mind hearing the story directly from the horse's mouth. No offense intended, Doc." He laughed, patting Beck's sleeve.

Beck proceeded to relate the events of the previous two weeks, his encounter with Eberhart at the hospital, his discovery of Lowery in the Wicomb section of town, his visit to the Caterpillar dealer, Carter's investigations and the foray into the Tip-Top premises that had culminated in triumph.

"Incredible!" Vincent declared when Beck finally ended. "That's some story. You ought to write a book about it, you know."

"Well, I hadn't thought of it," Beck answered, "but maybe I will some day . . . On second thought, I doubt if anyone would believe it."

He stroked his beard for a second, a look of amusement playing across his eyes.

"Anyway," he continued, "the only loose end remaining in the case is the oriental connection. Chet found a letter in Japanese at Tip-Top on Tuesday and took it to a professor at the university to have it translated. We believe that all the jewels were being smuggled to Japan by a man named

Mikiachi Goto. He runs an import-export business on Dorchester Street. We discovered that he fled the country yesterday morning, eight hours after Tip-Top was mopped up. We figured the Feds would be interested, so Chet turned over everything we know to the FBI. It's in their hands now, so we have nothing to do with that end of the case any more."

"Very good," Vincent responded. "I'm sure he won't be back any time soon."

"Chief," Beck continued, "I don't mean to change the subject, but I've got a very big favor to ask of you. Something that means a lot to me."

"Doc, if it's within my power to grant it, it's yours. Shoot."

Beck glanced from Carter to Bobby and finally directed his eyes toward Vincent. He held his breath a moment, then began speaking slowly, choosing his words.

"Chief, a week ago yesterday, one of your outstanding men, Officer Bobby Graham, saved my life."

Chief Vincent tried to find Bobby's eyes, but the big cop was studying a nick in the table top.

"And it didn't happen through pure accident," Beck continued. "No, Bobby didn't rely on luck. Rather, he used the intellect G-d gave him and the training that *you* gave him. In fact, Bobby was on the scene in the first place only because he cared about the welfare of another human being.

"Chief, I know the department reserves its highest honors for men who have performed the most heroic feats. I believe that Bobby's bravery fulfills that criterion, and you would be rendering my conscience an inestimable service if you would award Bobby a Silver Star."

Vincent seemed to hesitate, causing Beck to question whether he had overstepped the bounds of his prerogative.

"What do you say to that, Bobby?" Vincent asked pointedly.

Bobby raised his eyes and glanced helplessly from Vincent to Beck and back to Vincent again. He looked like he would have preferred to crawl under the far end of the long table and hide.

"Sir, I was jus' doin' my job, that's all," he managed to squeak.

No one spoke for fifteen seconds. Vincent drummed his fingertips on the table, inspecting each of his visitors in turn. Finally, he addressed Beck.

"Doc," he said sternly, "I figured you out a long time ago."

Beck was nonplused, confused by Vincent's words.

"Nothing you do surprises me any more," Chief Vincent continued. "On the contrary, it helps me stay one step ahead of you. That's why I have already arranged for Silver Stars to be awarded to Officer Robert Graham and Officer Chester Carter at the Graduation and Commendation Exercises this morning!"

"Wha—" Chet and Bobby stammered simultaneously.

"Chief! That's tremendous!" Beck beamed. Jumping up, he grabbed Vincent's right hand and pumped it vigorously.

Vincent stood, grinning from ear to ear. "See, Doc, you're not the only one who can stage a coup. You almost fouled up the whole plan when you tried to change our meeting to this afternoon."

"Chief, I owe you one," Beck responded.

"Now I've got to get ready," Vincent continued, "so I hope you'll excuse me. You two men ought to spruce up a bit. Would you like to use the private facilities next to my office?"

Chet and Bobby, still speechless, fidgeted uncomfortably.

"Sir," Carter spoke up, "that's okay. We can use the men's room across the hall."

Vincent swung around toward Beck and exclaimed with feigned annoyance, "Doc, have you ever witnessed such insubordination? I just ordered these two officers to follow me into my office, and they want to go across the hall. Someone ought to report them."

He winked as a blush spread across Carter's face.

"And one more point, Officer," Vincent addressed Carter with mock seriousness. "I don't like my men sitting idle. You put a lot of work into solving this case, but now that the battle's over, what are you going to do with all that time on your hands?"

Suddenly, Carter looked alive, his self-consciousness evaporated, as if he had finally discovered himself back on familiar turf. He peeped gingerly at Beck, as though on the horns of a dilemma.

"Go ahead, Chet," Beck reassured him, "I'll keep the Chief off your back."

"Sir," Carter respectfully addressed his commander, "the battle is not over, despite what you may think. The trial is set for Judge O'Brien's court. We've got only three months to prepare the case, and it won't be easy. If we lose, the offenders will be back on the street, and the lives and property of citizens will be more at risk than ever. Sir, if you ask me, the fight has just begun!"

Vincent glanced sharply at Beck. The latter stood with his shoulders back, glowing with pride. For eight years, he had remolded Carter, converting him from a typical cop, whose job was completed once an offender was arrested, to an integral element of the broader justice system responsible for removing criminals from society. It was one thing to arrest a suspect, Beck had taught Carter, but an entirely different matter to make the arrest stick.

"You can't fool me, Chief," Beck said. "You know he's right. Every case looks easy, until you confront one of those vandalistic lawyers. Then all common sense goes out the window. Unfortunately, I'm afraid we've got an uphill fight."

"And if we lose this trial, we lose everything," Carter added ominously.

Vincent appeared sobered by Carter's concluding portent. He turned to Beck in farewell.

"Well, good luck, Doc," he said as they shook hands. "But if I know you, the trial's as good as won."

As Vincent turned to leave the room, Beck replied quietly, "I have serious doubts, Chief."

The five men filed out in silence.

17

"IT'S HARD TO BELIEVE THAT THREE MONTHS HAVE ALready passed since the arrests," Dovid said.

He was sitting in a brown armchair in the Beck's living room, sipping "yummy drink," a nutritious concoction of milk, orange juice, raw eggs and crushed ice that Rusie had invented years ago.

"It certainly is hard to believe," Rusie agreed. She had dragged a chair from the dining room and placed it next to her husband, who was rocking gently in the Lazy Boy.

"How'd it go today, Binyamin?" she asked. "As you can see, Dovid, I haven't had a chance to speak to Binyamin yet."

"Not bad," Beck replied, "considering it was just the first day of the trial. Most of the time was spent on jury selection. You should see the woman that O'Brien appointed as foreman."

"Oh," Rusie said, "you didn't tell me that Judge O'Brien would be trying the case. You like him, don't you?"

"Salty Sam?" Beck answered. "He's worth his weight in gold. The man's got a lot of common sense, and he doesn't let legal technicalities stand in the way of justice. We found out quite a while ago that the case was on his docket. Sorry I didn't mention it to you earlier."

"And what about the jury foreman?" Rusie referred to

her husband's earlier remark. "A woman, I think you said. What's so special about her?"

"Well," Beck replied, "I have to trust O'Brien's judgment. He's been in this business long enough to be able to read his jurors pretty well. To me, she looks like a scatter-brained peacock. She wears more makeup than Geronimo on the warpath, and she's got this beehive of dyed blonde hair piled up on her dome. She doesn't weigh more than ninety pounds—a real skinny-ma-link. Couldn't hurt a fly. She also carries around an oversized feather fan, which she's always working back and forth like a flag flapping in the breeze."

"Sounds dramatic," Rusie commented. "I hope you're not speaking *lashon hara*."

"You're right," Beck said, "I shouldn't be speaking ill of her. She could be a very kind and generous woman, and even if she's not, who am I to criticize another human being? Besides, as I said, O'Brien usually singles out sensible jurors to appoint as foremen, so she must have some good qualities to recommend her."

"You weren't so charitable toward the defense counsel," Dovid interrupted.

"Grimm?" Beck said in disgust. "That charlatan? I don't have the right to criticize another person without just cause. But Horace Grimm gives me ample cause. You see how fast he abandoned Lowery when the money ran dry. And he knows he's in for a fat cut if he can get those four crooks off the hook. I'm sure Henley has guaranteed him a handsome prize."

"It's sort of ironic, isn't it?" Dovid commented. "I mean, Grimm originally was defending Lowery, and now he's defending the parties who actually tried to kill Lowery."

"I told you, Dovid," Beck retorted, "Grimm travels whichever road is greener. He's not interested one iota in justice, civil rights or any of the other protean slogans that he squeezes and stretches to fit the particular case he is working on."

"Was Chet in court today, too?" Rusie maneuvered the conversation away from Grimm.

"Of course," Dovid replied. "And he really looks sharp wearing his new Silver Star."

Beck cast a chagrined look at his wife.

"What's the matter?" Dovid asked. "Did I say something wrong?"

"No, Dovid," Beck responded. "It's just that every time I think of Chet's Silver Star, I'm reminded of how thoughtless I was when we met with Chief Vincent. I recommended Bobby for an award, but I forgot all about Chet."

"Oh, don't berate yourself," Dovid remarked. "Chet works with us so closely, it's easy to overlook him when credits are due."

"I know," Beck moaned. "That's just the problem. People always take their best friends for granted."

"Like I take you for granted, Binyamin," Rusie addressed her husband. "I should thank you more often for providing our material needs. Every time I pull in the driveway, I should thank you again for the greasy work you do on the car to keep it going. And that's not to mention the thanks I owe you for bringing home all the Torah that you learn, so we can discuss it and teach it to the children."

Beck fidgeted uncomfortably. After Dovid left, he promised himself, he would tell Rusie how much she meant to him.

"You're right, Rusie," he said. "Not about the work I do. I mean you're right that the friends who are closest to us and do the most for us are the ones we fail to thank sufficiently. Our best Friend—the One in Heaven—is the Friend who benefits us the most, yet we forget about Him all the time.

"Right now, we should take time out and thank our Friend for the next breath of fresh air we inhale. Then we'll let out the carbon dioxide and take in another breath, and thank Him all over again for that second breath. And then a third one and a fourth one. It should go on forever, until we take our last breath. Each breath is literally a lifesaver!

"And just look at Hashem's *chessed*! The substance that we are most immediately in need of—fresh air—is the substance that He furnishes most abundantly and at no cost. The next most vital substance—water—is not as abundant as air and is not free. Food, being even less critical, is still less plentiful and costs even more. The *Ribono Shel Olam* is supplying us all the time, exactly in proportion to our needs.

"It is a staggering fact! The Master of the Universe, the Power who manages the complex affairs of the vast world, humbles Himself, so to speak, to serve this lowly speck of protoplasm named Binyamin Beck. In reality, Hashem is my only true Friend, and I should spend my life thanking Him for the millions of kindnesses He showers upon me."

Beck finished his speech with a flair that left a spell of silence in the room. Each person was absorbed in thought.

"You two are lucky, you know," Dovid finally noted.

"What do you mean?" Rusie inquired.

"You have each other to practice on. You can use each other to bring yourselves to the realization that we humans are always dependent on Someone, always obliged to thank our closest Friend."

"It's true," Beck said. "That's one of the great benefits of marriage. Too bad people don't capitalize on that opportunity more often."

"Which brings us to another topic," Rusie commented. "Dovid, we have a girl we'd like you to meet."

Dovid sat up alertly, and plunked down the empty glass he had been holding.

"Who is it?" he asked.

"Devorah Dickman," Rusie replied.

"You don't mean Charles Henley's stepdaughter, do you?" he said with concern lining his features. "After all these years of living with a crook, she's bound to have picked up some nasty *hashkafos*, don't you think?"

"Now, Dovid," Beck interrupted, "you've never met her, and you know nothing about her. She's spent a lot of time in our home the last three months, and we've gained a lot of respect for her. The truth is, she was ready to become *frum* even before Henley was arrested. That was just the final straw. She rented an apartment in the Spiegel's house across the street, and she's done a lot of growing since then."

The Becks looked at Dovid expectantly. The young man's dark eyes reflected his confusion and dilemma.

"Dovid," Rusie urged gently, "Devorah is constantly calling me with questions about *kashrus*, *Shabbos* and all the other details of Torah life. I see in her a rare level of devotion and commitment that would make any Jewish husband proud. Besides, Dovid, she possesses beautiful *midos*. She is so generous and exhibits a genuine, inner concern for the happiness of other people. It is precisely because she is so strong inside that Henley's influence never rubbed off on her. We really don't think you have anything to worry about."

"She also has a lot of common sense," Beck added, "and a keen intuition. I'm sure she saw right through Henley from day one."

Beck held his peace. Dovid, he knew, needed time to weigh their advice. Rusie stood up and left the living room. She returned a minute later with a pitcher to refill Dovid's glass.

"Thanks, Mrs. Beck," Dovid said, placing his hand over the top of the glass, "but I'm going to pass. Believe me, it's tempting. Just like Devorah Dickman is tempting. But I think I'm going to pass on both the drink and Devorah, too."

Beck was perplexed. Dovid was being stubborn, he thought to himself, making an ogre out of an imagined phantom. Rusie and he had several times remarked to each other how pure Devorah was in thought, speech and action. She seemed to have countered Henley's profligate immorality by fortifying her own sense of decency and virtue.

No, Beck meditated, the intellectual approach had not worked. He would have to resort to the big guns and take aim straight at Dovid's ego.

"Dovid," he remarked, "we told Devorah about you. She's very interested in meeting you. We even showed her your picture."

Beck watched in suspense as a faint blush rose on Dovid's cheeks above the top of his trimmed beard, while he struggled inwardly to recover from this potent salvo. It was a cheap shot, Beck recognized, but more than one man had been roped in by an appeal to his ego.

After a lengthy silence, Dovid managed to croak, "I'm sorry, Benny. I can't help but be suspicious of her background. She's been surrounded by Henley and his unscrupulous cronies for too long now. Maybe I'm wrong, but I'm afraid that Devorah will always carry her background with her, hidden in the remote corners of her mind, no matter how much she plasters it over with the purity of Torah living."

"Dovid," Beck addressed the young man in serious tones, "we won't pressure you, but as a friend to a friend, will you do us a favor? Will you agree to meet her just once?"

Dovid glanced from Beck to Rusie and then down to the empty glass in front of him. He began slowly wiping the condensation from the sides of the glass.

Finally, he said with halting reticence, "Please don't

misunderstand me. I realize you two only want the best for me. You know how much I appreciate everything you do."

He seemed to hesitate, torn between his intellect and his emotions, confused by the conflict between his own rationality and that of his loyal friends.

"Okay," he said at last, "I'll agree to meet her, but only on one condition."

"What's that?" Beck asked.

"As a friend to a friend," Dovid answered, "promise me you won't mention Devorah to me any more after we meet this first time."

"You've got it, Dovid!" Beck said, barely concealing his delight. "In fact, I'll make it even easier for you."

"What do you mean?" Dovid inquired.

"Well, the truth is, I'd like you to attend our meeting tomorrow night with Cunningham. He agreed to come to the Patrol office and review all of the testimony we'll be hearing in court tomorrow. Hopefully, we can help him assess our strategy and discuss possible tactics for the next day. Now, if you will allow me to take advantage of your good nature, I'd like you to stop by here first and help me shlep another two boxes of steering wheel locks from my basement to the office. Meanwhile, Rusie will see if Devorah can be here when you arrive. You can meet her, talk to her for two or three minutes, and then we'll leave."

"No fuss, no mess, no pain, eh?" Dovid remarked. "I appreciate your consideration. What time?"

"Chet is telling Cunningham to arrive at the office at eight-thirty in the evening."

"Great, Benny. How about if I show up here at the house around eight?"

"You're a champ."

As the threesome rose, Rusie reached over to the coffee table and picked up Dovid's glass.

"Thanks for the refreshment," Dovid said, stretching the stiffness out of his legs. "I love to visit your home, Mrs. Beck. Each time there's a new edible delight in store for me. Palace for the Palate. That's what the Beck's home should be called."

"You're welcome," Rusie said demurely. "And you know we always enjoy your company, too."

They accompanied Dovid to the front door. Beck surreptitiously caught his wife's attention and raised a finger to his lips to instruct her to remain quiet.

"See you in court tomorrow morning," Beck said as Dovid stepped outside. "And thanks again for agreeing to help me with the boxes tomorrow night."

He closed the door and turned around to face his wife.

"What's the matter, Binyamin?" she asked. "I was just going to remind him to put on a fresh shirt before he comes."

"I figured you were going to say something like that, Rusie. After twenty-five years, I've learned a *little* bit about how you think. But you would only have made him uncomfortable. Besides, if I know anything about the male psyche, Dovid will arrive all spruced up and looking like a million bucks, even if he doesn't expect this *shidduch* to go anywhere."

"Okay, if you say so. It's just that first impressions can make or break a *shidduch*."

"Oh, there's no question about that, Rusie. A couple should always try to put on a good act in front of each other— and not just the first time they meet. As long as they're married, even when they're ninety years old, each one should be the best possible actor or actress. Each partner should behave outwardly as a bigger *tzaddik* than he or she knows himself to be inwardly. After a while, in the process of tricking the spouse, he'll end up tricking himself into actually *becoming* a bigger *tzaddik*. By the way, Rusie, I hope I didn't misspeak when I volunteered you to make arrangements with Devorah."

"Of course not. In fact, let's go take care of that right now."

The two of them strode toward the kitchen.

"Mind if I get on the extension while you talk to Devorah?" Beck requested as he plugged a cord into a wall jack by the pantry.

"Not at all," she answered.

She dialed a number on the kitchen phone. He winked at her when they heard the ringing on the other end of the line.

"Hello," they heard Devorah answer.

"Hi, Devorah? This is Rusie."

"Oh, hi, Rusie. I was just thinking of you all."

"Oh yes? I hope it was in a favorable context."

"Absolutely," Devorah asserted. "Actually, I just finished reading the first three chapters in the book your girls bought me for my birthday yesterday. It's very interesting. I saved the card they gave me, too, to use as my bookmark."

"Well, I'm sure they'll be pleased to hear you are enjoying it," Rusie said. "You know, they didn't even show me the book before they wrapped it."

"Oh? The next time I come over, I'll bring it."

"Actually, Devorah, I was calling to invite you to drop by tomorrow evening. I'll be making *challos* for *Shabbos*, and you said you wanted to learn."

"Rusie, that's wonderful! I'd love to. What time?"

"Make it around seven-forty-five."

"It's a deal. See you then."

"Wait, Devorah. One more thing. It might be proper for you to put on a little eyeliner. A dab of Shalimar wouldn't hurt either."

"What? I thought we're making *challah*?"

"We are, Devorah. But don't forget it's *lekavod Shabbos*, so you have to dress appropriately. Besides, I just had a little prophetic vision that Dovid Berg will be coming by the house tomorrow evening at eight o'clock for a few minutes."

"Oh, you scamp!" Devorah squealed. "What else did you see in your vision?"

"That was it, I'm sorry to say. The screen went blank after that. Maybe someone pulled the plug. I've got to go now. See you tomorrow, okay?"

"Wouldn't miss it for the world, Rusie. Bye."

Rusie smiled broadly at her husband as she replaced the receiver, but her grin disappeared when she spied the furrows on Beck's serious countenance.

"What's the matter, Binyamin?" she asked. "Didn't I say the right words?"

"Oh, of course you did, Rusie. You were perfect—as always. I just hope we're doing the proper thing. In a way, Dovid is right. A *bachur* has to make a judgment beforehand whether a particular *shidduch* will work out, and if he feels that it won't, he has no business seeing the girl. The girl has to make the same judgment for herself, too. The depravity of the modern dating scene has made animals out of young people, and Jews must avoid such dating at all costs. The frivolous mixing of men and women heralds nothing but moral suicide."

They gazed at each other silently. Rusie unplugged the pantry telephone and began wrapping the white cord around the set. She laid it gently on the counter and then looked back at her husband.

"You know what I mean, Rusie?" he continued after a moment. "A Jewish marriage is holy, and building a Jewish home is a paramount mission in our lives. Miners blasting away a mountain to get at the ore don't play around with the dynamite beforehand. When men and women get together 'just for fun,' it's playing with dynamite. Dovid and Devorah should be introduced to each other only if we believe there's likely to be pay dirt."

He lifted the unplugged telephone from the counter and replaced it on the shelf.

"Rusie," he said, coming closer to her, "here's where I must rely on your female intuition. You don't think we're being caught up in the disgusting infatuation game that pervades modern romanticism, do you? We haven't gone overboard, have we?"

Her eyes fell to the toe of her shoe, which was scraping the worn edge of a cracked floor tile.

"I don't know," she said softly. "Maybe you're right. I don't think we've become frivolous, as you put it, but maybe we've shaved off our seriousness too much. I still think it's an excellent match, though. Devorah is such a gentle soul and so is Dovid. Intellectually, they're well-matched, too."

"Okay," Beck said, "that's how I feel also. But if we are the *shadchanim*, it behooves us to approach tomorrow night's introduction with clear heads and *shem shamayim* in our hearts."

Rusie raised her eyes to meet her husband's.

"I think you're the greatest," she said.

"You took the words out of my mouth," he replied.

18

"HI, DOVID," RUSIE CRIED CHEERFULLY AS SHE OPENED THE door. "Come on in. Nice to see you again."

Dovid stepped into the front hall and suddenly drew himself up tall, his nose sniffing the air.

"Mmm," he crooned. "Smells like *Shabbos* in here, and it's only mid-week." He smiled broadly at Rusie.

"Never hurts to prepare early," she said. "I heard you all had an interesting day in court today."

"I don't know if I'd call it interesting. I actually found it depressing."

"Cheer up, Dovid, Hashem's in charge," she said. "Binyamin's in the kitchen. I'll get him for you."

She led Dovid into the living room and turned on the table lamps.

"Make yourself at home, and please ignore the mess. I'm trying to get Rochel packed for her trip. By the way," she added, "take a look at that book on the coffee table. I think you'll enjoy it. It just appeared in the book stores last week."

She left Dovid and disappeared through the hallway to summon her husband.

"Oh, hi, Dovid," Beck called as he entered the room a minute later. "Hope you're ready for some heavy lifting. By the way, I've got someone I'd like you to meet."

Just then Devorah materialized in the living room doorway. Her long, blonde hair was gathered in a stylish ponytail. Her white blouse was tucked into a pink and white pleated skirt.

"Devorah," Beck began, "this is Dovid Berg. Devorah Dickman," he continued, turning to Dovid. "Devorah lives across the street."

"Nice to meet you," he intoned mechanically.

"Devorah is here helping Rusie make *challos* tonight," Beck explained with a nonchalance meant to break the ice.

"The Becks have told me a lot about you," Devorah said. "I am pleased to finally meet you in person."

"Thanks, it's nice to meet you, too," he stammered, forgetting that he was repeating himself.

An awkward moment passed, and then Beck offered, "I see you picked up that new book, Dovid. Like it?"

Overjoyed to find a neutral subject, Dovid gushed, "Oh yes, it's fascinating and very well written. In fact, I was going to ask your wife if I can borrow it when she's finished reading it. I'm afraid I messed up her place, though. This birthday card fell out when I opened the book."

"That's okay," Devorah immediately replied. "It's my book, actually. My darling friends, the Beck children, gave it to me yesterday, and I brought it over to show Rusie. You're welcome to borrow it, though."

"Oh, I'm sorry," Dovid said uncomfortably. "Looks like you are in the middle of the book."

"Don't worry," she said. "I know exactly where my place is. And really, if you'd like to borrow it, I have plenty of other things to read at home. You can return it to the Becks when you're done with it."

"No, no, that's okay," he said quickly.

"Listen, Dovid," Beck interjected, hoping to leave the two of them alone, "I'm going down to the basement to get those boxes ready. Can you help me in a few minutes? I'd prefer to be in the office before Cunningham arrives."

"I'm coming right now," Dovid replied quickly, with obvious relief in his voice. "Two pairs of hands work faster than one. Nice meeting you," he muttered for the third time, nodding to Devorah.

"Same here," she replied.

Dovid scrambled down the steps two at a time and found Beck already surveying two large, white cardboard boxes beside the workbench.

"You call that a meeting, Dovid?" Beck demanded with obvious disappointment.

"Benny, please don't jump on me. I've never reacted that way before. I'm sorry, Benny, but I need time to think."

Beck examined Dovid's countenance. He wasn't certain what Dovid was saying, and he doubted whether Dovid himself knew what he was saying. He sympathized with the young man, and decided that silence would be the best response for the moment.

"Look, Dovid, let's just carry these boxes up and leave, okay?" Beck said quickly. "I'm sure Devorah's back in the kitchen helping Rusie now."

Beck tucked in the flap of the heavy box and bent over to lift one end, while Dovid seized the other side. They maneuvered it up the stairs and set it in the living room.

"Let's cart the other one up," Beck suggested, "and then we'll ferry them both out to the car. I already made room in the trunk."

When they arrived at the ECCP office, Beck backed up the car as close as he could to the main door. There were no other vehicles in the lot, so he parked on a slant to facilitate their access.

"I wish Chet were here already," Dovid commented. "We could use some help."

"We'll manage," Beck assured him. "Let's get this cargo upstairs and put on some coffee before they arrive."

They braced themselves to carry the first of the boxes up the three flights of stairs.

"Hit the light switch as you pass, would you, Dovid?" Beck called. "We could break our necks in the dark."

As Dovid backed himself through the main doorway of the building, he raised an elbow and flipped a switch on the wall. The staircase was instantly bathed in light. They struggled with their load, step by step, until they ascended to the third-floor landing. Stabilizing the box on his knee, Dovid extracted a key from his pocket and unlocked the office door. They stumbled inside and grunted with relief as they dropped the box to the floor.

"What's this?" Beck said in surprise as the box flap popped open. He raised a book from the stack of bright orange locks in the box.

"Hey, this is Devorah's book, isn't it?" he exclaimed. "The one you were just reading at my house?"

"Sure is," Dovid replied, taking the book from Beck.

Dovid opened the front cover and immediately spied a crumb-stained scrap of green paper tucked into the flap of the jacket. He slipped out the paper and read its message: "Hope you enjoy this. Just return it to Dr. Beck when you're finished. No rush. Devorah."

Balancing the open book in his palm, Dovid threw an accusing gaze at Beck, who immediately raised his hands as if he were being frisked.

"I promise you, Dovid, I had nothing to do with this. She must have slipped it in when we went down to the basement for the second box."

Dovid glanced down again at the note. He removed it from the book and closed the cover, then ambled over to his desk and gently slid the book onto the desktop. Fingering the note, he sat down in his chair and rested his chin in his right palm.

"It's her birthday present from your children, isn't it?" Dovid asked. "Shouldn't she read it first?"

His question was a smoke screen, Beck realized, a convenient asylum where he might dodge his underlying dilemma. No, thought Beck, it was not the book that was troubling Dovid.

He approached the young man and laid a hand lightly on his shoulder.

"Rusie and I wanted you to meet her, Dovid. We felt we had an obligation to both of you, and we were thrilled when you agreed to be introduced. But we had nothing to do with this book."

Dovid remained silent.

"I'm sorry if we pressured you too hard or hurt you in any way, Dovid," Beck spoke with sincere empathy.

"You didn't hurt me, Benny. You and your wife are the best friends I've ever had. I know I can trust you with my life. I'm just confused right now, that's all."

Beck decided not to respond. He knew Dovid needed time to cogitate. They both fell silent.

Beck crossed the room and sat down in his chair. He turned on his desk light and began reading a crime prevention newsletter that had arrived in the mail the day before. He soon realized that the words were entering his eyes without registering on his brain. He sat back in his chair and swiveled around to face Dovid.

Dovid looked up and stared straight at Beck.

"She's extraordinary, no?" Dovid asked ingenuously.

Beck averted his eyes to the ECCP recruiting poster on the far wall, and began stroking his beard. Dovid had obviously been touched by Devorah's sincerity and thoughtfulness, but Beck sensed that Dovid was still uncomfortable speaking about her good qualities. Beck wanted to encourage the young man.

"What do you mean by extraordinary, Dovid?" Beck asked.

"I don't know, Benny," Dovid fumbled. "I guess I mean . . . well, she's so cheerful and considerate, and it all seems to come so naturally to her."

"Dovid," Beck replied, "Rusie and I discovered Devorah's good qualities several months ago. Everyone has some faults, of course, and I'm sure Devorah is no exception. But one must always concentrate on the *midos tovos* in other people, while learning to accept their shortcomings. Nowhere is this more critical than in the relationship between husbands and wives. It will be your lifelong task to search out the depth of goodness in your mate, whoever she may be, and nourish its further growth."

Beck stood up and returned briskly to Dovid's side. He tugged Devorah's note out of the young man's fingers and read it again.

As he flipped the paper back to Dovid, he added, "If Devorah is the one, I don't think you'll have to search very far to find the good *midos*."

Just then, a car door slammed.

"It's Chet and Owen Cunningham," Beck said, peering out the window. "Do you mind running down and asking Chet to help you carry up the other box? I'll put on the coffee meanwhile."

As Dovid exited, Beck slipped a coffee filter from a dispenser and inserted it into the grounds cup. He filled the tank with water and flicked on the switch.

"Thank You, Hashem," he muttered, as the brew began trickling into the carafe. "With Your help, I think I finally loaded all the ingredients. Now it's up to Dovid to do the filtering, and it's time for Rusie and me to back off. Please help him, and may his decision be as rich and pure and aromatic as this refreshing beverage."

"Hmm! There's a wake-me-up smell," Cunningham said as he stepped boisterously into the room. "Long time, no see," he quipped, extending a hand to Beck.

"Right," Beck returned. "At least three hours. Have a seat. Sugar and creamer are already on the table. Help yourself."

A minute later, Chet and Dovid tramped heavily through the doorway and deposited the second cardboard box of locks on the floor.

"Say, why didn't you guys take the elevator?" Cunningham teased, tilting his chair.

"Listen," Carter shot back in jest, "you lawyers never lift anything heavier than a pen. I should've made *you* haul this thing up here."

"Okay, gentlemen," Beck mediated. "Let's get down to business. We're all tired, and tomorrow is not going to be any picnic."

"You can say that again," Cunningham responded as everyone found a place at the table.

Beck began tapping the eraser end of his pencil on an ivory colored note pad in front of him while he surveyed the other three men. Dovid and Chet were still panting from their exertion, and both had collapsed into their chairs like wet washrags.

Cunningham, who was sitting opposite Beck, looked even more tired. His loosened tie was hanging limply from the open collar of his white shirt. His thinning, black hair was a mess, and a very noticeable five o'clock shadow darkened his face. The truth was, Beck reflected, Cunningham was under considerable pressure to win this trial, and today's proceedings had not gone well.

"Well," Cunningham addressed everyone, after sipping

from a styrofoam cup. "Here's the way I would sum up the case so far."

He displayed his right hand, curling the index finger around to meet his thumb in a big, round zero.

"That bad, huh?" Beck commented.

"Yup. Our best shot would have been Mrs. Stein. She got a good look at Damon Hughes, and she made the initial I.D. on him the first time he robbed her. By the way, did you know she was a portrait artist?"

"No, really?" Beck said in surprise. "No wonder she described his face to Chet with such detail."

"Exactly," Cunningham continued. "Unfortunately, that's all water under the bridge. She may have recovered physically from the stabbing, but mentally she never made it back to the real world. Her daughter put her in the Golden Acres Home several weeks ago. She'll probably stay there until she dies."

Beck was never comfortable prejudging other people's futures. There was always ample room for Hashem to intervene. But he said nothing.

"Can't you use her I.D. from the first robbery?" Dovid asked. "Even if she's not present in the courtroom, everything is documented."

"Ha!" Beck laughed. "You're speaking like a man with common sense. You forget that we're dealing with the American system of criminal *in*justice."

"He's right," Cunningham said with a smile. "The accused has a right to face his accuser, blah, blah, blah . . . No, in my opinion, our only chance to nail Hughes is with Mrs. Bernstein's I.D. But I have to warn you gentlemen that she is a pitifully poor witness, and Grimm will shred her to pieces. I know how he operates, and 'it won't be purty,' as they say in Topeka."

"I wonder why everyone loves Mr. Grimm so much,"

Beck said facetiously. "I have to give him credit, though. He was pretty effective in neutralizing the conversation that Chet and I witnessed at Tip-Top the night of the arrests. The man obviously knows how to try a case."

"Oh, there's no doubt about that," Cunningham replied. "Technically, Dr. Beck, you were trespassing, and that undermines your testimony. But what's much more damaging—and Grimm harped again and again on this point—is that you never once heard any of the defendants admit to robbing any of the victims. Of course, any sensible person could surmise that fact, but legally it's just hearsay. O'Brien has no choice but to sustain Grimm's objections."

"Bah!" Beck spluttered, slapping his palm flat on the table.

"Well, how do you think I feel," Cunningham said with irritation, "standing up there and letting myself be browbeaten by that oversized vulture? Even after twenty-two years of trying criminals, it still knocks something out of one's fortitude."

Cunningham began puncturing his empty styrofoam cup with the point of a pen. A drop of leftover coffee trickled slowly out of one of the bottom holes, like mud oozing out of a fumarole.

"So what do we do now?" Beck asked.

"The infamous question," Cunningham responded. "I'm not normally a pessimist, but we are really in a bad way. I never expected this to be easy, but I had hoped at least to be able to present a set of facts, build a case and tweak the jury's emotions a bit. Grimm's not letting me do it, though. I'll be honest with you. At this point, we'll be lucky merely to convict Ritondo of possession of stolen goods. He's the owner of Tip-Top, and the jewels were found on his property. However, the other three are going to walk. That's my prediction."

The four men sat speechless around the table, like stupefied fishermen surveying huge holes ripped in their empty nets. Beck began tapping his eraser again.

Suddenly, Dovid jumped up.

"Wait a minute!" he exclaimed. "I've got an idea. Have you ever thought of putting Lowery on the stand as a witness for the State? I'm sure he has plenty to sing about, and maybe we can get his cooperation by promising to dismiss the VOP on his prior conviction."

Cunningham looked at him. "I don't mean to belittle your suggestion," he said, "but that was one of the first things I considered. It won't work, however, because Lowery's credibility is practically nil. Aside from the fact that Lowery's been living in a slum for several months now, without a steady job, he's also got a criminal record, and Grimm can show that he never got along with the gang. In other words, he's got a lot of gripes and prejudices that have nothing to do with the crimes, and that's precisely the picture that Grimm will paint. Anyhow, Grimm knows too much about Lowery's past, since Lowery was formerly his client. Wouldn't you agree, Dr. Beck?"

Everyone turned to hear Beck's concurrence, but the latter was staring at a cobweb in a corner of the ceiling.

"What's the matter, Benny?" Dovid said. "You look like you're in outer space."

"Benny!" Chet shouted. "Wake up!"

"Wha-what?" Beck startled. "Oh, sorry. What were you saying?"

"Been a long day, huh?" Cunningham said. "I was just venturing the opinion that Lowery would not be a credible State's witness. Would you agree?"

"Hm," Beck mused. "Ordinarily, I would certainly agree with you. But you just said something about Lowery living in a slum, and it triggered my thoughts. Owen, do you think you could put Lowery on the stand, and set him up to pit his integrity or courage against that of Horace Grimm?"

"Dr. Beck, what in the world are you talking about?" Cunningham reacted in dismay. "Everyone knows that Lowery has no integrity to speak of."

"Oh?" said Beck rhetorically. "And Mr. Grimm, I take it, is the very paragon of integrity?"

"Well . . ." Cunningham hesitated.

"Listen," Beck continued. "We know where the truth lies in this case. We just have to find a way to liberate the truth from the straitjacket in which American jurisprudence has smothered it. I've got a plan."

"Uh-oh," Carter ribbed.

"Quiet, Chet," Beck ordered. "Look, let's put Lowery on the stand, let him spill all the beans about how the gang operated, whom they hit, what they did with the credit cards and every other incriminating fact. Next, focus on Lowery's courage in bucking the gang. And then, Owen, wind up your questioning by casting Horace Grimm's own courage in doubt."

"Say, that's good," Dovid enthused. "Then, when Grimm crossexamines, we will have reduced the whole issue to a question of who is more believable—Mark Lowery or Horace Grimm. With *siyata dishmaya*, the jury will opt for Lowery."

"Now, wait a minute, wait a minute," Cunningham insisted. "Are you guys nuts? How on earth am I going to show that Grimm is a coward? Just because he dumped Lowery as his client? Besides, Grimm's not the one on trial, and he'll immediately object when I touch the issue of his manliness. You're asking me to prove the impossible. In fact, the whole thing could do us more harm than good."

Beck picked up his pencil and aimed the sharpened lead at Cunningham. Staring him straight in the eyes, he said, "Owen, I'm not asking you to prove a thing. All you have to do is raise the *question* of Grimm's courage. Just plant the idea in the jury's mind. Lowery will be the one to *prove* it actually."

"I must be on Mars!" Cunningham exclaimed. "You're speaking riddles. How can Lowery prove a thing?"

"For your information," Beck replied mysteriously, "Mark Lowery has at his disposal a resource that none of the rest of us has access to. Leave it to me, Owen. You do your part, and I'll make sure Lowery does his. *Im yirtzeh Hashem*, victory will be ours!"

Cunningham flopped back in his chair, still staring at Beck, and scratching nervously at the emerging stubble on his chin. Doubt and uncertainty fairly leapt from his dark eyes, but he said nothing.

Chet reached over and slapped Cunningham lightly on the back. "Don't worry," he said, "whatever Benny's got up his sleeve, it's bound to work. He hasn't failed yet. Trust me."

"Now hold on, Chet," Beck corrected, "neither success nor failure is in the hands of *any* of us. You know good and well Who's controlling this trial."

Cunningham abruptly heaved forward in his chair. As he seized the table, his hand smacked hard against his empty cup. It rocketed forward and impaled itself unceremoniously on the pencil point still extending from Beck's hand. Beck startled in surprise, and the speared cup flipped out of his hand onto the floor.

"Someone's controlling the trial?" Cunningham exploded with incredulity.

"Sure," Beck began, "don't you rea—"

"Wait! Wait! Just wait a minute!" Chet shouted, jumping up and waving his hands wildly, like a frightened matador facing a maddened bull and trying vainly to call time out. "Owen! Benny didn't mean a thing, I promise you. Don't get him started, *please*! I'm too tired for this now. I'll explain everything to you later. Please! *Pretty* please, with sugar on top?"

The vehemence of Carter's importuning was enough to stall Beck's *mussar* machine before it gained steam.

"Okay, okay," Beck conceded. "It's not my fault if no one's interested in the truth. That's the trouble with you crime fighters nowadays."

Cunningham sat in stunned silence, obviously befuddled by secrets beyond his ken.

"Also," Beck added, "it occurred to me a minute ago that we've overlooked one big factor in this case."

"What's that?" Cunningham asked.

"Rav Feinman," Beck responded.

"Refinement?" Cunningham croaked, more nonplused than ever. "Dr. Beck, you're a strange bird, if ever I met one. We just want to win this case. Who cares whether it's a refined win or a sock-'em-in-the-teeth win?"

"Rabbi Feinman," Beck corrected. "We never make any critical moves without his knowledge and guidance. I mean, we're proposing to let Lowery off the hook on the VOP. I would feel a lot more comfortable if Rabbi Feinman agrees to our decision. Also, if my scheme works, Grimm's name will be worth less than manure on a peat farm."

"Since when do you lose sleep over Grimm's reputation?" Carter asked.

"Chet, I know that Horace Grimm may be an enemy of the truth . . ." Beck paused and suddenly turned serious. "But he's still a human being."

Carter returned Beck's steady gaze for a full ten seconds. An unspoken river of understanding, respect and mutual support flowed between them.

"What time do we start tomorrow?" Dovid broke the stillness.

"Nine-thirty," Cunningham eked out, still mystified by Beck's statements.

"Whew!" Beck huffed. "Not much shut-eye for me, I'm afraid. Dovid, will you please reach Rav Feinman and set up an appointment for me to talk to him tonight. He's never available before midnight, but I have no choice."

Cunningham stood up, shaking his head. "Listen, gentlemen, I'm just a simple prosecutor by trade. You guys travel in higher circles. Dr. Beck, I'm on board with you, but only because I trust you not to be rash. Chet, shall we go?"

He gathered his papers and stuffed them hurriedly in a legal folder. Extending his hand to Beck, he said, "See you in the morning."

Beck accompanied Cunningham and Carter across the room and held the knob as he opened the door for them.

"Thanks for believing in me, Owen," he asserted as the two men departed. "I won't let you down."

He closed the door gently, but he did not turn around. This was one profession, he pondered to himself, that stimulated one's *bitachon*. It was clearer to him than ever that the *kehillah's* safety was entirely in *Hakadosh Baruch Hu's* hands. Certainly one could not rely on the wiles of the criminal justice system. He would have to *daven* especially well tonight, he thought.

Suddenly, he felt Dovid's eyes piercing his back.

"A penny for your thoughts," Dovid invited.

"You know what I find so frustrating, Dovid?" Beck replied. "Everyone in that courtroom knows those crooks are guilty. O'Brien knows it, Grimm knows it, and we know it. Yet we must steer the facts of their guilt—the light of truth—through a sinuous obstacle course that has been purposelessly thrown up to quench every beacon of *emes*. It's a microcosm of the whole wide world."

"How so?" Dovid prodded.

"Don't you see that *sheker* never wins out, Dovid? Ultimately, if it's not unmasked in *Olam Hazeh*, it will certainly be exposed in *Olam Haba*. That is the consummate response, the ultimate answer, to the question of *rasha vetov lo*, the prosperity of the evil. If glory, success or any form of good is conferred upon crookedness in this world, it is only for the purpose of entangling the perpetrator further in his crookedness. His seeming success goes to his head, steals away his humility and lures him into deeper evil. *Aveirah goreres aveirah*. And the whole account will have to be paid in full, with triple compound interest, in *Olam Haba*.

"Of course, most of the time it never gets that far, because we often observe the downfall of *reshaim* even in *Olam Hazeh*. I'm not saying that Grimm is a *rasha*, but one thing's for sure—he's no staunch purveyor of the truth!"

With that, Beck walked back to the table and began wheeling the chairs back to their respective desks. All at once, he spied Cunningham's used coffee cup lying on the floor, his pencil piercing its rim.

Bending over, he grasped the eraser end of the pencil and held it up toward the fluorescent ceiling light, twirling it slowly and examining the lanced styrofoam.

"Sometimes, falsehood meets its demise in the most unusual manner. Very often, wickedness spears itself on the same lies it attempts to foist on the world."

He set the cup down and firmly planted his hands, palms down, on the table, leaning the full weight of his shoulders on his extended arms.

"Dovid," he addressed the young man, "a feeling of confidence and *emunah* is washing over me right now. Tomorrow's going to be a glorious day."

19

A LUSTROUS SAFFRON SUNBEAM BORED THROUGH THE round window set high in the cafeteria wall. It glanced off Binyamin Beck's foil-wrapped tuna sandwich, launching rainbow sparkles of light into Owen Cunningham's squinting eyes.

The large clock on the wall had already reached one o'clock when Beck and Cunningham sat down to eat. Two young men in soiled aprons were clearing trash and other vestiges from the lunch hour mob.

Beck was grateful for the break from the trial. He had been on pins and needles all morning, listening to the ebb and flow of the testimony. Now, as he enjoyed his brown bag lunch, he surveyed the courthouse cafeteria, but he recognized none of the people lingering at the tables. A poorly dressed young woman was sitting with a teenage boy in a far corner, both of them munching Fritos and hot dogs. Three tables to Beck's left, an elderly, dignified lady was sipping a soda and leafing through some portfolios. Most of the other tables were empty, save the black and white checkered oilcloths waiting to be scrubbed.

"You're absolutely positive about Grimm's history?" Cunningham asked as he wiped condensation from the sides of a half pint milk carton.

Beck washed down a mouthful of sandwich with a gulp of ice water.

"Oh, definitely," he replied. "Some of the older magpies in the police department told me about Grimm. You know, the cops—especially the old guard—can't stomach cowards, draft dodgers, student protesters and the like. It seems that when the Korean War broke out, Grimm received a draft notice, and within a week, he fled like a traitor to Canada on the pretense of studying law at McGill University. In the decades that have passed, his faintheartedness has mostly been forgotten, but the old-timers still rib him about it. He's super-sensitive when the subject arises."

Beck took a large bite from his sandwich, inadvertently squeezing a sloppy wedge of tuna fish and mayonnaise out the other side. He caught the errant mass in his palm and directed it to his mouth.

"Excuse me, Owen," he apologized, "while I get some napkins."

Beck traipsed across the cafeteria to the empty food line and pinched several paper napkins from the top of a pile near the closed register. One napkin he used immediately to wipe the remnants of mayonnaise from his fingers. He retraced his steps across the room, and as he slid into his chair opposite Cunningham, he noticed that a round-headed man had taken a seat at the next table. The man was wearing a tweed sports jacket and sky blue golf cap, sitting with his back to them.

"I noticed you didn't call Mrs. Bernstein to the stand," Beck remarked, biting off the end of a dill pickle.

"I just couldn't bring myself to do it," Cunningham explained. "When I saw her this morning, I knew immediately she would never stand up to Grimm. He would have squashed her between his fingers like a rotten banana. Did you see the way he was waving that gold fountain pen around like Zorro brandishing his sword? That's his trademark. It's just for show, of course, but that type of display would have shriveled Mrs. Bernstein into a shadow. Besides, her I.D. was not that solid, if you recall."

"I know, and I'm just as happy you spared her," Beck said gratefully. "By the way, what time do we have to be back in court?"

"Theoretically, we're supposed to have an hour for lunch," Cunningham replied. "But I think O'Brien will reconvene as soon as everyone returns, because I took longer than I should have this morning."

"Oh, you were terrific, Owen," Beck complimented the D.A. as the latter squeezed open the flaps of the milk carton.

"You mean *Lowery* was great," Cunningham asserted. "All I did was throw him the questions. You could tell from his answers that he is intimately familiar with how the gang operated. That will certainly help convince the jury."

"True," Beck said, "and I think you ended at precisely the right point. You got all the facts out in the open, without bringing anyone's personality or prejudices into question. The jury will have the whole lunch hour to ruminate over Lowery's damaging testimony."

"However," Cunningham cautioned, "the acid test will come as soon as we resume. That's when I'll be departing the world of facts and probing into Lowery's intentions and conduct. I'm warning you, Dr. Beck, I'll be sowing a minefield that could blow up in our faces. It's going to hand Grimm a grand opportunity to upset the whole apple cart by tearing into Lowery's credibility. Lowery's got a lot of skeletons in the closet, and Grimm knows about most of them. I don't know what sort of magic trick you've planned for him—but it better be good!"

"Don't worry, Owen," Beck said evasively, "Lowery knows how to defend himself."

"I wish I were as optimistic as you, Dr. Beck. I've enacted this strategy many times before, but I only chance it when I'm fairly certain of the outcome. Besides, this jury is not your run-of-the-mill collection of dumbbells."

"I'll second that," Beck concurred, "but that might work in our favor, don't you think?"

"Are you kidding?" Cunningham scoffed. "One intellectual in a flock of illiterates can ruin the whole show. Ask any judge—it's always the college types who bring in the acquittals. They abandon all common sense in their fascination with legal acrobatics, and they get hung up on technicalities. I've always said, hand me a jury of uneducated construction workers, and I'll hand you a conviction."

"As a rule, I wouldn't argue with you," Beck conceded. "But how about Annabelle von Streichen?"

"Miss Peacock? Our foreman . . . er . . . foreperson? . . . Sorry. I've got to get the parlance straight . . . Now there you've got a good point. That woman may look like a made over pantomime, but mark my words, underneath that circus facade lurks a canny intuition that will penetrate any mendacious ploy we might throw up. And if there's anyone who can horsewhip that jury into line, it's Miss Annabelle. She's the one to play to, all right."

"It's getting late," Beck remarked. "My wife's sandwich was delicious, but I've still got to thank the One who brought that fish and tomato and bread into existence. It'll take me about three minutes to say my grace after meals, so you can either hang around, or else I'll meet you back in the courtroom."

Cunningham stared blankly at Beck. He was just about to reply when the man in the tweed jacket pushed his chair back and rose to leave.

"Owen!" Beck declared when the man was out of earshot. "I didn't recognize that fellow until now because he had his back to us, but I spied him talking to Grimm in the corridor this morning! They were too far away for me to hear, but I saw Grimm hand him some cash."

"Oh, G-d!" Cunningham groaned. "Are you serious? I had forgotten how tough Grimm can play. I wonder if we spilled anything."

"We certainly didn't do ourselves any good."

"How could we have been so stupid?"

"Listen, Owen, what's done is done. Now, you cheer yourself up, and go in there fighting!"

Cunningham nervously cleared the trash off their table as Beck *bentched*. Then they both hurried through the stately hallways to Judge O'Brien's courtroom.

As they entered, Beck noticed that, except for the judge and jury, they were the last to return. Horace Grimm's round torso was squeezed tightly between the arms of a polished oak chair behind the defense's table. He was dressed impeccably in an azure business suit, the tip of a monogrammed handkerchief peeking from a breast pocket. A pile of papers and notes on the table in front of him were topped ostentatiously with a gold fountain pen. Beck recognized the implement as a newly popular version of the old cartridge pens of the Fifties and Sixties. During examination of a witness, or when addressing the jury, Grimm waved it back and forth effectively as a symbol of success and authority.

Sitting next to Grimm in a rogue's lineup were Charles Henley, Jack Ritondo, Damon Hughes and Robert Eberhart. Each man's wrists were coupled in front of him by handcuffs, and each wore a set of heavy leg irons. Henley was the only one of the lot who was dressed neatly, and the only one whose face bore any semblance of equanimity and confidence. The others wore scowls that vacillated periodically between worry, anger, fear and enmity. Six hefty marshals dressed in gray and brown uniforms and gray Mounty felt hats, stood like towering obelisks next to the wall by the prisoners, the heels of their black boots planted firmly against the oak paneling.

Mark Lowery was already seated in a wooden armchair behind the prosecutor's table, studiously avoiding eye contact with the prisoners on the other side of Grimm. On the table in front of Lowery was a cream colored pad of paper sandwiched inside a clean, white plastic cover.

Chester Carter stood next to Lowery, chatting with him. Beck had observed that Lowery harbored an inbred fear of his erstwhile associates and, consequently, had assigned Carter the job of escorting Lowery continuously during the trial.

A trim woman with brown hair and a petite gold wristwatch was sitting at the clerk's table positioned beneath, and immediately in front of, Judge O'Brien's imposing bench. She was copying something into a ledger.

Beck resumed his seat next to Dovid Berg on the first bench in the gallery. He surveyed the courtroom in a nervous but unsuccessful attempt to locate the man in the tweed coat. Meanwhile, Cunningham strolled through the opening in the railing and eased himself into an armchair next to Lowery.

Beck leaned toward Dovid and whispered, "Everything set?"

"It's a go," Dovid confirmed.

Beck stared at Carter until he caught the policeman's eye. Carter turned slightly to the left to shield that side of his body from Grimm's view and flashed a furtive thumbs up signal to Beck. The latter allowed himself a sparing smile as he nodded a faint acknowledgment.

Just then the jury began filing through a side doorway into the jury box. Beck counted them while they assumed the identical seating configuration they had used throughout the trial. There were four men and eight women, ranging in age from the mid-twenties to the upper seventies. By and large, Beck reflected, they had been fairly attentive during the exhausting testimony. A few jurors had taken notes, but most simply watched the proceedings like a judging panel at a chess match.

"Annabelle refuses to abandon that fan, doesn't she?" Beck breathed in Dovid's ear.

Funny, he thought, they had all begun to refer to the foreman by her first name. She was certainly a character. Today, her lips were painted a stop sign red, and her face appeared caked with an unusually thick layer of oily makeup. Enough to grease the wheel bearings in his car, Beck mused to himself. Every strand of her platinum blonde hair seemed to be appointed to a reserved slot in the swirling cotton candy that frosted the top of her head. Her carnation-pink chemise dress adorned with sequined swirls cascading from the shoulders, would have been stunning in a more elegant environment. Much too showy, Beck considered, for the sordid business of deciding which of two parties was telling the bigger lie.

"You're right," Dovid whispered back. "She must have plucked a grandfather peacock to get that fan. And she wields the thing around like Babe Ruth used to sling his bat at home plate when pointing at the outfield."

"Hah!" Beck chuckled softly. "She's such a tiny little woman. Next to her that fan looks absolutely gigantic."

At that moment, the clerk jumped up and stood erect.

"Judge Samuel O'Brien," she announced. "All rise."

O'Brien strode quickly into the room from his chambers and lowered himself into his dark brown, leather upholstered judicial chair. His freshly combed hair melted into prominent sideburns, framing a handsome face that appeared a decade younger than its fifty-eight years.

With an alertness in his bearing, O'Brien invited Cunningham to resume the examination that had been interrupted for lunch. As Cunningham called his witness back to the stand, Lowery arose with his white notebook and advanced to the seat beside the judge's bench.

Cunningham sidled up to the witness stand and placed a hand on the rich oak molding forming the border of the stand. He looked from Annabelle von Streichen to the rest of the jury, and then to Lowery.

"Mr. Lowery," Cunningham opened, "until now we have dealt with your knowledge of the operation of the robbery ring. We're going to shift gears at this point and explore your relationship with the defendants. I understand that some difficulties arose between you and—"

"Objection, Your Honor," Grimm sang out emphatically, hoisting his weight to a standing position. Beck was surprised at the heavy man's alacrity.

"Sustained," O'Brien immediately responded. "Mr. Cunningham," he admonished, "you will refrain from leading the witness."

Cunningham clenched his fists, then turned back to Lowery and instructed in a conciliatory tone, "Please tell the court about your relationship with the defendants."

Lowery swung his gaze from Cunningham to Grimm to Carter, and finally to Beck. The latter attempted mightily to beam packets of support and confidence to the frightened young man. Lowery, he realized, had little experience with the phenomena of trust and loyal friendship, and even though they had tried to bolster the young man, Beck was unsure whether he would respond to the treatment.

"My 'lationship, huh?" Lowery spoke hesitantly. "Ya cain't have no 'lationship if dey's tryin' to kill ya. Sissy almos' done me in on th' crane. Ah know he done it on purpose.

Ain't none of 'em gives a mess 'bout bumpin' sum'un off. So whatcha 'spect, ah's gonna love 'em er sumpin'? Ah hates 'em, course."

Beck saw Cunningham look sideways at Grimm. For a tense moment, Beck tightened his muscles, praying fervently that Grimm would not object just yet. If Grimm would just give the prosecution another minute to open the trap a little wider . . .

"If you hated them so much, as you put it," Cunningham continued, "why did you join them in the first place?"

"'At's a lie! Ah never stuck up no one. Ah hung 'round 'cause Puppy was there, at's all. An' ah needed a job."

"But didn't you rob Woody's Restaurant last year?" Cunningham pressed.

"Yez'r, but ah tol' ya it was th' on'y stickup ah done, 'cause mah frien' dare me, but ah promise mahse'f ah wou'n't do no more, an' ah bin keepin' mah promise."

"Well, Mr. Lowery," Cunningham said, "that sounds very brave of you. What did the defendants have to say about your promise?"

"They say ah's chicken but ah ain't, tha's what ah tol' 'em. Ah tol' 'em hain't right to hurt peoples an' they shoulda make a promise like me an' don' hurt no peoples no more but they don' care an' Puppy don' care if'n he stab an' kill that ol' lady so ah tol' 'em they better stop an' tha's why they try to kill me but ah stood up to 'em an' tol' 'em ah wou'n't break mah promise even if'n they kills me."

Lowery had steadily gained confidence as his run-on sentence energized him like a self-priming pump. He finished with an inflection of finality that left no room for doubt as to his determination. Cunningham was crowing, and he paused to allow Lowery's courageous resolve to permeate the courtroom.

"How old are you, Mr. Lowery?" Cunningham asked,

turning back to the witness stand.

"Ah jes' turn eighteen."

"Have you ever thought of joining the armed forces?"

"Objection!" Grimm snapped himself erect, like a hare instinctively sensing a lurking fox.

O'Brien's eyes widened slightly, as he inquired, "What is the basis of your objection, counsel?"

Grimm composed himself and explained patronizingly, "Your Honor, my dear colleague, counsel for the State, is pursuing material that is not relevant to these proceedings."

O'Brien turned to Cunningham, inviting a rebuttal.

"Your Honor," Cunningham responded, "the State believes that this question contributes significantly to understanding the witness's character and, consequently, the credibility of his testimony about the defendants as well."

It was one man's opinion against the other's, Beck thought apprehensively. He began scratching his arm nervously, praying fervently for *siyata dishmaya*.

O'Brien tilted back in his chair and stared at Grimm for a second. Then he leaned forward again.

"Overruled!" he announced.

"Atta boy!" Beck cheered quietly, striking his right fist into his left palm.

"Ssh!" Dovid cautioned.

"That's Hurdle Number One," Beck whispered, ignoring Dovid's shush. "One more to go."

Ostensibly to gather some notes, Cunningham perambulated a crescent path from the witness stand to his table and back to the front of the courtroom. It was just for effect, Beck realized, a ploy enabling him to strut in front of the jury and flaunt his victory.

Addressing the witness again, Cunningham repeated, "Mr. Lowery, have you ever thought of joining the armed forces?"

"Yez'r, ah bin to th' recruitin' office th' day of mah birthday, but they say ah needs a high school graj'ation fust, so's ah's goin'a night school afta' th' summa'."

Cunningham paused again, shifting his feet so that he was half facing Lowery and half facing the jury.

"Here comes the bomb!" Beck whispered. His heart began pounding in anticipation. "Oh, Hashem, *please* help us!"

"Mr. Lowery, considering the danger of serving in the military, wouldn't it be prudent to try to avoid it, or even to leave the country, if necessary?"

O'Brien stiffened suddenly, as his eyebrows flew up. He glanced sharply at Grimm with a look of expectation.

"Ob—" Grimm started to utter, then broke off abruptly in the middle of the word.

Beck, with his white fingers tightly interlocked, shot a frantic look at the defense table. Grimm had frozen halfway out of his chair. His bulbous nose was rosy red, and streaks of blush played over his bowling ball face. Beck could see glistening beads of perspiration sprouting on his skull underneath the thinning white hair.

All at once, Beck observed Grimm begin to relax. As the rotund man lowered himself again, his red nose turned upward, and his physiognomy assumed a well known expression of sardonic smugness that reflected his inner arrogance.

"The Lord hath delivered him into our hands," Beck muttered, quoting from one of the nineteenth century Darwin debates. "His own egotism forced him to take the bait."

Beck smiled broadly when he saw Cunningham peer in his direction.

"Go ahead, Mr. Lowery," O'Brien finally instructed with a look of bewilderment. "Answer the question."

"Naw," Lowery said simply, "Ah wou'n't run 'way f'um th' army jes' 'cause a' th' danger. Ah ain't no coward, is ah?"

"What a capper!" Beck exclaimed with relish as he watched Grimm struggle mightily to maintain his reptilian grin.

Cunningham once again faced the jury and studiously directed his eyes over each member, like a giant laser beam branding a message onto its target.

"No more questions, Your Honor," Cunningham said demurely. He strode back to his place at the table.

"Counsel, do you wish to crossexamine?" O'Brien asked Grimm with a twinge of consternation rising in his voice.

"Yes, Your Honor, I do."

Grimm planted his hands on his table and slowly pushed himself to a full standing position. He grasped the gold fountain pen in his right hand and ambled toward the front of the courtroom. Lowery's face suddenly darkened, and his shoulders drooped slightly. Beck wanted to buttress his confidence, but he could not catch the young man's attention.

Grimm waddled to a stop in front of Lowery and inspected him intently. Lowery cringed and shriveled down another notch. Grimm then sidled over to the jury box and raised his pen, its nib aimed at von Streichen, like a conductor directing a concertmaster before the first symphony notes are struck.

"Ladies and gentlemen of the jury," he intoned in a booming, resonant voice. "The witness has suggested to the court that he is the paragon of courage and valor. Yet he was convicted of robbery little more than a year ago, and himself admits to that cowardly act."

"But ah tol'—" Lowery began.

"Order!" O'Brien commanded instantly, banging his gavel down hard on the bench. "Mr. Lowery, you will refrain from talking out of turn. You are to speak only when the counsel asks you a question. Is that understood?"

"Yes, y'ahna," Lowery said faintly. He withered back in his chair, his remaining spirit crushed by the unsparing sternness of O'Brien's lecture.

Grimm turned around to face the jury again, hitched his nose a millimeter higher and raised his baton once more. As if in a hypnotic echo, von Streichen elevated her feather fan an inch and dialed her wrist action up to high speed. The sequins on her dress flashed turquoise and violet reflections of the peacock hues.

"Furthermore, my friends," Grimm resumed his attack, "the witness lived for nearly a year with full knowledge of the alleged crimes he has ascribed to the defendants. Never once did he inform the police, even anonymously, nor did he seek help from any other quarter. Such shrinking from duty hardly seems appropriate behavior for a hero such as the witness has made himself out to be. Ladies and gentlemen, this is not heroism at all, but baseless *cowardice!*"

Forming his puffy lips into a half sneer, Grimm thrust the fountain pen forward toward von Streichen to punctuate the word "cowardice." Beck noticed von Streichen's rouge start to crack from perspiration, but she did not flinch from Grimm's *coup de main*. Rather, her expression remained as stoic as a rock, and only the precision oscillations of her feather revealed that she was still alive.

Grimm faced about and marched determinedly toward the witness stand. Beck fulminated with a mixture of anger and helplessness as Lowery cowered backward.

"Now, young man," Grimm trumpeted, tugging his jacket as straight as possible over the curvature of his belly, "as for your so-called attempt at military service. The many decades of peace which this great nation has enjoyed have spoiled and softened you children in the young generation.

I vividly recall in my youth the sacrifices many of us endured."

Grimm glanced at the judge, who in turn looked quickly at Cunningham. The prosecutor stared back stonily, like a master returning a slammed ball in a ping-pong tournament. No objection was forthcoming. O'Brien shrugged perceptibly, a flash of confusion on his countenance.

"Continue, counsel," he directed Grimm.

"Yes, Mr. Lowery," Grimm resumed his sermon with gathering brimstone in his voice, "many of us endured years of hardship to obtain the education we would need to contribute productively to society. It was an ideal that you dropouts would not understand."

Grimm glued his eyes firmly to Lowery's, like a torpedoist zeroing the cross hairs of his periscope on a doomed frigate. Then he straightened up and pranced back to the railing in front of the jury box.

He stepped up close and grasped the thick railing opposite Annabelle von Streichen with his left hand. They stared determinedly at each other, oblivious to the avian plume interrupting their line of sight every half second like a giant metronome intervening between the conductor and his score. It was a test of wills that filled a breathless twenty seconds.

Suddenly, Grimm let go of the railing and took one step back, pointing his gold pen skyward like a ballistic missile.

Without removing his gaze from von Streichen, he thundered, "No, Mr. Lowery, it is *we* who are the brave—*we* who invested our all, *we* who raised ourselves by our bootstraps, *we* who poured into ourselves the resources that now enable us to defend innocent men from dissembling scoundrels and perjurors!"

Neither Horace Grimm nor Annabelle von Streichen budged an inch. Silence ruled the courtroom.

Finally, his eyes still locked on von Streichen, Grimm added with vituperous scorn, "I would venture, Mr. Lowery, that you cannot even read the notes that are sitting in front of you."

With that, he swung around and stalked swiftly back to the witness stand. Laying his pulpy left hand next to the white notebook on the stand, he fixed his eyes on Lowery and said facetiously, "Can you?"

Lowery looked forlornly at Grimm before lowering his gaze to the notebook. He slowly peered up and glanced around the courtroom. His woeful eyes caught sight of Beck, like an apprentice parachutist beseeching his sergeant for moral support before his first jump. Carefully, Beck nodded his head up and down just once.

Lowery extended a steady hand to the notebook and snapped it open with a vigor that startled Grimm. There, crouching on the clean paper, were a half dozen large, ugly brown cockroaches waving whiplike antennae in the air. They instantly scattered in all directions, scurrying for the nearest hiding place.

The flap of fat under Horace Grimm's chin collapsed into the circumference of his throat as his lower jaw tumbled down like an avalanche. His eyes began to bulge out of their sockets, while the rolls on his cheeks assumed a moribund purple cast. He seemed paralyzed in a trance, his left hand pasted next to the notebook, his right hand still seizing the fountain pen and beginning to tremble.

Suddenly, one of the larger roaches spied the darkness of Grimm's sleeve and scampered up the underside of his arm.

"Argh! Gagh! Hch!" Grimm choked, his gullet working up and down in paroxysms of ghoulish palsy.

"Oh, Hashem!" Beck pleaded. "Don't make him bring up his lunch. That's too much for him to bear."

At that moment, a violent spasm seemed to invade Grimm's body and wrenched his hand off the witness stand. He staggered backwards toward the jury box, his left arm swaying aloft like a cobra dancing to a flute. As he twirled around on leaden feet, the offensive roach sprang from his sleeve into his open palm, which reflexively snapped shut on the creature.

The mess on Grimm's fingers was the final straw. The flabby man's eyes rolled upward in his head, his hands sprung to his chest, and he fell heavily against the jury railing directly in front of von Streichen. The cartridge end of Grimm's gold fountain pen was compressed forcefully between his weighty chest and the hardwood rail, and a fine jet of ink streamed out. Its destination was the reddest locus of Annabelle von Streichen's powdered cheek.

"Aiy!" she shrieked.

Her diminutive figure twisted back and forth like a windsock in a hurricane, as she sprang to her feet, the precision ink jet inscribing a bold Z down the length of her spotless chemise. Immediately, she wielded her feather with a scarecrow arm and began striking Grimm's colorless pate in a quixotic effort to beat it off the rail. Slowly, the fat man slumped to the floor in a dead faint.

20

A PLEASANT EVENING BREEZE GENTLY SWAYED THE FADED yellow curtains through an open kitchen window. Beck's eye followed a sinuous crack in the plaster wall as it descended from the top of the window frame and faded behind a fog of steam rising from a gallon pot of spaghetti that Rusie was stirring on the range.

Rusie muttered, half to herself, "The older girls are in the dining room putting bibs on the little ones, so I think I'll give this another two minutes to boil. We should be able to eat soon."

She extracted a large wooden spoon from the pot and laid it on the counter.

"Thanks very much for drying the *milchig* dishes, Binyamin," she said, glancing at her husband.

"Uh-huh," he acknowledged, as he wiggled another clean cereal bowl out of the brown dish drainer.

Rusie stirred the pot once more and stepped back from the stove.

"Excuse me, Binyamin," she said, reaching in front of him. "I need to get a potholder from the drawer."

"Huh?" he said absently.

Her right hand resting on the drawer knob, she looked up at him.

"Are you all right?" she asked worriedly.

"Huh? Oh, yeah, I'm fine. I was just thinking about the trial. I'm glad it ended today. I really can't afford to take more time from work."

"Well, you figured it would take three days, didn't you? You were right."

"That's true," he admitted. "If you had asked me yesterday, I would have predicted that we would lose. As it turned out, we got twenty-five years on Henley, fifteen on Ritondo and Eberhart, and forty on Damon Hughes because of the stabbing. *Baruch Hashem,* everything fell into place. Except I still regret having put Grimm in such a compromising and shameful position."

"Don't feel guilty," she consoled. "Remember, you had Rav Feinman's *psak.*"

"By the way, did I tell you what Chet and I are planning to do for Lowery?"

"No, what?" she asked.

"Well, you know Chet was the one who took Lowery over to Wicomb this afternoon during the lunch break. We wanted the roaches to be fresh, so to speak. Chet told me that Lowery required all of about sixty seconds to round up half a dozen of the creepy crawlies, and then they zoomed back downtown to the courthouse."

"Ugh!" Rusie grunted, shuddering for an instant.

"Anyway, while they were driving, they struck up a conversation. Chet learned that Lowery's uncle used to operate an electrical appliance repair shop, and for the last three summers, Lowery has worked there. It seems he has a real aptitude for tinkering. Unfortunately, the uncle died recently, and that's when Lowery got the job with Tip-Top through Damon."

"Oh, that sounds interesting," Rusie remarked. "But what's it have to do with you and Chet?"

"Well, it so happens that Annabelle von Streichen owns a computer business. We'll ask her to hire Lowery to work in the service department. I think he can make it."

Rusie opened the drawer and rummaged inside. She withdrew a red and white checkered potholder.

"That's wonderful," she commented approvingly as she walked back to the stove.

Beck slid the dried bowl onto a cabinet shelf and grabbed another one out of the drainer.

"Most criminals don't deserve any breaks at all," he declared. "But I'll have to admit that Judge O'Brien was right about Lowery. He sized up the boy accurately."

"And *you* sized up Horace Grimm's nature accurately," Rusie said, her back to him.

"Oh, no, Rusie, it wasn't me at all. The whole thing was *hashgachah pratis*. In fact, this entire mystery, from the original series of robberies to von Streichen's final announcement of the guilty verdict, was one long chain of *hashgachah pratis*. Do you realize how many so-called 'coincidences' we encountered, and how many supposed 'lucky breaks' we received? It was all Hashem."

Rusie lifted the lid with her potholder and a billow of steam emerged from the cauldron like a genie from a bottle.

"You know, Rusie," Beck mused, "*bitachon* often comes easier to a downtrodden person, because he has no one but Hashem to turn to for help. It's the accomplished person who readily falls into the trap of thinking that he is the maker of his own success. That's the big *nisayon* of victory. But in this case, Hashem's Hand was so evident every step of the way, it would be impossible to shed our *bitachon* and think that we were the champions of our own triumph."

"Sort of like the story of *Purim*, isn't it?" Rusie replied as she turned the burner off.

"Exactly."

Beck suddenly stopped wiping the bowl and stared absently at the back of his wife's blue and gold *tichel*.

"Say!" he exclaimed. "If you spell Henley in Hebrew—*hei-nun-lamed-yud*—it's the same numerical value as Haman!"

"Wow!" she exclaimed, turning quickly to face him.

"It really was a *Purim* story, wasn't it?" he enthused.

Rusie trod lightly to her husband's side and stood next to him, tugging the corners of the potholder in her hands.

"Binyamin," she said humbly, raising her soft eyes to meet his, "I'm not trying to present myself as Queen Esther, but if you had listened to me at the outset, you would have fingered Charles Henley right off the bat."

Beck's grin collapsed into a defensive scowl. He tossed his towel on the counter and stared dumbly at his wife.

"Binyamin," she added gently, "I certainly don't mean to say 'I told you so.' I know how hard you worked on this case and how you agonized over the pain and suffering of all those victims. But I felt in my bones that there was something sinister about Henley the first time I talked to him."

"Okay, I'll concede the point to you," Beck said with a hint of irritation. "But the police can't act on a feeling in your bones. A woman's instinct might not lie, but it won't stand in court. They need good, solid evidence." He punctuated his conclusion by stabbing the air with his finger.

"I know, I know," Rusie soothed. "Of course, you're a hundred percent right," she added, ending the debate.

Beck clenched his fists, digging his fingernails into his palms. Rusie, he conceded to himself, had the upper hand, but her modesty had compelled her to yield the battle before it began. He was abashed that even in victory she had taken care not to hurt his pride. She had won the war for both of them—the war against his own contentiousness, the war against the self-centeredness which looms as the archenemy of matrimonial bliss.

Just then, the doorbell rang.

"You kids stay where you are," he ordered as he passed the dining room. "I'll get the door."

The brass knocker began resounding insistently.

"Hold your horses," Beck muttered. "Give me a chance."

When he unlocked the deadbolt, the door almost flew open in his face. Devorah came bounding in, the yellow ribbon in her ponytail hopping up and down as she danced on her tiptoes with excitement.

"Hey, what's all the hysterics for?" he said. "If your grin gets any wider, your face is going to disappear."

"Hi, Dr. Beck," Devorah bubbled. "Is Rusie home?"

"Sure. In the kitchen." As she bounced off, he added, "You look like you just won a million bucks."

"*More* than a million, Dr. Beck. *Much* more."

She left Beck holding the door. His nonplused face gave way to gaping curiosity as he heard shrieks and squeals of delight coming from the kitchen.

Making his way to the scene of the commotion, he stood in the kitchen doorway. There was Devorah, jumping up and down, hugging Rusie and turning her in a circle. Snatches of words and phrases reached his ears, but they were so smothered by the screeching that he could not make heads or tails out of the affair.

"Hey, what's going on?" he demanded. "Did *Mashiach* come, or something?"

By now, all the children had clamored into the kitchen. The room resembled Grand Central Station at rush hour.

Rusie looked over at Beck, and between Devorah's bear hugs, she whooped, "Dovid called Devorah. He wants to meet her. And for a little longer than last time."

This revelation triggered a new round of squeals and antics as the children rushed Devorah *en masse*. She dropped Rusie and dashed out of the room with the girls draped all over her. Beck listened as the din receded to some far corner of the house.

The tiny kitchen suddenly seemed cavernous in size, husband and wife abandoned as two lonely figures in its center. The absolute silence contrasted starkly with the pandemonium of the minute before. If they had not known each other so intimately, they both would have found the hush intolerably awkward.

Beck looked deeply into his wife's eyes.

"So?" he finally uttered in total confusion. "So? It's just a meeting, you know."

"Just a meeting?" Rusie repeated softly, raising her inflection as though Beck had uttered the most outlandish statement of his life. "Just a meeting? Binyamin, don't you know what this means?"

Beck stared at his wife in dismay, his mouth hanging open. She looked down at the floor and fingered the potholder in her hand.

"Rusie, it's just a meeting," he repeated. "The way she's carrying on, you would think they're already engaged. Don't you think she ought to wait and see where this ends up?"

Rusie raised her compassionate eyes again to meet his, and hesitated an instant.

"Oh, Binyamin," she said with tender sympathy, "what do you know about female intuition?"

He was speechless. It was the last parry he had expected from her.

He thought a moment, shook his head in resignation and answered, "Not much, I'm afraid. Not very much at all."

GLOSSARY

apikoress: apostate
aveirah: sin
Avos: Patriarchs
baal teshuvah: penitent
bachur: youth
Beis Hamikdash: Holy Temple
baruch Hashem: thank Heaven
bechirah: free will
bentch: to bless [Yiddish]
bikur cholim: visiting the sick
bitachon: trust
brachah: blessing
brachah acharonah: concluding blessing
briah: creature
challah: Shabbos loaf
chas veshalom: Heaven forbid
chassan: bridegroom
Chazal: the Sages
chessed: kindness
daven: pray
eishes chayil: women of valor
emes: truth
emunah: faith
erev: day before

frum: observant [Yiddish]
gashmius: material things
gedolei Yisrael: leaders of Jewry
gedolim: leaders
Gemara: part of the Talmud
gemillas chessed: kindness
geulah: redemption
Gomel: prayer of thanksgiving
goyim: gentiles
Hakadosh Baruch Hu: the Holy Blessed One
Halachah: Jewish law
hashgachah pratis: providence
hashkafah: perspective
hishtadlus: effort
Im yirtzeh Hashem: if G-d wills i
Imahos: Matriarchs
kashrus: state of being kosher
kavanah: concentration
kedushah: holiness
kehillah: community
Kiddush: blessing of sanctification
Klal Yisrael: the Jewish people
kvelled: beamed with pride [Yiddish]

lashon hara: slander
lekavod: in honor
maakeh: protective fence
Maariv: evening prayers
machmir: strict
mashal: parable
Mashiach: the Messiah
mayim acharonim: post-meal finger washing
mechadesh: renew
mechilah: forgiveness
menorah: candelabra
mentch: proper person [Yiddish]
mesiras nefesh: dedication
midah (midos): character trait(s)
Midah keneged midah: tit for tat
Midrash: homiletics
milchig: dairy
Minchah: afternoon service
minyan: quorum of ten
mitzvah: commandment
Modeh Ani: prayer upon waking
mussar haskel: lesson
mussar: ethical instruction
mutar: permitted
Navi (Neviim): prophet(s)
neshamah: soul
ness: miracle
nisayon: test
Olam Haba: the world to come
Olam Hazeh: this world
parnassah: sustenance
posek: halachic authority
psak: ruling
rachmana litzlan: Heaven save us
rasha: villain
rebbi: Torah teacher
refuah sheleimah: a full recovery
Ribono Shel Olam: Master of the Universe
Rosh Chodesh: New Month
sakanah: danger

s'char: reward
seichel: intelligence
sefarim: books
Shabbos: the Sabbath
Shacharis: morning prayers
shadchan: matchmaker
shaliach: messenger
sheker: falsehood
shem shamayim: the name of heaven
Shema: daily confession of faith
shidduch: match
shiur: lecture
Shmoneh Esrei: the Eighteen Benedictions
shomer Shabbos: *Shabbos* observer
shomer mitzvos: observant
siyata dishmaya: the help of Heaven
sukkah: *Sukkos* booth
tachlis: goal
tafkid: purpose
tefillah: prayer
teshuvah: repentance
tichel: kerchief
tumah: spiritual defilement
tzaddik: righteous person
tzaar gidul banim: the pain of childrearing
tzeddakah: charity
tzitzis: fringes
tznius: modesty
umos haolam: gentile nations
Yam Suf: the Sea of Reeds
Yemos Hamashiach: the Messianic days
yetzer tov: good inclination
yetzer hara: evil inclination
Yiddishkeit: Judaism
yirah: fear
zemiros: songs
zrizus: diligence